An Empty Seat

D.G. PARTINGTON

PAGE PUBLISHING, INC.
New York, NY

First originally published by Page Publishing, Inc. 2019

ISBN 978-1-64424-830-0 (Paperback)
ISBN 978-1-64424-831-7 (Digital)

Printed in the United States of America

Chapter 1

Having poured herself a cup of coffee, she walked into her office to start work like any other day. Without warning, however, today would be a very different kind of day, a life-changing day. She sat at her desk, drinking her coffee, and reading her emails when the phone rang. "Bay Realty and Management Company, Madison speaking."

A familiar Russian accent greeted her in his usual abrupt manner, "Listen up, Nikolai here."

Madison sarcastically responded to the caller and said, "Good morning to you too." Ignoring his request to listen, she continued talking, "I was just thinking about you. I got an email from Andersen Plumbing regarding a bill. It was very reasonable and under the amount you've authorized me to spend on repairs, so I paid it."

"That's what I pay you for. Now be quiet. Connie called me this morning. She's sending over a purchase agreement for the office complex on Oakwood. It's an all-cash deal, and I'll be closing in a month."

Madison refused to lower herself to his level and cheerfully said, "That's fabulous. I know you've had that property on the market a long time."

The caller completely ignored Madison's comment and continued with his train of thought. "I'm going to use Bernie Sharp to do the closing, a Jew, but he's the best in the business. I'll call you next week with the details. You need to have your bank prepared to give my buyer a cashier's check for the two hundred and fifty thousand dollars in security deposits. I don't want any problems closing the deal at the last minute. Got that?"

Madison quickly answered him just to shut him up and avoid the usual aggravation. "No problem, and congratulations. I'll wait to hear from you."

Responding back in his standard rough manner, he said, "Enough now" and hung up the phone before Madison could get her goodbye in. Madison muttered out loud, "Goodbye to you too, Nikolai," but the sound of the dial tone drowned out her words. "And good riddance," she added, glad to be off the phone with him.

Nikolai Gusev was one of several clients whose properties Madison managed. While he was not the wealthiest that she represented, he was definitely the most difficult to deal with. His conversation was always short and abrasive, and at times even abusive. He once spoke of his past, relating how as a child of eight years of age, his family had been slaughtered in front of him by the Nazis during the Russian occupation. He escaped by hiding behind a woodpile, practically freezing to death while waiting for the Germans to leave. He was now well into his eighties, and when he recalled the incident, it seemed to be fresh in his memory. Perhaps the brutal way in which his family was killed was the cause for his savage behavior. Maybe it was the result of the six years he spent in prison charged with being an accessory to murder that molded his personality.

Madison read about the murder years earlier when it made front page news. Nikolai was charged in a murder-for-hire scheme. Allegedly, he wanted his business partner murdered in an act of vindictiveness. According to the papers, Vladimir Petrov, the partner, borrowed money from the business without Nikolai's consent. Even though he was paying it back over time, this betrayal allegedly infuriated Nikolai. He was accused of setting up Vladimir's murder.

After six long years of appeals, Nikolai's lawyer created enough reasonable doubt that Nikolai had not hired John Anthony for murder. Instead, the attorney proposed that Anthony fabricated the entire story to frame Nikolai when he refused to pay Anthony blackmail money. The lawyer was successful in obtaining Nikolai's release, and Vladimir's murderer was never found.

Madison first encountered Nikolai's violent side during a trip to his business for his signature. While talking to Nikolai in his office, Madison glanced out the glass partition to the factory floor and noticed a man walking down the aisle toward them.

As Nikolai waved the man to come inside his office, he sent Madison out. Standing on the opposite side of the glass enclosure, Madison focused her attention on the workers at their machines to give Nikolai and the man privacy. The employees, who faced Nikolai's office, kept their eyes glued to their machines.

Within a few minutes, shouting could be heard. It became louder and louder. Not once did the workmen turn their heads. They knew better than to look up and suffer the consequences. Curiosity and concern got the better of Madison. She turned to look into Nikolai's office just in time to see his hands around the man's throat attempting to squeeze the life out of him. The man's face was turning blue from a lack of oxygen and was about to pass out. Nikolai let go, and the man slumped to the floor. Madison stood there frozen, not knowing if she should help him or run.

A minute passed, and Madison feared he might be dead. The visitor regained consciousness and stumbled as he stood upright. He then bolted out of the office. To say she was scared to go back in was an understatement. Rather than return, Madison poked her head inside the door and nervously said, "When the papers are notarized, just mail them back in the envelope I gave you."

Sprinting out of there so fast, she could have broken the world record for speed. She fled to her car where she sat trembling. Seeing someone's life on the line shook her up. When she regained her composure, she drove directly back to her office. It was a day she would always remember.

Having turned forty just one month before, this tall, slender woman whose blonde hair still retained its childhood color could have easily passed for thirty. From the outside, it looked like she had it all. Having grown up in an upper-class family, Madison was privileged, and it showed. It was the way she spoke and carried herself that gave an onlooker the feeling she was well-heeled. Madison never flaunted it though. She'd been raised with humility, and not a day went by that she didn't say to herself, "There but for the grace of God go I."

By no means was it a perfect upbringing. Madison had been adopted at birth by the Mitchell family. Her father was alcoholic and a former Navy captain of an aircraft carrier. James Mitchell, her father, was a total control freak both at work and at home. He treated his children and his wife like the subordinate sailors under him, expecting complete obedience and compliance at all times. One night, after Madison had gone to sleep, her father came in her bedroom to kiss her good night. Her toys were strewn all around the room like in any other five-year-old's room.

When he tripped over a stuffed animal, he woke Madison up and made her clean up her toys while he stood by, watching till the job was done.

By contrast, her mother was passive except when James was out to sea. In his absence, her mother took the opportunity to exert control, perhaps to compensate for the lack of it when he was around. It took many years for Madison to overcome the pathology of the family dynamic. At times, in adulthood, her fear of being controlled by men reared its ugly head. One example was that she took martial arts classes to learn self-defense, and while the purpose of the classes was protection from physical threats, Madison subconsciously took it a step further. She wanted to be able to maintain control with men.

Madison read the remaining emails in her inbox while sipping her coffee. When done, she logged on to her bank's website and into her business account to see which transactions had cleared.

Next, she checked the escrow account where the security deposits for Nikolai's property under management were kept. That balance was zero. "What? What's this?" Madison screamed out loud in astonishment. "I'm a quarter of a million dollars short!" The account was wiped out. "How could this be?" Madison couldn't understand how that was possible. In a panic, Madison scrolled down the debit column only to see that two days prior, the money had been withdrawn by a check numbered 9999. This was the bank's way of designating money withdrawn directly from an account using a bank check instead of a personal one. She clicked on the check, and the image appeared. It was made out to cash, and the signature was Frank Jensen's.

Frank Jensen was Madison's business partner. Frank and Madison had known each other for years, going back to when they both worked for the Trident Real Estate Company selling homes. Then the downturn hit late that year, and houses were going into foreclosure in record numbers. That's when Frank and Madison decided they needed to take a different tack.

They seized the opportunity to open their own company, and instead of selling houses, they went into managing commercial buildings and shopping centers. Frank asked a former client, Nikolai Gusev, if they could manage his office complex. Having done business with Frank in the past, Nikolai agreed.

Madison needed to get a hold of Frank to find out what earthly reason he could possibly have for taking out the money that belonged to their client. She picked up the phone and called Frank's cell. It went directly to voice mail. Trying Frank's business line, she didn't get a response there either. Madison rhetorically asked, "Frank, how could you not answer your phone? What if a tenant's pipes broke?"

As a partner, her real estate license and reputation were on the line as well as her obligation to replace the missing money. Her inability to reach Frank was cause for panic. Since she couldn't reach him by phone, her only option was to drive to Frank's place. She grabbed her handbag and headed over to his condo.

Madison's home office was only fifteen miles away from Frank's, but given the urgent need to get there pronto, it seemed like forty. She was so anxious to find out where the missing money went that she ran a red light.

Passing a cop car hiding behind some bushes on the side of the road, she looked back in her rearview mirror. "Please don't pull me over. Please don't pull me over. Please don't pull me over," she chanted. Luckily, the cop must not have seen her, and she avoided being stopped and ticketed. Watching her speed, she finally reached Frank's condo twenty minutes later. Madison grabbed the first parking spot she could find. It was half a block away. She jumped out of her car and ran down the street to get to his place as quickly as possible.

Once inside the foyer, Madison pressed his unit number, ringing the buzzer repeatedly. It was futile. There was no response, and Madison had no way of getting in the lobby to go directly to Frank's door. She looked at her watch, hoping he might come home at any moment and thought maybe she should wait for him. She stood there impatiently, tapping her toe and looking at the time every few seconds. After a couple of minutes, the lobby door swung open to let a man exit the building. With a big smile on her face and acting like she lived there, Madison grabbed the open door and breezed in. She pressed the up button on the single elevator before noticing it was on the sixth floor. Madison waited a minute, but in her anxious state, she decided not to wait any longer and made a dash for the stairs.

Upon making her way to the stairwell, she could hear voices and the elevator door opening. She ran back to catch it. An elderly lady with her two dogs stepped off as if in slow motion, followed by a mother pushing a baby carriage and a toddler in tow who refused to get off. The mother took an extra thirty seconds to grab his hand and move on. Exasperated, Madison stepped into the elevator, and the doors started to close, but a gentleman put his hand in to keep it open so he could get on. He then pressed the button to hold it open for the woman with groceries running to catch it. After what felt like an eternity, the doors finally closed.

The man pushed the number 5 before asking the other passengers what floor they needed. The number 10 could be heard, and Madison asked for 14. Standing at the back of the elevator, she shook her head and rolled her eyes. The fact that the elevator would make two additional stops before she could reach Frank's floor drove her crazy. She desperately needed to get to Frank's apartment and to hear his explanation of the missing 250 thousand dollars. The elevator finally arrived at the fourteenth floor, and Madison ran out the second the doors opened. Frank's unit was located halfway down the hallway, just past the stairs.

She sprinted to his unit and began knocking on the door. Her knocking turned into pounding when no one answered. Next, she jiggled the doorknob and was startled when the door opened slightly. Madison stepped back, expecting Frank to answer it, but no one was there. Madison grabbed a hold of the knob and pushed the door all the way open into the living room.

"Frank?" Madison called out. "Frank, are you in here?"

Still no answer. She walked into the kitchen expecting to see some indication that he'd been home, but there was no sign of dirty dishes or of food having been cooked. Everything was neatly in its place. She went to check out the bedroom, hoping maybe Frank had one of his late-night booty calls and was still asleep. Just as she was about to enter the room, Madison heard the front door open. *It must be Frank,* she thought and stopped dead in her tracks to turn around to go to him. As she turned, Madison felt a sharp blow to her head and heard a cracking noise, then she fell unconscious to the floor.

Chapter 2

"Frank! Frank! Are you here?" Madison asked while touching her hand to the right side of her head. "Ouch!" she yelled then touched it again. "Ow, my head hurts. Why are you wearing a white coat?" Am I in heaven?" she asked.

"Nurse, give her two milligrams of morphine," the man in the white coat ordered.

"Who are you? Where am I?" Madison questioned.

"You're in the hospital. I'm Dr. Alex Chandler," he replied. "You came into the emergency room last night with a skull fracture and a contusion to your brain. I'm the neurosurgeon who's been treating you since your arrival." Madison wondered how she had gotten there. Dr. Alex explained that paramedics brought her in by ambulance. "A neighbor heard a noise and found you on the floor in a pool of blood. You're lucky you're doing as well as you are," he told her.

Madison, not realizing the severity of her injury and anxious to go home, asked him how quickly she could be released. "In several days," Dr. Alex told her. "We have to observe you and get follow-up CT scans to ensure that your brain contusions don't worsen." Madison was about to put up a fight when the door to her room opened, and a middle-aged heavyset man in a jacket barged into the room. There was a gun in a holster under his arm that was visible from his open lapel. He reached inside, and for a second, Madison thought he was going to shoot her. Instead, he flashed a badge.

"I'm Detective Malachek. I want to speak with the patient," he announced, sounding like a drill sergeant talking to new recruits at boot camp.

Exerting his authority, Dr. Alex snapped back, "She just regained consciousness and needs her rest."

"Well, I couldn't very well speak to her if she was unconscious now, could I? I'll be quick."

Dr. Chandler wasn't very pleased but motioned to the nurse to leave the room and warned the detective, "Just for a minute, that's all."

The detective waited till Dr. Chandler exited the room before he began his questioning. "Can you tell me your full name?"

Madison obliged the detective. "Yes, it's Madison Grace Mitchell. MGM for short, like the casino." Madison let out a giggle. The morphine was kicking in, and she was feeling euphoric.

"That's good. Very funny," Malachek said and waited till Madison stopped laughing. "Did you know Frank Jensen?"

"Yes, of course I know Frank. He's my business partner. What did he do now? Screw someone out of their commission?" she asked.

"He's been murdered." Detective Malachek didn't mince his words.

Sobering up, Madison repeated the detective's words. "*Murdered*. Murdered as in dead? No, no, that's not possible. No, no, no." Madison became more hysterical with each no.

Dr. Chandler came rushing in and told the detective to leave. "All right, but I'll be in touch," he told Chandler. "I'm leaving my card. See that she gets it," he commanded.

Having made it clear that his investigation was not finished, Detective Malachek left the room. Dr. Chandler leaned over Madison and told her that she needed to get some rest if she wanted to be discharged anytime soon. By now, the morphine's effect was in full swing, and Madison's eyes involuntarily closed shut as she drifted off to sleep.

Madison remained in the hospital for several days recuperating from her head injury. On the third day, during patient rounds, Dr. Chandler came to Madison's room to give her the latest progress report. "Your scans look good, and you can be discharged today. Do you have someone to pick you up and stay with you tonight? Otherwise, I can't let you go home."

Madison ensured him that she would arrange for a friend to pick her up and stay with her.

She reached for the phone on her nightstand to call her best friend, Cathy, to come get her.

"The discharge nurse will notify you when you can go home. Should be late afternoon. She'll be in to take your final vitals and give you discharge instructions. I can give you a prescription for pain if you think you'll need it." Dr. Chandler proceeded to give her initial instructions to follow. "I want you to take it easy these next few days. Don't make any major decisions. You've been through a rough time, and I'm going to want to see you back in my office in two weeks."

As Dr. Chandler continued writing his notes, Madison threw the covers off and sat up on the side of the bed. Dressed in a hospital gown, her bare legs dangled over the side of the bed. The business card from Detective Malachek was sitting on her nightstand. Madison picked it up and read it. "Somebody left a business card on my night table. It's from a Detective Malachek, LAPD."

"Yes, that's for you," Dr. Chandler said. "He was here the first day you regained consciousness. He asked you several questions and, understandably, you became very upset, so I asked him to leave. He said that he would talk to you at a later time."

"Talk to me? Talk to me about what? I don't remember any detective."

"I'm sorry to bring it up, but apparently, someone you know by the name of Frank has been murdered."

"Murdered," Madison repeated as she put her hand up to her mouth in bewilderment. "I thought I was dreaming. I don't remember any detective.

"Please don't worry," Dr. Alex said. "You suffered a right temporal and frontal lobe injury, and loss of short-term memory is not uncommon. In time, your memory will improve," he reassured her.

Feeling anxious at the thought that she couldn't remember an important detail like the murder of her partner, Madison asked, "When will it return?"

Dr. Alex was reluctant to give Madison an exact time frame, couching his answer. "It varies from patient to patient. I've had patients come back to me for their two-week checkup, not remembering that they were hospitalized, but soon after, their short-term memory improved."

"Is that what happened to me? I lost my memory?" Madison asked.

"It's too soon to tell. But be encouraged that over time, most patients' short-term memory can return." He paused a moment to let Madison wrap her head around what he had just said. "I also want to make you aware that a common side effect of a frontal lobe contusion, like the one you sustained, can be mood swings, but again, that can improve with time."

Madison picked up the business card again and briefly stared at it, hoping to jar her memory.

"Oh my God, Frank is dead." Madison started sobbing.

Dr. Chandler walked over to her and put his hand on her shoulder to console her. "You have my deepest sympathies for your loss," he said. Just then, his beeper went off. He looked down and exclaimed that it was the emergency room calling him. Dr. Chandler apologized for having to leave her alone and excused himself to rush to the ER.

Chapter 3

When Cathy got to the hospital, she immediately went to Madison's room. She was alarmed to see her friend in a hospital bed and confused as to why she was never called before today. The answers to her questions would have to wait since the discharge nurse came in and asked Cathy to wait in the patient lounge while she took Madison's vital signs and prepared the discharge papers. An hour passed before Cathy was allowed into Madison's room. The nurse left so Madison could get dressed in private and talk with her friend. She returned a short time later with Madison's discharge instructions. She asked Cathy to bring her car around to the front of the hospital and wait for Madison to be wheeled down to the lobby.

Cathy drove up to the main entrance and promptly got out to help Madison into the front seat. As they drove away, Cathy eased into asking Madison for the answers to her questions. "Madison, why didn't you call me? I had no idea you were hurt!"

"I knew you were litigating a very important case, and I didn't want to stress you out any more than you already were," Madison replied.

"You're more important to me," Cathy told her. "Besides, I could have gotten one of my partners to take over. What exactly happened?"

Madison started at the point when she was at Frank's condo but couldn't remember the reason why she was there. She talked about being hit over the head and learning of Frank's death from the doctor but couldn't remember much more than that.

"Oh, Madison! I had no idea. I'm so sorry. Let me get you home. We, uh..." Cathy was at a loss for words. "We can talk about this later."

Cathy pulled into the driveway to Madison's darkened house. It was late evening by the time they arrived home. Fortunately, the EMTs who brought Madison to the hospital had picked up her purse containing her identification and her keys.

"Give me your house keys and wait here while I turn on some lights and open the door."

Cathy was such a good friend. She mothered everyone whether they needed it or not, and right now, mothering was exactly what Madison needed. Once inside, Cathy insisted Madison head right for bed. For a change, she didn't argue with Cathy and did as she was told. Madison was happy to be home and to be able to sleep in her own bed. "I'll be up to check on you as soon as I lock up."

"Uh-huh" was all Madison said. In the time it took Cathy to check the doors and close the shades, Madison had managed to get into her pajamas and into bed. When Cathy came upstairs to check on her as promised, Madison was fast asleep. Cathy shut off the overhead light and quietly closed the bedroom door.

Around three in the morning, Cathy was awakened out of a dead sleep by a loud bang she heard coming from Madison's room. Cathy jumped out of bed and ran down the hallway to Madison's bedroom. She didn't waste time knocking but threw open the door and rushed in, fearing that the noise she had heard was Madison passed out on the floor. The bathroom light was on, and Cathy could hear the toilet flushing. In an effort to avoid embarrassing Madison, she called out, "Honey, are you okay in there?" Without waiting for an answer, Cathy continued, "Do you need any help?"

Madison didn't answer. Cathy walked into the bathroom and saw Madison standing in front of the mirror, looking dazed and smacking her lips. Cathy once again asked if she needed something. Madison just stood there continuously smacking as if she was tasting something foul. Cathy was worried that something was terribly wrong and in a strong tone of voice, she called out, "Madison."

Concerned by Madison's bizarre behavior, she asked, "Honey, is your mouth hurting you?" Seemingly snapping out of a trance, Madison slowly turned and looked at her. Cathy told Madison that she was smacking her lips.

"I'm fine," Madison said matter-of-factly. "I had to pee. You can go back to bed now."

Cathy was, to say the least, relieved. In those few seconds, Cathy had imagined all kinds of medical emergencies Madison might be experiencing. "Okay honey, good night. I'll be here in the morning to check on you."

When you're awakened in the middle of the night, it feels like the morning comes sooner than usual. It was now seven in the morning, and Cathy had to get up and get ready to go to work. She was feeling guilty about having to leave Madison all alone, but being a litigating attorney, she was due in court at 9:00 a.m. She showered, dressed, and checked in on Madison to find her still asleep. She went downstairs to the kitchen and left Madison a note to say she would call later that day when she was out of court.

Madison had slept soundly, and when she woke up, the clock read ten fifteen. She couldn't believe she had slept so late. She got on her robe and went downstairs to make a pot of coffee for her and Cathy. She found Cathy's note by the coffee maker and read it. "I'm lucky to have a friend like her," Madison said out loud.

While the coffee was brewing, she went into her office to do some work. Her laptop had been left open from that horrendous day she went to Frank's. The screen saver was running, and when she hit the enter button, the page to her bank opened up, displaying a timed-out message. Madison logged into her bank account and for some unknown reason, went directly to her escrow account. It still showed a zero balance, of course. "Why is it zero?" Madison asked herself. Images flashed in her mind as memories started coming back.

"Oh my God. That's right. I'm missing money, and Frank is dead, and I'm supposed to deliver a cashier's check to Nikolai Gusev." Alarmed, Madison shouted, "What am I going to do?" expecting an answer to come to her. She sat back in her chair, her hand covering her mouth in disbelief.

The coffee maker sounded a beep several times, reminding Madison that she had made coffee. She sat at her desk, frozen in thought. "What should I do?" she questioned. Madison played out several scenarios in her head. Without any solutions on the horizon, she got up to go to the kitchen to get a cup of coffee. She returned to her office and sat staring at her bank account's balance of zero.

The phone rang, interrupting her concentration. It was her business line, and she had to answer the call. "Bay Realty and Management Company, Madison speaking."

"Hello, Madison. I'm interested in buying a house. Are you available to help me?" the voice on the other end asked. Madison put her troubles aside for the moment, and in her best professional voice, responded, "Yes, I'd be happy to help you find a home. With whom do I have the pleasure of speaking?"

The male voice didn't give his name but simply said, "I'd like to know what houses you have for sale."

Madison told him that it was a buyer's market, and there were many listings to choose from. "What price range were you thinking?" she asked him.

"Between three and five," the man replied. Looking for clarification, Madison asked the potential customer if he was looking for homes between three and five hundred thousand dollars or three and five million dollars? After all, LA was very expensive.

"Three and five dollars, honey," the voice replied.

"Who is this?" Madison demanded. She was in no mood for joking around and was just about to hang up the phone when she heard the voice on the other end say, "Shep."

Madison paused in silence. She began to shake her head left and right. It was a mannerism she did when she was annoyed.

"Shep!" Madison repeated. The ice in her voice could have caused hell to freeze over.

"Hey, blue eyes, how are you?" he asked.

Cold and distrusting of Shep and his motives, Madison flatly answered, "I'm fine."

She left it at that, not caring how he was or interested in niceties. Hearing from Shep was the last thing Madison needed on her plate. Ben Shepherd, or Shep, as he was called by his friends and enemies, was bad news. He belonged in Madison's past, and that's exactly where she preferred to keep him. It had been many years since she last heard from him; he was traveling, playing poker for a living. Shep continued on as if they were still BFFs.

"I just arrived in town to play in the Western Poker Series. Entry fee is ten thousand dollars. Are you going to be playing in it?" he asked.

Without hesitation, Madison snapped her response, "No, I don't do that anymore."

Shep repeated her response, "You don't do *that* anymore?" accenting the word *that* with mockery and a sexual overtone. Surprised at her response, he tried to tempt Madison into playing by telling her, "Top ten winners get a seat to play for eight million dollars in prize money, winner takes all. Imagine what you could you do with eight million dollars."

Still resisting, Madison replied, "I don't play poker anymore. Besides, I'm out of practice."

Amazingly, Shep backed off.

This was totally out of character for him. He was a man who was extremely persistent and used to getting his way. With his GQ looks and a smile from ear to ear, he was, to sound old-fashioned, a lady killer. He knew how to turn on the charm without seeming phony.

"Well then, how about dinner? You still do *that*, don't you?"

Once again, he emphasized the word *that* to poke fun at Madison. "Yes," she said.

"Great, then I'll pick you up about 7:00 p.m."

"No. Yes," Madison blurted out in what sounded like a state of confusion. Perhaps her head had begun to hurt, or maybe it was Shep who had her all mixed up.

"Yes, I still do dinner, but no, not with you."

"What are you afraid of, baby?"

"Are you challenging me? You were always doing that."

He laid on the charm. "I'd just like to see you again," he told her. Shep was confident that he could get her to agree to go to dinner with him.

Madison thought about it for a moment. "I still like a good challenge. I'll have dinner with you. But just dinner."

"That's my baby. I heard about a great restaurant called The Circle. I'll come get ya at seven."

Having given in to the dinner challenge, Madison asserted herself by letting Shep know she would meet him there. Shep was always pushing the envelope and trying to persuade the other person to his point of view. He told her that if he drove, she could drink and not have to worry about driving. Madison stood firm and repeated that she would meet him there.

"Is drinking another thing you don't do anymore?" Madison ignored his jab and got one in by telling Shep that the restaurant was very pricey and that she hoped it wouldn't be a problem for someone looking to spend three to five dollars on a house.

Both Shep and Madison laughed, and for a split second, it seemed like old times. The conversation ended with Shep agreeing to make the reservation and meet her there.

She hung up the phone. While Shep's call was not welcomed, it was a momentary distraction for Madison. By now it was late morning, and reality started to kick in again. Madison still didn't have a clue as to how she was going to handle getting a quarter million dollars or where to find the missing money.

Madison asked herself, *What would Cathy advise?* Not only was Cathy her closet friend but also her lawyer. In the past when Cathy helped Madison with her real estate transactions, Cathy had always told her honesty is the best policy. Thinking that Cathy's advice was the best course of action, Madison reasoned the only solution for her was to tell Nikolai that the money was gone, and the closing will have to be delayed. Madison would have rather suffered the worst torture one can imagine than to have to make that phone call.

Picking up her office phone, she gripped it so tightly that the veins in her hand popped out. She looked at them then slammed the phone back down into the cradle. Calling Nikolai Gusev was not as easy as dialing the numbers. Stopping for a minute to gain her nerve, Madison redialed. This time, the number went through, and a female voice sounding very businesslike answered the call.

"Gusev Manufacturing," she announced. The woman proceeded to ask, "How may I help you?"

Madison, in a monotone voice, replied, "This is Madison Mitchell. I'd like to speak with Nikolai Gusev." Nikolai's abrupt manner had rubbed off on Madison. She skipped saying hello and got right to the point.

Nikolai's receptionist had been trained to screen his calls. "What is this in reference to?" she asked.

Madison answered, "I manage his office complex," to which the receptionist responded, "Just one moment please."

Madison cleared her throat in preparation for talking with Nikolai. She secretly was hoping he was too busy to speak with her. Unfortunately, he promptly answered the call, and from his tone of voice, it was glaringly apparent he was annoyed. "Yes, what is it?"

Hearing his voice made an already nervous Madison even more on edge. Hesitant to break the news, she spilled out that it was about the closing, practically stuttering as she spoke.

Sounding even more irritated, Nikolai asked, "What about it? I told you I would call you and give you all the details. Is this what you interrupt me for?"

There was no way to sugarcoat the truth, so Madison plunged right in. "No. It's about the rent deposits. They're missing."

Without taking a breath, Madison rattled off the rest of the bad news as fast as possible, just to get it over with. "My partner, Frank Jensen, withdrew the money from our escrow account, and now he's dead, and I don't know where the money is." All the while, Madison was thinking, *This is not really happening.* She couldn't bear the thought of pissing off Nikolai Gusev. Was he going to choke her like the man in his office so long ago? There was a very pregnant pause coming from the other end of the phone. "Nikolai, are you there?" The phone went dead.

Chapter 4

She dialed the number repeatedly for at least twenty minutes without getting through and began to think that the company's phone must be out of order. That was the only explanation that would explain why Nikolai hadn't responded to Madison's declaration. Driving over to see Nikolai was another option, but Madison was getting fatigued, and Dr. Chandler had warned her not to overdo it and to rest. She took the busy signal as an omen. It seemed that fate had bought a slight reprieve, and maybe tomorrow would bring another solution. Madison decided now would be a good time to take a nap so she would be wide awake for that evening's dinner with Shep. In addition, she definitely didn't want to confront Nikolai in person with the bad news so fresh in his mind.

Madison snuggled up on the living room sofa, and it didn't take very long at all for her to fall asleep. About two hours into her nap, the phone rang, jarring her out of her deep sleep.

Disoriented, she answered the phone with a simple "Hello." It was Cathy on the other end. "Madison, hi, I just got out of court. How are you feeling?"

In her best perky voice, she told her friend, "Just great."

"So glad to hear it. I was concerned about you all day long. Anyway, I'm done for the day, and I'll be bringing dinner over in a little bit. Are you in the mood for Chinese?"

Madison declined the offer and assured her that there was plenty of food in her freezer. She didn't want to be mothered by Cathy and receive a lecture on why she shouldn't be going out for the evening. After repeated assurances that she wouldn't overly tax herself, Madison was able to fend off a visit from Cathy.

Luckily, Cathy's call woke Madison up. She needed to get ready for her dinner date and use the additional time to retrieve her car, still parked at Frank's condo. She showered and picked out something to wear. She chose a simple black dress. Madison, with her blonde mane and curvy figure, couldn't help looking seductive without trying. She called for an Uber ride to pick up her car. With a final check in the mirror, she turned the lights on in her living room and headed out the door to catch her ride.

If traffic was light on the expressway as it was tonight, the restaurant was a thirty-minute drive from Frank's condo. She picked up her car and headed to the restaurant. Twenty minutes into the drive, a car came up on Madison's bumper and stayed there, tailgating. The car, being so close to her bumper, made her nervous. She looked into her rearview mirror and began swearing out loud as if the other driver could actually hear her. The driver, a male, pulled out from behind her into the lane next to her Benz. Slowing down until they were dead even, he shot her a menacing glare. Then suddenly, he cut in front of her, almost hitting her front end. Her gut reaction was to swerve to the right to avoid getting hit.

Fortunately, she had been driving in the far right lane and ended up on the shoulder. Madison had narrowly avoided going through the guardrail and plunging five hundred feet into the canyon below. She felt a combination of terror and anger and let loose a string of expletives that would make the Godfather blush. Sitting on the side of the expressway, she felt the other driver was purposely trying to scare her. The thought crossed her mind that maybe Nikolai put him up to it but dismissed the ideas as being paranoid. Madison veered back onto the expressway, driving a little more cautiously than before.

She arrived at the restaurant and valet parked her car. Madison handed her keys to the valet and walked up the steps to the front door, whereby she was greeted by a doorman dressed in a black tuxedo. He opened the double doors for Madison and said, "Good evening, miss."

Madison walked inside and looked around to see if Shep had arrived but didn't see him. She went over to the hostess desk and said, "I'm meeting a friend here by the last name of Shepherd. Has he arrived yet?"

The hostess checked the guest list and confirmed the reservation. "Shepherd, 7:00 p.m, party of two. No, Mr. Shepherd hasn't arrived yet. Would you like to be seated at your table while you wait or perhaps visit the bar?" Madison chose to wait in the lobby instead. It was so exquisite that you could dine right there and not mind that you weren't seated in the main dining room. The high-back white leather chairs trimmed in black adorned the marble floor, setting the stage for a memorable night. The tall white columns throughout had gold leaf filigree at the top that were carried over to the coffered ceiling. The white ceiling beams sectioned the room into three cozy waiting areas, each containing a large six-tiered Venetian glass chandelier.

The bar was located only a short distance from the lobby and was twenty feet long and made of beautiful mahogany. It was skillfully manned by two bartenders working as fast as they could to serve the customers.

As she sat waiting, several couples and a group of six handsomely dressed businessmen came in and were seated. To keep herself entertained, she checked out what the other women were wearing and silently evaluated whether each woman looked good in the dress they had on.

After twenty-five minutes of playing fashion police, Madison was getting impatient and had grown tired of looking up every time the door opened to see if it was Shep.

By this point, seating in the lobby was completely full, with couples enjoying themselves, laughing and drinking glasses of wine. She read the emails on her cell phone and even played Candy Crush.

The door to the lobby opened, and Madison could feel a wave of energy enter. Bigger than life, very charismatic, and with raw sexuality that got your attention, Shep had finally arrived. The Italian-cut suit he wore didn't hide his muscular build but only enhanced it. The women seated next to their dates sneaked glances at this gorgeous

Adonis. He stood six feet, three inches tall with a cleanly shaved head and a day-old stubble. His cologne permeated the room like pheromones. He walked straight over to Madison, who had just stood up in preparation to leave. Without missing a beat or apologizing for being late, he greeted her with a kiss on her cheek and a "Hey, gorgeous, nice to see you."

Just as Madison was about to say something to him, Shep walked over to the hostess and gave his name, telling her that he had a reservation at seven.

The hostess looked at her watch and told him, "I'm so sorry, sir. I waited a half hour before giving away the reservation, and we have several guests yet to be seated."

With that huge smile that could melt ice, he said, "Traffic was heavy." He paused for a second to gauge her reaction. It was amazing to watch him in action. The hostess didn't have a chance. She blushed and was dazzled by him. Shep leaned on her podium and put his hand over hers. "So, beautiful, tell me that you can still seat me. I know you can pull it off," he told her.

The hostess looked down at the seating chart then looked up at him and asked, "Would a booth be all right?"

"You're a doll. I knew you could pull it off." The hostess led Shep and Madison to one of the best tables in the restaurant. It was a booth overlooking a pond with a fountain in the middle that was lit up, casting its lights on two white swans floating in the water.

Chapter 5

"Good evening and welcome to The Circle. My name is Emile and I'll be your waiter this evening. May I start you off with something from the bar?" The waiter was impeccably dressed in a crisp black shirt, black pants and a white apron tied around his waist. His accent was hard to pin point but it lent itself to the European ambience of the restaurant.

Shep gestured to Madison with an open hand looking for her to give the waiter her order. "I'll have a club soda please with a slice of lime." Looking at Madison in shocked amazement, Shep gave the waiter his order for a black Russian.

The waiter courteously responded back with a "Very good, sir.", and then asked if there was anything else they needed before he left the table.

When the waiter was out of earshot, Shep, staring into Madison's eyes, told her how incredible she looked. "You're even more gorgeous than when I last saw you. The years have only enhanced your beauty." Not wanting to react to his words, Madison's eyes blinked non-stop in an effort not to say a word and especially not to gush. Even though she never really got over the hurt and anger he had caused her, it was very difficult to resist his good looks and charm. Over time, she had just moved on with her life. Shep continued complementing her until, in a very undiplomatic way, he commented on her drink order. "Club soda. Are you in a program?" She knew exactly what he meant by "program", and told him no, it was just that she had a very tiresome day and if she drank she might just fall asleep right there at the table. Shep continued pressing the subject. "In the old days you could put away five or six on two hours of sleep. You've really changed."

Taking a shot back, Madison said, "And it appears you haven't."

Not wanting to get into an argument, Shep pointed out that he was in town for only a short while, so why not leave things in the past, but not before adding one more comment. "I thought you were over that by now."

Madison could see the waiter approaching with their drinks; she took the opportunity to let the topic go.

After this initial confrontation, the two of them mellowed out. While Shep drank his black Russian, and Madison sipped her club soda, they started to reminisce about the past. Actually, it was Shep who dominated the conversation as he filled her in on what he had been doing these past few years. He talked about traveling to different cities to play poker, never seeing more than the inside of casinos and hotel lobbies. He went on and on telling her all about the bad beats and how the "donkeys" lucked out. It seemed, at least according to Shep, that any player who called his bets and raises, even though the odds were against them, and then wins the hand was a "donkey."

As he gave a play-by-play description of his most memorable poker hands, whether he won or lost, Madison sat still with a far-off look in her eyes as if she wasn't present. She was also rubbing the fingers on her left hand together in a rhythmic motion over and over and over. Shep kept on talking till he took notice and asked, "Madison, are you even listening?"

She sat silently for a few more seconds before snapping to. "What? Did you say something?"

Shep snapped, "I said a lot! I guess whatever you were thinking about was more important."

Emile returned to inform Shep and Madison of the dinner specials and to take their order. Each dish he described sounded more delicious than the next. There was a five-pound lobster dinner for two that was tempting, but the pair said they preferred a non-seafood meal. Shep ordered a glass of Malbec to go with his dinner. Emile said, "Very good, sir," and left with their dinner order. The pace of dinner was leisurely, and eventually, Emile and another waiter arrived. They were each carrying a dinner plate covered with a silver dome. Emile set one in front of Madison and politely said, "Madame, your Veal Oscar," while the second waiter set the other plate in front of Shep and said, "Sir, your bone-in rib eye."

Simultaneously, the two waiters lifted off the silver domes and, in unison, recited, "Bon appétit."

Emile asked if there was anything else they might need and mentioned that he would check back shortly. Madison remarked that the presentation was unique and the service was impeccable. Shep concurred that it was impressive. They savored their dinners, and while Madison dined with Shep, the days of being a couple were long past.

She talked about her real estate business, how it had grown, never mentioning the missing money or Frank's murder and the near-miss fatal accident. She wanted to forget her troubles for the evening as much as possible because in the morning, they would still be there for her to deal with. As the conversation continued, a vibration of sexual tension could be felt between them. Shep had always exuded an overpowering magnetism, and if you were the target of his attention like Madison had been, you couldn't help but fall under his spell. Madison could feel his eyes upon her the entire evening and repeatedly reminded herself that it appeared he hadn't changed.

During dinner, Shep's phone buzzed, letting him know he had a text message. He excused himself as he read it and replied back to the sender. After hitting the send button, his attention quickly returned to Madison. The conversation changed from poker to current events. Madison became more lighthearted, laughing at times. Aware that her feelings were softening, she avoided looking directly into his eyes, afraid of being drawn in.

Emile reappeared at their table. "May I take your plates?" he asked. Shep nodded yes, and Emile went about removing them, stacking the plates up his arm proficiently and leaving with them. Having cleared the table, he returned with a crumber and swept the table clean of any food that may have dropped on the starched white tablecloth. He placed a dessert menu in front of Madison and Shep and asked if they would like a cappuccino.

"Cappuccino sounds good," Madison said. "But no dessert for me." Shep ordered the same, and Emile left to get their coffee.

Shep had spent the past few hours having dinner with Madison and never once mentioned the poker tournament that brought him to town or tried pressuring her into playing. It was all too good to be true. Then as if on cue, Shep brought up the tournament.

"This tournament coming up is going to be a big deal. They're expecting a couple thousand players. It's eight million dollars in prize money." He stopped talking for a second, like an experienced salesman, letting the possibility of winning eight million dollars sink in. When she didn't say anything, he asked her point-blank, "So you haven't been playing poker?"

Madison emphatically responded, "Absolutely not!"

He pressed on. "Don't you miss the excitement or money, the good times?" His voice went up when he spoke the words *good times*.

The inference to their sexual relationship was very obvious, but Madison wasn't going to acknowledge the intense sexual feelings they had shared, nor the high she got when playing poker. In the past, her attraction to cards was as strong as her attraction had been to Shep.

Without skipping a beat, he continued the pitch. "Do you remember the time we sat down at a low stakes game? Had to be our usual playing time, like nine, nine thirty, you know, after dinner. We'd been grinding away for hours not making much money, getting bored as hell. I think it was around midnight when we decided to play a higher stakes game, three hundred, six hundred. We'd made a bet between the two of us. Whoever had the most money by 6:00 a.m. would give the loser fifty percent of their winnings. I was ahead till that player called an all-in and threw a twenty-dollar gold coin in the pot. We both made the call, and you won the hand. The next day, we went to the pawnshop and found out it was worth ten thousand dollars, and I had to cough up my fifty percent." He was enjoying reminiscing about days gone by.

"Ah, those were exciting times. Money flowed easily, and you were the hottest thing in the room. You still are." He fell silent momentarily and took a drink of his cappuccino, allowing his compliment to resonate with Madison.

While he had been absorbed talking about the past, Madison couldn't help focusing on their sexual relationship. Shep was not her first sexual encounter, but he was the best lover she had ever had. A man like Shep, good-looking and confidence enough for ten men, had plenty of experience with women. His repertoire enabled him to become an expert at pleasing a woman.

Memories of the two of them in bed making love came rushing over her like a tidal wave. Her stomach had chills running through it, and she felt a warmth between her legs. Madison took a last sip of her cappuccino to dispel the thoughts and softly replied, "Thank you."

She looked down at her watch and saw that it was very late. She told Shep that it was good to see him, but it was time for her to leave since she had an early start the next day. He honored her request and asked for the bill. As the pair walked out into the lobby, Shep walked over to the hostess and gave her a kiss on the cheek and said, "Good night, honey, thanks for the great table."

Madison had never seen a face turn so red. The young woman looked as if she'd been lying under a tropical sun for hours and had a second-degree sunburn.

The two of them made their way out of the restaurant and down the steps. Shep asked Madison where she parked, and she told him that she had used the valet service. The valet was not in sight, so Shep waited with her. The valet returned with another patron's car and then went over to Madison. She handed her claim check to him to bring her car around. A couple of minutes later, the valet, instead of driving back with Madison's car, came running back. He explained that when he went to get her vehicle, he noticed the rear tire was flat. "Ma'am, if you have a spare tire, I'll be happy to change it for you," he offered.

She thought to herself, *What an idiot I am* as she replied to him, "Yes, I do have one, but it's in my garage. I took it out when I was moving furniture last week."

Shep instantly took charge and tipped the valet generously. He asked for Madison's keys, saying that he would drive the lady home and then get the car tomorrow. The valet handed over her keys, and as a courtesy, brought around Shep's car. Madison laughed and called Shep her "shining knight." Both seated and buckled in, Shep asked Madison for her address to put in the navigation system. She didn't want her address in the nav's memory, making it easy for Shep to pay her a future visit. Flustered about how to respond to his request, she told him, "That won't be necessary. I can give you directions."

"It'll be more convenient," he told her. Picking up on her hesitation, he convincingly added, "Don't worry, I'll delete it, if that's what you're worried about." Madison unwillingly gave him the address and looked out the window while the voice on the navigation system spoke the turn-by-turn directions.

Chapter 6

Ten miles down the interstate, there was a sign for the casino. Shep pointed it out. He waited to hear what Madison's response would be. She didn't say a word.

"That text I received during dinner, it was from a friend who asked me to come by the casino and bring him the money I owe him." Madison was tired and feeling the effects of her recent injuries. She hadn't set foot in a casino since her relationship with Shep ended five years ago. Entering one now was the last thing she wanted to do—and especially with him. She had had enough dredging up of old memories for one evening. Shep, true to his nature, persisted in an effort to get his way.

"He's on a heater, baby, and can't leave. It's just the next exit, and I'll be in and out." Madison stood her ground. "I really need to get home."

Shep put the pressure on. "It's on the way to your home. I'll make it quick." She didn't have the energy to argue with him any further and said okay.

Putting his turn signal on and moving into the exit lane, he followed the signs to the Garden's casino. The parking lot was jam-packed. The first available spot was located a long distance from the main entrance, and he took it. Taking his key out of the ignition, he got out of the car but noticed that Madison was still buckled in her seat. He popped his head back in the door and asked, "Aren't you coming in?"

Preferring to stay put, she told him, "No, I'll be fine. Hurry back."

He pointed out that it was too dangerous to leave a beautiful woman sitting all alone in a parked car and that anything can happen. Shep had persuaded her that she would be safer with him. Feeling manipulated, Madison unbuckled her seat belt, opened the passenger door, and entered the casino with Shep. When they got inside, they headed straight for the poker room. Bright neon signs pointed the way.

They passed aisle upon aisle of slot machines, and the overwhelming sound of *ding, ding, ding* coming from the machines caused a ringing in Madison's ears. The blackjack tables were filled with players, drinking and cheering when they won, moaning when they lost. The disappointed cries from players who lost their bets at the roulette wheel rang out. Players at the craps tables shouted out their bets, "Give me five on yo, I want ten on number eight." The casino was buzzing with activity even though it was a weeknight. It seemed like nobody had to go to work the next morning. Cigarette smoke permeated the air, reminding Madison what it was like to be in a casino. There was a certain excitement being there while at the same time, she felt a disdain for the people sucked into the ephemeral experience of winning.

Reaching the poker room, Shep went over to the desk and asked where the ten twenty Texas Hold 'Em table was. The hostess promptly replied, "Table fifty-five, six rows down on your left." Shep and Madison walked past row upon row of poker tables all lined up like desks in a busy New York office until he came to table fifty-five.

His friend, Sam, spotted him first. Sam got up from his seat, walked over to Shep, and gave him a man hug. "Hey, bro. Thanks for coming," he said.

Shep reached into his pocket and pulled out a wad of hundred-dollar bills and handed it over to Sam. They talked a couple of minutes about the action at the table. Shep looked back at Madison, who was patiently waiting for him to leave. "Gotta run," Shep said.

Sam asked him to join him for a drink. "Better yet, why don't you play? There's an empty seat."

It was tempting. The allure of the cards was overwhelming. Shep walked over to Madison and gently put both hands around her arms and whispered in her ear, "I'll stay just long enough to double up, and then we'll go. I promise."

To seal the deal, Shep kissed her hard on the lips. It had been five years since Madison felt tingling like that. Before she could object, he raced off to buy his chips, leaving her standing there, a mountain of Jell-O. She took a seat at a nearby table, still feeling his kiss upon her lips.

As the sensation wore off, she took out her phone to check for messages. Madison went back to playing Candy Crush while waiting for Shep. She waited patiently for over an hour before going over to Shep and tapping him on the shoulder. She leaned over and quietly reminded him of his promise. "You said just long enough to double up. Looks like you've done more than that."

It was déjà vu. Walking away, Madison could hear the dealer say to Shep, "The action's on you."

He had to decide between going after Madison or playing the hand. Shep looked at his cards for a few seconds then put them down. In a deep voice, he said, "Raise."

Madison went to the lobby of the casino and called Uber for a ride. *When you're a gambler, the poker cards are your first love, and everything else comes second.*

Chapter 7

In spite of being exhausted, sleep refused to come. Madison tossed and turned, stressing about how she was going to replace Nikolai's money. The memory of Nikolai choking a man in his office played over and over in her mind followed by the thought of his murdered partner whose killer was never found. Madison was frightened that this might be her fate.

She looked at her clock and two hours had passed without falling asleep. When Madison was a young child and too scared of the dark to sleep, her mother had taught her to repeat the Lord's Prayer until she fell off to sleep. It worked, and the young Madison would be out like a light. As a grown woman, Madison gave it a try.

"Our Father who art in heaven..." Madison murmured. The prayer had the same effect on her, and soon she was fast asleep.

The next morning when Madison awoke, she went into the kitchen to make coffee then into her office while it was brewing and sat down at her desk. That would be the only routine thing she did that day. The reality of the missing money was as fresh on her mind as the first day she learned of it. Having told Nikolai the truth about the money being gone was a first step but definitely not a solution. With Frank gone, and not a clue as to where the money had disappeared to, she wondered how she was she going to get her hands on such a large sum.

Racking her brain, one thought came to mind. Her retirement account surely must have had over two hundred thousand dollars in it. Perhaps she could withdraw the funds or at least borrow against it.

Madison looked up the number for Dan Greene, the agent who handled her 401k, and called him. Luckily, Dan was in his office and available to take her call.

"Dan, good morning, it's Madison Mitchell. How are you?"

He replied that he was doing well. "I saw Frank's obituary in the paper. How are you holding up?" he asked.

Madison politely replied that she was taking it one day at a time.

"I was sorry to read about Frank's sudden passing. If there's anything I can do, please don't hesitate to ask," he offered.

"Thank you for your concern," Madison responded back. "I'm okay for now."

Upon hearing that she was all right under the circumstances, Dan asked her, "What did you want to talk about?"

She didn't know where to begin. Not wanting to show the desperation in her voice, she casually said, "With Frank gone, the business is going to change. I wanted to know how much money was in my retirement account."

Dan said to hold on a minute while he pulled up the account. He came back on the phone and said that the market had been up and that he had her money in very conservative funds to avoid a loss of principal. Madison wanted to shout, "Just tell me how much my account is worth," but she kept her cool all the while Dan was talking. Finally, he gave her the answer she was looking for. "There's well over two hundred thousand dollars. Two hundred and sixty-six thousand to be exact." Hearing that it was more than enough to pay off Nikolai, Madison was home free.

Madison took a deep breath and told him that she wanted to withdraw some money. Surprised, Dan asked her if she was retiring to which Madison said no. He started to give her a lesson on early withdrawal before legal retirement age and how she would incur penalties and taxes, etcetera, etcetera. She put her hand up to say "Stop," acting as if Dan could see her, and in her most assertive voice said, "I just need it for an emergency."

Taken aback, Dan said in a slow southern accent, "Oh well, in that case." He stopped talking, leaving Madison lingering. "In addition to all the reasons I mentioned, there's more. It's not impossible, but it won't be easy."

Madison's nerves were doing somersaults. Somewhat relieved to hear that it wasn't impossible, Madison sat back in her desk chair and relaxed a little. Asking what she would need to do, Dan replied, "I said it's not impossible, but it's going to take at least six months." Her heart sank, and all the nervousness she had been feeling returned. He went on to explain that her retirement account was held by her company, and unlike an individual IRA, there were more federal regulations that had to be followed. To add to her troubles, he spelled out that she would now have to go through a legal process for a proper dissolution of the company's assets. Hopefully, Frank had a will, he added. Dan continued to advise Madison that all this takes time, and if Frank didn't have a will, then settling the company's business would be an even longer process.

Madison had tuned Dan out when he had said six months and never heard a word he said after that. Feeling even more despair than before, she thought to herself, *Just shoot me now.* She thanked him for his time and said she would get back to him.

Madison disconnected the call and placed her arms on her desk, resting her head upon them. She wanted to cry. The tears in her eyes started to bubble to the surface. She hated crying. It reminded her of her brother's merciless teasing when she would cry as a child. Ever since then, she stifled the desire. Instead, to stop the tears from coming, she closed her eyes and pictured happy situations from her past and dwelled on positive thoughts. Mentally transporting herself to the beach, she imagined that she was lying on a chaise under the Caribbean sun, getting a tan in her bikini-clad body as the sound of the turquoise-colored ocean lulled her to sleep, and for the moment, she forgot the awful reality of her situation.

Regaining control of her emotions, Madison pushed her chair closer to her desk and asked out loud, "Okay, what's next?" Remembering that she had made coffee, she went into the kitchen to get a cup. In an attempt at humor, she grabbed for a cup and said to herself, "I definitely need a black cup of coffee today." With her cup in hand, she returned to her office to ponder her options. She sat down in her desk chair, and with her elbow on the arm, she put her hand to her forehead and once again went back to the drawing board to think about other solutions that might have been available to her.

Madison drew a big, fat blank. She wondered if there was anyone else she could call. Cathy's name instantly came to mind. Not wanting to disturb her if she was in court, Madison texted her to see if it was a good time to talk. Cathy called her immediately and asked, "What do you need, girlfriend?" Madison explained that she wanted to borrow a very large sum of money. "Just how large are you talking about?" Cathy asked. Too apprehensive to respond, Madison hesitated a moment. Then she got out the words. "Two hundred and fifty thousand dollars."

Shocked, Cathy couldn't imagine why Madison would need such an enormous amount of money. "What's wrong? Is it your head injury, the hospital bill?" Cathy asked. Madison explained that the escrow monies belonging to her client had gone missing. Frank had written a check and withdrawn the funds, and now, with his death, she didn't know where the money was or how to replace it.

Cathy was a litigating attorney and knew how serious this was. She was alarmed and worried for her friend. Madison could be charged with embezzlement if she didn't come up with the money and find herself in jail. Cathy explained to Madison that right now, she was financially strapped. She had used all of her savings and took out loans to buy into her law practice when she became a partner in the firm. Cathy was most apologetic and told Madison that she would do anything in her power to help, including taking out more loans. Madison felt so badly for putting her friend on the spot and told her things would turn out okay. She thanked Cathy for always being there for her and that she considered her more like a sister than a friend. They said goodbye, and Cathy said she would see what she could do to help come up with the money.

Madison blamed herself for not having any savings of her own. She thought, *I'm house rich and cash poor. If only I hadn't spent all my money on real estate.* Then it dawned on her that she could refinance her properties.

With renewed hope, Madison searched her contacts for mortgage brokers. She had worked with many of them over the years but was looking for one in particular named Jeff Morgan. He was sharp and creative. When it came to financing, if anyone was going to be able to help her, it was Jeff.

She picked up the phone to call his number. Before she could dial the first digit, a call was coming through, and she answered it. "Good morning, Bay Realty, Madison speaking."

The voice on the other end responded with, "Hey, doll, good morning to you." It was Shep, and Madison didn't have time to deal with him, nor did she care to. She was pissed off with him for keeping her out so late at the casino and then, to add insult to injury, she had to find her own ride home. Madison minced no words telling him that she was extremely busy, and he was the last person she would make time for. "Look, I understand, and I'm sorry," came his response. "But you still need to get your car, and I was going to come over and pick you up."

She did need to get her car and, if he was able to drive her to the restaurant, that would be a big help. "I can be there in forty-five minutes," he told her. Resigned to having to see him again, she curtly said fine then added, "I need to shower and dress and give you directions."

"That won't be necessary. I've still got it in my NAV system," he told her. "See you soon. Goodbye."

"Bye," Madison said.

Rolling her eyes, Madison had caught him in another lie; just like he wasn't planning on leaving the casino after dropping off the money, he never had any intention of deleting her address either. She popped into the shower and took her time getting ready. Madison was buttoning the last button on her blue denim shirt when she heard the doorbell ring. Shep, unlike his usual tardy self, showed up on time. In his own small way, he was trying to make things right between them. They went into the garage to get the spare tire and placed it in the trunk of Shep's car. Together, riding to the restaurant to retrieve her vehicle, the air was filled with tension.

Aside from being mad at Shep, Madison's mind was on her troubles. They manifested themselves physically, and she felt a constant pain in her stomach. Her neck and shoulders were in a knot from all the stress. In her mind, she ran idea after idea on how she could get her hands on a quarter of a million dollars. Each time when she came up empty, she grew more anxious.

Finally, in an effort to get her mind off her problems, she made small talk with Shep, asking if he still lived in the same condo where they had lived together in Las Vegas. He told her that poker had been very profitable for him and that he was able to move to a nicer part of town.

Then, like the night before at dinner, he flattered her, complimenting Madison on her looks and how she had kept in shape. He sounded sincere. But Shep was good at that.

Madison wondered if this time he was being genuine. While she didn't want to start anew with him, she couldn't help feeling a warmth for him like she did when their relationship originally started. He had that effect on women, and when he honed in like he did with Madison, there was no escaping.

Once they arrived to The Circle parking lot, Shep jumped out of the car and began changing her tire. "You know these spares are only good for fifty miles, so you're going to have to get a new tire as soon as possible."

"I will," Madison promised. As he worked, he mentioned he would be in town for a few days. "I'd like to get together with you again, how 'bout it?" He lowered his head just a little as he spoke, giving him a sheepish look, but that broad smile and full lips were more wolf in appearance. Madison was caught off guard and smiled then simply said, "I'm kinda busy right now, but we'll see. Thanks again for your help." Shep let it go, and they parted in peace. At least for now.

Chapter 8

Wanting to get home as quickly as possible and make the call regarding refinancing her property, Madison wasn't going to take the time to get another tire. She got in her car and drove directly home. Once inside her house, she threw her keys on the hall table along with her handbag and grabbed her cell phone on the way into her office. She dialed the number to California Home Lending, picking up where she had left off just before Shep had called.

When the receptionist answered the call, Madison asked to speak with Jeff Morgan and was told that Mr. Morgan was in a meeting and was unavailable to speak with her. Madison, desperate to talk with him, asked how long he would be. "I'm not quite sure," came the answer, "but I can put you through to his voice mail if you like." Madison left him a detailed message but wasn't going to wait around for his call. She went back to her contact list of mortgage brokers and searched for Amy Patterson's number. She was another mortgage person that Madison had dealings with and liked very much. She located Amy's personal number and placed the call.

When Amy answered the phone, Madison said, "Hi, Amy, it's Madison Mitchell."

"Hello, Madison. How are you?" Amy's voice was cheerful, and just hearing it lifted up Madison's spirits.

"I'm fine. I suppose you heard about the death of my business partner, Frank Jensen?" When Amy said no, that she hadn't heard a word, Madison briefly filled her in and accepted her condolences. Madison then explained that she needed to refinance her property.

Amy was involved in making the original mortgages on several of her properties. She asked which one she wanted to refinance. "Is it your personal residence or one of your investment properties that you're looking to refi?"

Madison told her it was one of her rentals. Still upbeat and cheerful, Amy continued on, "Okay, we can refinance the rental property, but the interest rate is a little higher than if it was your primary home." Madison could care less at this point about what the interest rate was. It could have been 50 percent, and she would have gone ahead with this plan just the same.

The only thing she cared about was how fast she could get her hands on the money. Fearful of Amy's answer, Madison cautiously asked, "How long will it take to get it done?" to which Amy replied, "I can get it closed in thirty days, maybe twenty if I push real hard." Madison thought to herself that it might be enough time if she was lucky, and given that her back was up against a wall, it would have to do.

Somewhat reassured, she said to Amy, "Let's do it!"

"All right, I'm going to need some information." Amy asked her the standard litany of questions required when applying for a mortgage. Then when she asked if Madison wanted to get cash out, there was a pause, to which Madison said, "Yes, definitely, that's why I'm doing this." Amy continued her line of questioning, asking how much the property was worth and the dollar amount of the remaining mortgage balance. Madison had all the information at her fingertips. After answering all of her questions, it turned out that Madison would only be able to get fifteen thousand dollars by refinancing. That amount was a drop in a very big bucket and wasn't going to help. Madison then asked how much money she could get if she refinanced all of her properties. Amy took down the information. "I'll get back to you in about twenty minutes."

After saying goodbye, Madison sat back in her chair. She tapped her fingernails on the desk in a monotone beat. She did this for a couple of minutes then looked at her watch, expecting the twenty minutes to have passed. "I need to keep busy," she told herself. She picked up a pile of papers sitting on the corner of her desk, planning to clean, when the phone rang. *Could this be Amy calling back so soon?* she hoped.

"Hello, Madison." It was the unmistakable voice of Nikolai.

Dreading what was to come, Madison politely said, "Hello, Nikolai. How are you?"

He responded back with, "More importantly, how are you?"

She didn't catch his drift and asked, "What are you talking about?"

"I heard you had a little run-in last night."

Confused, she asked, "How did you know about that?"

Nikolai responded, "A little birdie told me."

Suspicious that Nikolai may have had something to do with the menacing driver, she was about to ask him if he was involved. There was the sound of a click; he hung up on her. This caused Madison to become more desperate than ever to get Nikolai his money. She didn't know where to begin coming up with a quarter of a million dollars.

Her eyes strayed to a picture on her desk of Frank, taken when they were vacationing together in Napa Valley Wine Country. She focused on his picture, recalling happier times in her life. Although business partners, it was not unusual for them to occasionally vacation together. Madison picked up the silver frame and held it in her hand, wistfully remembering the day it was taken.

It was the weekend they had closed on a huge real estate deal. They had been working on it for eight months, and it earned them the largest commission check they ever received. To celebrate, Madison suggested they go out to dinner at one of Los Angeles's five-star restaurants.

Frank had an even better idea. He thought that instead, they should drive up the California coast to Napa and Sonoma counties and spend a long weekend in the Wine Country. Feeling exuberant, they high-fived each other and agreed to meet at 4:00 a.m. the next morning. Frank picked up Madison at four on the dot, and by noon, they were sipping wine.

Sterling Winery was located on top of the Mayacamas mountain range. They had ridden a tram, like the ones in Switzerland, to reach the tasting room.

After sampling several cabernet sauvignons, merlots and pinot noirs, Frank and Madison went outside to the patio to sit at one of the many wrought iron café tables. They ordered a glass of the winery's award-winning Reserve Chardonnay and enjoyed the breathtaking view. The color of the sky was a robin's-egg blue with white clouds that looked like puffs of smoke providing a beautiful contrast.

In the distance was the lush canopy of trees on the surrounding mountain tops. The sun was overpoweringly bright, but the warmth it provided was a fair trade-off. It was an idyllic setting and a perfect photo opportunity. Madison, wanting to take advantage of it, asked Frank to pose on the rock wall surrounding the patio. A woman walked by and offered to take a picture of the two of them. Frank wrapped both his arms around Madison's shoulders and, embracing her, gave her a kiss. That picture was the one she was now holding in her hands.

While grasping the sides of the frame, a strange feeling fell over her. She was about to put the picture back on her desk when unfamiliar images came flowing into her mind. She saw Frank lying naked in bed, an arm with a heart tattoo, and then the images went blank.

She couldn't understand where these visions were coming from. It couldn't have been a memory because he didn't have a tattoo. Feeling shaken as if her body had been taken over by someone, she threw the picture down.

Madison glanced at her office clock. Only ten minutes had gone by since she had talked to Amy. Madison was losing it. She decided not to wait for Amy's call and dialed her number.

Amy answered the phone, and fortunately for Madison, she had finished crunching the numbers. Madison took a deep breath, fearing the worst, and said, "Okay, tell me what you got."

Amy, not knowing how much Madison needed, eagerly replied, "I can get you seventy-five to eighty-five thousand dollars." She expected Madison to be excited. Amy waited to hear Madison's response before she continued. Still six figures short of the two hundred and fifty thousand dollars that she needed, Madison felt sick to her stomach. Instead of saying that would work, she told Amy that she would get back to her and abruptly hung up the receiver.

This time around, Madison couldn't control the tears from coming. No amount of positive thoughts could stop the crying. She laid her head down on her desk and howled. All the stress she had kept hidden below the surface the past few days came out in her tears. She gasped as the tears pooled around her head. There was no solution to the dilemma she found herself in.

The news of Frank's death, the potential of losing her business after all her years of hard work, the veiled death threat from Nikolai all played into her emotions. The breaking point was Shep's return, reminding her of the past she had finally put behind her.

Chapter 9

Still sitting with her head resting on the cold, hard glass desktop, she thought back to when she had first met Shep. Seven years ago, she and five of her girlfriends had flown to Las Vegas to celebrate Cathy's birthday. Arriving at the Bellagio, they had assembled in the lobby like a group of sorority sisters going to their first fraternity party.

They were young, gorgeous, horny, and so loud that the guests all the way on the other side of the expansive lobby turned around to see what all the racket was about. It was Madison and her friends checking in. They were feeling high from the airplane drinks and the excitement of being in Las Vegas.

After settling into their rooms, they met in the lobby bar to start the birthday celebration. The alcohol flowed, and several hours later and a bar bill for six hundred dollars, the girls headed back to their rooms to get dressed for a night of dancing and more drinking.

Since the action in Las Vegas didn't heat up till 11:00 p.m., they planned on meeting up around nine to grab a bite to eat and then go clubbing. They stayed up all night partying and drinking.

At dawn, Madison and her friends, with their shoes in their hands, looking disheveled and exhausted, were obviously very drunk. They dragged themselves through the hotel lobby on their way to the elevators to their rooms. Too tired and too drunk, no one said a word.

They slept in till early afternoon and somehow managed to wake up in time to catch some sun poolside. Cathy suggested that this evening, they hit the casino before they go clubbing and leave the drinking till later. They all agreed that would be wise.

Later that evening, dressed in their hottest-looking dresses, hems three inches below their panties and wearing heels that were more like stilts than shoes, the girls headed to the casino.

As they walked three abreast and in two rows, all eyes were on them. They laughed and giggled their way to the craps table. The guys were eager to move over and let the ladies squeeze in and play. "You can stand next to me, there's plenty of room," said a good-look-ing man in his forties, dressed in jeans and a blazer, shifting to his right to make room for Julia on the rail. He rolled both dice, and the numbers four and six landed faceup. The dealer placed the marker on the number ten. Players rushed to place their bets hoping to win side bets before the shooter rolled a seven. The next roll of the dice came up six, and players took their winnings as he continued rolling. He kept rolling winning numbers, and the players at the table cheered loudly as they were paid on their bets. On the eighth roll of the dice, a five and a two came up. He had crapped out. The players let out sounds of disappointment while others said, "Good run, man," and clapped their hands.

He passed the dice to Julia, who placed them in the palm of her hand and threw them hard against the back wall of the table. The dealer said "Nine" and proceeded to place the marker on the number nine. As Julia rolled the dice, the men around the table were shouting out, "Come on, honey, you can do it," and "Daddy wants a new pair of shoes."

Each time she rolled the dice, she would lean over the rail to throw them. Her low-cut dress gave the men on the other side of the craps table a view of her breasts. They cheered her on, hoping her turn would never end, but unfortunately, it was short-lived. The dice passed from player to player while the guys flirted with Cathy and her friends nonstop. The laughter was loud and continuous. While Madison waited her turn to throw the dice, she glanced over to a blackjack table. Frank had often told her how much money he had won playing that game. It caught her interest, and she decided to try her luck. She told her friends to come get her when it was time to leave and walked over to the table. The guys at the craps table all let out an "Aw" as she left and shouted out, "Don't leave."

Madison put her chips on the blackjack table and was dealt two cards. She had a vague idea on how to play the game, winning some hands, but mostly losing. After several losses, she was dealt a ten of hearts and a two of spades, making a total of twelve.

Frustrated, she sat there looking at them, then looking at the dealer and saying out loud, "I don't know what to do." A voice from behind her said, "Take another card."

She told the dealer, "Hit me." It was a nine of hearts, making twenty-one and winning the hand for her.

She turned around to thank the person for his tip, and looking up, she saw this gorgeous man standing over her shoulder. Madison had never seen anybody so handsome in person; she literally couldn't believe her eyes.

He exuded such sexuality, and in the flash of that second, she wondered what it would be like to kiss him. He sat down next to her, put out his hand, and introduced himself, "Good evening. I'm Ben Shepherd." Reaching for his hand, she could feel the heat emanating from it, making her that much more excited.

To hide her nervousness, she overcompensated by becoming assertive and faking confidence in her voice. "I'm Madison Mitchell. Nice to meet you." That was how she managed to deal with the likes of Nikolai and other strong personalities she came across. Ben took out a roll of hundred-dollar bills from his pocket and bought chips to play with. She also bought more since she was now down to twenty-five dollars from the two hundred she originally started with.

Within a few minutes, Ben Shepherd made a move. His opening line wasn't very original, but she didn't care. She wanted the opportunity to talk with him and to smell his cologne as he leaned into her. "So what brings you to Vegas?" he asked. She thought about telling him it was her friend's birthday, but that sounded so boring. Instead, she chose to be humorous. "I always wanted to get married at the Elvis Chapel."

"Where's the lucky groom?" Ben asked.

"I haven't met him yet," Madison teased.

She went on to ask him what he was doing in Vegas. He told her that he was originally from Switzerland, but now Vegas was home and that he liked to play poker. "Ben, do you play for a living?" she asked. He admitted to being a professional poker player then added that his friends called him Shep.

Madison gave him one of her smiles that drew attention to her full lips, perfect white teeth, and then her turquoise blue eyes. "Oh, we're friends now, are we?"

She was becoming more irresistible by the minute, and it seemed that the tables were turned. He was now more nervous talking to her than she was when he first sat down. He kept his cool, and leaning closer to Madison, Shep whispered in her ear, "I'd like to be."

Ignoring the tingling sensation in her stomach, she looked at her cards, asking Shep what she should do. He pointed out her next play, and within a short period of time, she started to win. Instead of being down hundreds of dollars, she had won almost a thousand bucks and was bitten by the gambling bug. The more she won, the more she was hooked.

Shep asked Madison where she lived and, since she had just met him, hesitatingly told him Los Angeles. He told her that he periodically played poker nearby at the Commerce Casino.

Suddenly, the noise around them grew louder than it had been. Her friends rushed up to Madison, and all five were talking at the same time, telling her how much fun they had and how much money they won. Their plan to stay sober until later didn't work out, and they were tipsy and silly.

"Come on, girlfriend, time to go dancing," shouted Cathy as she did a side to side body wave. Madison picked up her chips and put them in her purse. Turning toward Shep, she took one last whiff of him and told him, "It was nice playing with you, and thanks for the lesson." He hadn't gotten her phone number, and before he could ask her for it, she went off with her friends.

Their first stop on their list of nightclubs was Rain, located in the Palms Casino. They danced and drank until Vanessa suggested they go to Tao in the Venetian because that's where the Hollywood stars hung out. They got in the very long cab line at the Palms and rode to the Venetian. Tao was everything they had heard it would be. A seat at a table cost a thousand dollars and included a bottle of Cristal champagne. Fortunately, they were young and hot and had no trouble getting drinks paid for by the guys draped around the bar, looking for action.

They danced with a group of guys from Germany then danced with one another and even danced with other women. It was an incredible party scene, and everybody was letting loose. Electronic music was playing nonstop, and everyone was either hammered or high on drugs.

While standing at the bar, Cathy heard someone talking about a movie that just came out that had been filmed at a local nightspot, the Voodoo Lounge. In addition to being the setting for a movie, the club was awesome and had the best views of Las Vegas. Since Cathy was the birthday girl, and anything she wanted that night was hers, she rounded up her posse to check it out.

They arrived at the Rio Casino where the Voodoo Lounge was located and took the elevator up fifty-one stories to the rooftop. It was jam-packed with beautiful women, each one more beautiful than the next, and great-looking guys. This was the place to be and to be seen. The girls headed over to the bar, and it wasn't long before some guys bought them drinks. Cathy and Madison headed straight for the outdoor lounge to see the beautiful Las Vegas skyline.

They stood there for a minute taking it all in but quickly went inside to find their friends, who were already on the dance floor. Cathy began dancing, and Madison went to the bar and ordered a martini. Handing the drink to her, the bartender shouted so he could be heard, "That'll be twenty dollars." Madison reached into her purse, preparing to pay. A voice from behind her said, "I got it." She turned around and saw a man hand the bartender the money. Madison thanked him, and they began talking. They stood there, squeezed in at the bar, drinking and making small talk. He made a comment about the Voodoo Lounge being the best place on the strip to pick up the prettiest women. If that was supposed to be a compliment, Madison didn't take it that way. She was polite but determined that she wasn't really interested in him. Madison looked around to see if one of her friends was nearby to rescue her, but they were some-where on the crowded dance floor. She thanked him again for the drink and excused herself to go to the ladies' room.

When she returned to the lounge, she eluded him and went outside to the rooftop to sit. All the drinking she had done at the other clubs was catching up to her, and she didn't want to get sick and throw up.

The lounge was higher than all the other hotels, and the view seemed even more spectacular than before. It was windy being so high up, and she felt chilly, especially in a skimpy dress. She hugged herself to keep warm, but then she felt a jacket slipping onto her shoulders.

"This will keep you warm," the voice said. It was Shep. She was surprised to see him, almost suspecting he followed her there but delighted just the same.

"Once again, Shep to the rescue," she said, to which he replied, "At your service, Mademoiselle." She knew in that moment that this guy was going to be trouble, delicious trouble, and that she wouldn't be able to help herself. He sat down next to her.

"What a beautiful view. This is one of my favorite nightspots," he said.

Curious what he was doing there and trying to determine if he came in hopes of seeing her, Madison asked him why he wasn't at the poker table. He explained that he had had an extremely lucrative day and had learned the hard way to get up from the tables when he was ahead.

He asked her if he could buy her a drink. Madison declined, saying that she came out to sober up. Their conversation was superfi-cial, and Madison wanted to make it real. She wanted to know more about this guy, like when did he come to the States, how he got into poker, and why he played for a living. She realized that he must be able to read people well in order to be successful at poker and asked him if he could tell when a player was bluffing or not. Humble in his answer, he said that he hoped so.

I wonder if he can read me? she thought to herself. Flirting with him as she tried to gain insight into him, she asked, "If I was playing poker with you, would you be able to tell if I was bluffing?"

He let out a laugh and with a broad smile said, "Definitely!"

Feeling hurt that she was so obvious, she asked him to elaborate. "You have a tell. Every time you're unsure of what to do, like at the blackjack table, you bite your lower lip. That's a dead giveaway that you don't have the nuts."

"The nuts?" Madison asked.

Shep explained the meaning to her. "The winning hand."

"Oh, okay, so you don't think I can put on a poker face, do you?"

"Not unless you change that habit," he shot back.

"I'm a quick learner." When he asked her if she would like to play some poker now, Madison took that as a challenge. Although not quite sobered up, she told him yes. They went to find her friends to let them know that she was leaving and would return to the hotel on her own.

Chapter 10

They grabbed a cab and went over to the Wynn. When they got there, Madison stopped in the gift shop and picked up a pair of sunglasses. She had seen poker players on TV wearing the proverbial sunglasses. Before they went in the poker room, Shep coached her on what cards to play as a beginner and the order of winning hands. He then took her to a low stakes table, figuring she was about to lose all her money.

She was dealt two cards and discarded them. She did this hand after hand patiently waiting until she was dealt two premium cards to play like Shep instructed her. In her hand, Madison held a king and a queen of diamonds. A player before her raised the stakes from two dollars to twelve. Another player threw his twelve dollars into the pot, and now it was up to her. Unsure of what to do, she looked over at Shep, wishing he could give her advice like he did at the blackjack table. With a smile on his face filled with pleasure watching his student, he wasn't allowed to coach her. She called and put out twelve dollars in chips.

The three community cards were an ace of diamonds, a six of diamonds, and a nine of clubs. The first player bet twenty dollars, the second player folded his hand, and the action was on Madison. She naively thought that the player who made a bet probably had an ace, but with two more cards to come and nine more diamonds left in the deck, she thought she'd gamble because, after all, she reasoned, that was what poker was all about.

She put her twenty dollars in chips out in front of her. The next card was a four of hearts, which didn't give her the flush she was hoping for. Without hesitating, her opponent made a hefty bet of forty dollars. Just as she was about to bite her lower lip, Madison caught herself and stopped. Instead, she put her hand to her mouth and sat motionless like the players she had seen on TV. She said "Call" and casually tossed forty dollars in chips into the pot. The last card to come was a two of diamonds, giving Madison the highest hand. There was now a hundred and fifty-nine dollars in the pot, with all the bets and blinds. Her opponent said, "All in," and pushed his remaining chips in front of him. Meanwhile, Shep, half amused, focused on Madison and the interaction with the other player. Madison looked at the board and then her cards to make sure she had a flush and said, "Call." She put out her chips, and the dealer counted them to see how much she had. Madison had two more chips than the other player, so the dealer tossed back two chips to her.

The guy turned over his cards, proudly showing that he had made two pair. It would have been the winning hand if three diamonds hadn't appeared. Madison turned over the king and the queen of diamonds, and the dealer said, "Flush," and pushed the chips in Madison's direction. She hid her smile behind her hands. The man, devoid of his chips and irritated, got up and left. Shep looked over at her and said, "Nice hand, well played."

Madison now felt initiated into the world of Texas Hold 'Em poker.

Excited about her win, she said "Thanks" and gathered up her winnings. "It's getting late, and I'd really like to go," she said. Shep readily agreed, and they left. On the way out, Madison told Shep, "I doubled my money, and thought I should quit while I'm ahead."

Shep was impressed with how quick a learner she was. He felt she had a natural talent for the game. Madison had put into practice what took him years to learn—to quit while you're ahead. She also proved that she had paid attention to what he had to say. Most women were artificial, wanting to be with him because of his good looks and what he could do for them. Madison was different; she seemed to be truly interested in him as a man.

He took her back to the Bellagio and suggested they have a drink. Even though she was feeling worn out from the lack of sleep the previous night, Madison didn't want the evening to end. She agreed to have one drink and then leave to get some shut-eye. It was 4:00 a.m,. and the lounge at the Bellagio was alive with people having fun as if the night had just started.

They talked about her experience at the poker table, and Shep conceded that he wasn't able to pick up any tells on her. Then he changed the subject. He wanted her phone number before she got away again. Reaching in his pocket for his cell phone, he asked her for her number. She spoke each number slowly, making sure he got it right while he added her to his contacts.

He told her that the next time he was playing at the Commerce Casino, he would call her. Grinning, he added, "I'll give you your second poker lesson." Madison finished her drink and said she needed to get some sleep, especially since she was leaving Vegas in a few hours. He said he would walk her to her room and assured her that he had no intention of coming in.

They reached her floor, got off the elevator, and walked down one corridor after another and around the corner until they reached her room. She got out her room key and, with her back turned to him, went to open the door.

"I'd like to kiss you good night, if I may." He was so polite she couldn't believe her ears. No one had ever asked her before if they could kiss her. Usually, she had to fend off her suitors to keep them at bay. She turned and looked at him then lowered her arms to her side while holding her key in one hand and her purse in the other. He cupped her face in his two hands and kissed her with such passion that she had never felt before. Her whole body was on fire; and the back of her neck became hot. The attraction to him was so powerful that she was seriously considering sleeping with him that night and risking never seeing him again.

Difficult as it was, she regained control of her emotions, realizing that a man like Shep had to be the aggressor until he allowed himself to be caught. He kissed her only one time for that was all he asked for. Releasing his hands from her face, he said good night and wished her a safe journey home.

Madison went in her room, dropping her things on the floor, and immediately sat on her bed. Stunned, she sat there reliving his kiss and the feeling over and over until she finally lay back on the pillow and fell to sleep.

Madison flew home with her friends, listening to their adventures that weekend, each story more outrageous than the next. She didn't chime in but remained somber, thinking what if she never saw Shep again. When asked by her friends why she was so quiet, she chalked it up to being tired. Cathy kidded her, saying, "Sure, we know it has nothing to do with the hunk you left with last night." Madison assured her friends that nothing happened. They kept on teasing her but let it drop when the stewardess served them their drinks.

As the days went by, Madison couldn't help thinking about Shep. She was finding it harder and harder to concentrate on her work. Every time her phone rang and showed "private caller," she hoped it was him, but it wasn't. Numerous times when she returned home and put her key in the lock, she paused and flashed back to standing with Shep in front of her hotel door, her face in his hands, and then his electromagnetic kiss.

Madison was being driven out of her mind, thinking about him every waking moment. She wasn't sleeping well or eating and was losing weight. Her clothes were baggy, and her face was gaunt. Madison wondered if she would ever see Shep again.

Two months had gone by, and one day, out of the blue, Madison got a phone call. It was from Shep, saying he was going to be in LA to play a tournament and wanted to see her. She was so excited at the thought that she instantly said yes. Later on in their relationship, Shep told her that he liked her straightforwardness and that she wasn't like most women who were into game playing.

On his first night in town, he invited her to dine with him at the casino restaurant. He told her that he had a tight schedule and could only spend a couple of hours with her. Madison made the drive to Commerce, anticipating their time together. She wasn't thinking about the dinner but when he would kiss her again. He met her in the hotel lobby attached to the casino. When he greeted her, Shep gave her a kiss on the cheek. Madison was disappointed, hoping that he would have taken her in his arms and planted a romantic kiss on her lips.

During dinner, Shep recounted details of the tournament. He spent very little time on the subject, turning the conversation to Madison. He wanted to get to know her better. Madison felt the same way, and they shared stories about where they grew up and their families. Dinner flew by, and Shep told her that he needed to get his sleep to remain sharp for the tournament the next day.

After dinner, Shep walked Madison to her car and said good night without touching her. Madison had expected the kiss she had been waiting for all evening. She had fantasized about how it would be if she ever saw him again, and now, without so much as a hug, she was feeling frustrated.

Madison didn't have a clue for why he avoided physical contact with her. Little did she know that Shep wanted nothing more than to make love to her, but being involved in a grueling tournament was akin to being a prize fighter the night before a title match. A boxer will abstain from sex to keep his focus on the fight and avoid distraction.

The tournament lasted three days, and Shep kept winning. He would call to talk with her but didn't come to see Madison or have dinner with her. Madison secretly wished he would bust out of the tournament so that they could be together.

The day of his final win, Shep called Madison to celebrate with him. She congratulated Shep but told him that she had flown to Colorado for a family emergency and didn't know when she could return. Disappointed, he invited her to come to Las Vegas the next month and stay with him. She flew there, and within the first hour of her arrival, they made love.

It was even better than she had imagined or anticipated. They didn't leave his condo the entire weekend until it was time for her to go to the airport. Exhausted from the marathon sex, Madison needed a vacation from her vacation.

In the next six months, they traveled back and forth to see each other. Growing tired of commuting, Madison quit her job and moved in with Shep in Las Vegas. When Madison complained that she didn't see enough of Shep, he taught her how to play poker so that they could spend more time together. Madison had become a very good player.

Aside from wanting to spend more time with Shep, Madison thrived on the challenge of the game and how it kept her active mind engaged. Best of all, she felt alive and in control of life, especially as her stack size increased.

She studied her opponents to determine their skill level and betting patterns, along with the mathematical chances of winning the hand with the cards she was dealt. When you put it altogether, she was hooked.

She also grew to love the lifestyle they shared together. There was never a dull moment.

They would hit the tables at nine and play until the early hours of the morning. They slept until noon and spent the afternoon making love. Sometimes they went to parties that lasted all night long, drinking heavily, dancing and talking about poker endlessly. They were living the dream. Ordinary life paled beside the exhilaration of their lifestyle.

In time, poker became an addiction just as if it were crack cocaine. She craved the action at the table, win or lose. Playing gave her a feeling of euphoria. No matter how many hours she played, she couldn't wait until the next night to get her fix.

A year into her exciting new life, the unthinkable happened. Madison got pregnant. She didn't realize she was a month late until she was rummaging through the bathroom closet and saw a box of tampons. It reminded her that she hadn't gotten her period yet.

Panicked, she went to the pharmacy and bought a pregnancy test kit. Not wanting to go home and see Shep, she chose a restaurant bathroom with private stalls and full-length wooden doors for privacy. She peed on the stick, and sixty seconds later, a blue cross appeared. To her dismay, it was positive.

She didn't want to go home, fearing Shep would be there, and she really wasn't ready to discuss this with him. Madison had nowhere else to go, but luckily when she got there, the condo was empty, giving her time to think.

She had always wanted children, but living life in the fast lane, she hadn't planned on having one now. How was she going to break the news to Shep? She didn't even know if he wanted kids.

That night at poker, she played terribly, losing hands she should have easily won. She was distracted by her situation. Her mind was on figuring out how to tell Shep the news and not on poker.

The more she thought about it, the more she came to the conclusion that there was no good way to tell him. At the very least, she decided that she should wait till he was in a good mood. Madison chose the following Sunday. It was going to be a day of relaxation for the two of them. They had plans to go to brunch and for a drive. Just as sure as the sun would rise on Sunday morning, she knew they would make love. Afterward, the timing would be right to broach the subject.

She never had any difficulty coaxing him to have sex. In fact, he was almost always the aggressor. Sex was still very exciting, and the novelty hadn't worn off but only intensified as they grew to know each other's pleasure points. Lying there, Shep and Madison enjoyed the intimacy following intercourse. She put her head on his chest, wrapped her arm around him, and straddled one leg over the top of his.

She let a few minutes pass before she began talking. "I have some news to tell you."

"I hope you're going to tell me you won back all the money you lost the other night. I saw your chip stack."

"No, it has nothing to do with poker. It has to do with us, the two of us."

Shep laid there in a state of blissfulness, not moving a muscle. Madison, in a very serious tone of voice, said to him, "There's going to be three of us."

Shep pushed her aside and jolted to a sitting position. Astonished, he blurted out, "What, you're pregnant?"

The cat was out of the bag, and there was no going back. "Yes, I'm pregnant," Madison replied. "You're going to be a father."

Chapter 11

Madison lifted her head up off the desk, drained and drenched from her tears. She slowly came back to reality when the snot coming out of her nose dripped down her face. Her shirt was wet, and she was getting cold. She dragged herself out of her chair to get cleaned up.

What she really wanted to do was to get into her pajamas, eat some dinner, and go to bed. Tomorrow would be another day and another chance to find a solution to her problem. Emotionally exhausted, Madison had no trouble falling and staying asleep.

The next morning, Madison woke up to a cloudy, rainy day that did nothing to help improve the mood she was in.

She went straight to her office, dressed in her pajamas to get down to business. There was an email from Jake Wilson, a fellow realtor, asking if she still had the book on real estate investing that Madison had offered to lend him. She emailed Jake saying that she would look for it when she had a chance.

While reading and responding to the rest of her emails, her doorbell rang. She opened her front door, but no one was there. Madison stuck her head out the screen door to see if maybe they walked away, but she didn't see anyone on the street, not even a UPS or FedEx delivery truck. Closing the screen door, Madison noticed a single long-stemmed rose lying on the doormat.

The rose was deep red, like the color of blood. She thought it might be from Shep. Madison picked up the rose, and drawing it to her nose to smell, she noticed that the other side was black in color. Shaken, she ran inside the house and slammed the door shut, carrying the rose with her. She dumped it in the kitchen trash can and stood there a moment. She thought to herself, *Could Nikolai have anything to do with this?*

Madison walked back to her office to continue working and put the incident behind her. The phone rang, and she picked up her pace to answer the call. It was Nikolai. He said that he was calling to tell her that he would be closing within three weeks. He warned her that she better be ready with the cashier's check, or there'd be hell to pay. Still wondering if Nikolai had sent the rose as a warning, Madison became frightened and told him, "Yes, but of course, everything is fine." She was afraid of him at this point and felt that she had to lie to protect herself. Madison absolutely didn't want to find out what his definition of "hell to pay" consisted of.

Rattled by his call, she made herself a cup of herbal tea and thought that now would be a good time to look for the book for Jake and to try to calm down.

Behind her desk were wall-to-wall bookcases that must have held four hundred books all neatly categorized by title. With her teacup in one hand, she thumbed through the titles with the other, looking for the book called *What Every Good Real Estate Investor Should Know*. She passed one title after another. There on the shelf, between two real estate books, was a book called *Ace on the River*.

For some reason, it was out of order. Maybe in the past, she had put it on the shelf with the intention of filing it in the proper place later. She took it out and sat down with it at her desk. Madison leafed through the poker book, reading the pages where she highlighted important concepts. For a brief second, she thought back to her playing days with Shep and said out loud adamantly, "I'm never going back to that again."

Madison put the book back on the shelf and returned to looking for the real estate investment book. She found it, and pulling it off the shelf, she placed it on her desk as a reminder to contact her friend and send him the book. Searching for the book had been the momentary diversion that Madison was needing, but now the seriousness of Nikolai's call was setting in.

"Maybe I should get a lawyer. I'm pretty sure he's going to sue me," she spoke to herself. "Or maybe I need to go to the police, but what can they do? He never really outwardly threatened me."

As she sipped her tea, the room became chilly, almost as if a ghost had entered. Bang! She turned around to see that a book fell off the shelf. Picking it up, she looked at it. It was *Ace on the River*" the book she had earlier returned to the bookcase. In her head, she heard Shep's voice say, "It's eight million dollars in prize money." Deciding this was an omen, she leaped up from her chair.

Chapter 12

Madison showered and dressed in record time. On the way out the door, she grabbed her keys and handbag and hopped into her car to head straight to the bank. Madison went inside, and without having to wait, she walked up to the teller and asked for her balance in her checking account. It was a paltry five hundred dollars. She was expecting a large commission check from a listing she had sold, but she hadn't received it yet. "What's the balance in my savings account?"

That was no better; it contained only seven hundred dollars. Madison told the teller that she would like to withdraw the entire amount from both accounts. The teller asked her how she would like it. "Hundred-dollar bills will be fine."

As she was turning to leave, Gwen, the bank manager, spotted Madison and went over to her. Offering her condolences, Gwen said, "I'm so sorry to hear about Frank."

Madison responded, "Yes, thank you, it was very unexpected."

Gwen added, "He was just in the bank the day before to withdraw a large sum of money. I'm glad I got to see him." Madison was taken by surprise by this news.

At first, she quizzically said, "Oh?" She was going to ask how much but stopped, wanting the information from Gwen without arousing suspicion. "Oh yeah, we had a big closing. Two hundred and fifty thousand dollars from the business escrow account, right?"

Gwen said yes and added that she was the one who had authorized the cashier's check. Madison made a "Hmm" sound and told Gwen that she had to run and that it was nice seeing her.

Madison was halfway to the door when she heard Gwen calling out after her, "Oh, Madison, Madison."

Madison stopped and turned around, giving Gwen a chance to catch up to her. "Do you have a sister?" Gwen asked.

A puzzled look came over Madison's face, and she replied, "No, but why do you ask?"

"Because the woman he was with looked so much like you she could have been your twin."

Thinking for a second about who it could have been, Madison shrugged her shoulders and volunteered that she didn't have a clue as to who he might have been with. "Oh well, it's been said we all have a double somewhere," Madison said.

They said goodbye, and Madison left the bank to drive the twenty miles from west LA to her destination. The morning rush-hour traffic was over, making the trip a thirty-minute drive instead of the usual hour and a half. By now the rain had stopped, and the sky was clearing up. Madison could see a little blue in between the rain clouds and thought it might turn out to be a sunny day after all.

The radio was turned to her favorite Pandora station, helping to block out her troubles. She had the volume turned up that when her cell phone rang, she almost didn't hear it. Pressing the mute button, she answered with a simple hello. A deep male voice on the other end of the call said, "I'm looking for Madison Mitchell."

Madison assumed it was real estate related, so speaking in her most professional and friendly voice, she said, "This is Madison Mitchell, broker for Bay Realty. How can I help you?"

"This is Detective Malachek, LAPD. Last time I saw you, you were high as a kite in the hospital. I hope you're feeling better." Madison replied, "Yes." She wasn't expecting his call and was not mentally prepared to talk to him. "I want to talk to you regarding Frank Jensen's murder" Malachek said.

Madison told him that she was in her car heading out of town for a few days. In actuality, she was planning on returning to LA late that evening. He told her that he was working the day shift for the next few weeks and to call him when she returned. He said he would text her the precinct number and his extension to reach him directly.

Madison said that she would call him and hung up the phone. She wasn't worried that she was a suspect but felt she wasn't ready to recall the night of Frank's murder. Since suffering a brain injury, she wasn't even sure she would be of any help or be able to recall much of what happened that night.

She finally arrived at the city of Commerce and pulled into the parking lot at her destination. Heading inside, she thought about how this was the first time in five years that she had been there. She went straight to the poker room in the casino and gave her name to the hostess for a seat at a table. Next, she got her chips and took a seat to wait for her name to be called. While waiting, Madison thought back to the past and how she always felt as though she was entering a lion's den to fight for a share of the territory in the form of chips.

Shortly thereafter, she heard "Madison, table thirty-five." Madison raised her arm to motion to the hostess that she was on her way.

When she got to the table, she placed her chips in front of an unoccupied seat and quickly glanced around the table to see who the other players were. They in turn looked her up and down, sizing her up.

She looked to see if anyone was a senior citizen. They usually played only the best face cards, so you had to have a good hand going up against them. Next, she looked to see if there were any professional players. They were usually young and wore hoodies and maybe sunglasses. These players would play any two cards that were dealt to them and tended to bluff more often. This made it more difficult to play against them. Then there were the players who were there because it was their day off from work, and they were looking for something to do. Playing against them could go either way because some were good players, and others were just plain lucky. Lastly, she wanted to know who might be a tourist. Frequently, they were the worst players, or what's called in poker language, a fish. They think they know how to play from watching televised professional poker, but they don't have a clue. It would be akin to watching baseball on TV then thinking you could play in the major leagues.

Once seated, the next thing she did was to check out how many chips each player had in their stacks. Feeling out of practice, some strategies came back to her.

She sat there patiently waiting for premium cards to be dealt to her, like aces, kings, and queens or a combination of them. She observed how players bet, and if they had to show their hand, what cards they played.

That was important information in the game of poker. Winning was a combination of skill, learned from playing over a long period of time and with all kinds of players, and just good old-fashioned luck.

Madison was dealt hand after hand. For over an hour, she discarded her cards, choosing not to play them. Her patience was wearing thin, feeling the pressure to turn her twelve hundred dollars into ten thousand. That would be enough to buy into the tournament, so she could try for the eight million dollars in prize money. This was all the money she had to her name, so she had to play tight, like the senior citizens who played cards using their social security money. She watched how each person at the table played. She imagined herself like an eagle perusing the landscape for its prey and swooping down to nab its dinner. Madison liked to give each player a nickname that would help her to remember how they played their cards.

Finally, she was dealt an ace of hearts and king of hearts. She decided to play these two premium cards and raise, making it twenty dollars for anyone who wanted to test their hand against hers. Two players called, and the action began. She was hoping only one player would call her because the chances of beating two or more was harder. The dealer dealt the first three cards to come. Cautiously, Madison checked her hand instead of making a bet. She wanted to see if anyone else would, providing her with a sliver of information about their cards. The second player checked as well, and Madison, keeping a poker face, breathed a sigh of relief.

The third player, who looked barely of legal age and wearing *the* hoodie, made a bet. Madison's sense of relief was momentary. She was wondering if the hoodie had made a pair or was it that he sensed weakness from her and the other player, thus taking advantage of the situation. The other player folded his hand, leaving Madison heads up with the hoodie. She felt the young man who made the bet was just bluffing. Her past experiences at the poker table taught her that young male players like to flex their muscle like a lion cub practicing to become king of the jungle. There was the possibility that he had a pocket pair or was hoping the next card to come would give him a winning hand. There would be two more cards dealt for a total of five. Madison calculated her odds of winning and called his bet by putting out her chips.

To Madison's surprise, the fourth card was dealt, and her opponent didn't make a bet. In a calm voice, Madison said, "I bet fifty," and placed the chips out in front of her. The other player called and put his chips in.

There was over three hundred dollars in the pot. Madison kept her cool, but internally, she was nervous. The last card was dealt, and Madison thought she had the winning hand with a pair of aces. This time, the "hoodie guy" bet a hundred dollars, and Madison was concerned he had a better hand than hers. Not someone to acquiesce easily, she boldly said, "Raise." Madison put out a stack of red chips to match his bet and increased it by one hundred dollars. Without hesitation, he matched her chip amount.

Feeling victorious, Madison showed that she had a pair of aces. The hoodie turned over his two cards, a four and a six. He made two pair, beating Madison's lonely aces. The dealer pushed the pot his way. Not only did the hoodie win, but he managed to humiliate Madison.

She was livid but had to show restraint and instead told him, "Nice hand." He should have never called Madison's initial raise with two low cards. It was a stupid move that ended up being lucky for the hoodie. Madison understood that poker wasn't always about having the best starting hand but the luck of the draw and the person you were playing against. It was still a bitter pill to swallow.

Determined not to let hoodie's stupidity have an effect on Madison, she told herself that each hand was different from the next and to be careful if she got into a hand with him again.

What made poker exciting was the anticipation of the two cards dealt to the player, and the insane amount of money that could be won in just one hand. The lure of winning big was the draw that brought players back to the table, time after time after time. Unfortunately, this was not the case with Madison right now. She wasn't playing poker for the thrill of it, like in the days when she lived with Shep. Instead, she was playing for survival.

Chapter 13

Having lost several hundred dollars of her twelve hundred in a previous hand, Madison had to make up her loss. She labeled the hoodie as a loose player and was determined to get her chips back from him and then some.

A new hand was dealt, and Madison looked down at her two cards. She was holding a six and a nine, only an unpredictable player like the hoodie would play them. A vision flashed before Madison's eyes. She saw a nine and two sixes being dealt.

There were already three players in the hand. The first was a young man about thirty years of age who had short hair and was clean-cut. The second player was a man in his fifties that had a scraggly beard and hair to match, and lastly, the hoodie, who put on a pair of sunglasses. Madison decided to call so that made a total of four. The aggressive hoodie raised, and Mr. Clean and the biker called.

She didn't know how the two of them would play, and Madison had to make a decision quickly. She asked herself if she was playing the hand because she felt her cards might win or was she playing them to get even with the hoodie. It was a combination of both, and Madison put in her chips.

Madison's vision was partially on point when the three community cards dealt were a six, nine, and a queen. The hoodie made a bet while the other two players folded. Madison casually put her chips in, hoping to do unto the hoodie what he had done to her.

The next card was a king, and he pushed even harder. Madison, concerned he might have a better hand than hers, studied her cards and took her time. To his surprise, she called. Since the last card hadn't been dealt, she wasn't home free yet. Madison silently said to herself over and over, "Six or a nine, six or a nine." The dealer put out the last card, and coincidentally, it was a six. Madison was first to act, and she made a very big bet. Hoodie had the two highest pair and raised her. In a show of dominance, Madison reraised him. He took a moment to look at her, arrogantly trying to figure out what she had. He felt he could easily read a player like Madison. She was a young, attractive female, and they were usually not very aggressive.

He called her bet, and she turned over a full house. He mucked his cards, and you could see the sickened look on his face. Madison had won back all of the chips she had lost and most of his stack. She had gotten the retribution she was hoping for and the respect she deserved.

Madison had more money than when she started and was well on her way to being able to buy into the main tournament. She continued playing for several more hours until she could no longer ignore her hunger pains. Madison headed out of the poker room, past the dinging of the slots, and over to the buffet dining room.

Forty minutes later, she was back in her seat ready for the next round. Only one player had left the table, and he had been replaced with a guy she nicknamed, "the Italian stallion." He had a big build with oversize biceps, and a T-shirt with a Harley Davidson insignia and cutoff sleeves that showed his multiple tattoos. When he greeted her, his accent placed him as being from New York.

He was the quintessential stereotype of a macho male right out of the movie, *Rocky*.

She had played cards with guys like this in the past. They think they're God's gift to poker and were usually very aggressive, especially against a female player. To them, women served two purposes, sex and to cook their meals. She learned early on that the only way to beat them at their game was to wait patiently till she had a good hand and let them do the betting.

She went back into poker mode, quiet, paying attention to how everyone played and waiting for two good cards. Her next hand looked promising, so she called. There was a lot of action with six players in the hand. She ended up losing that one. For the next hour, it was a seesaw; she was up, then down, up, then down again. She couldn't seem to get ahead.

Then finally, she got a pair of jacks. It wasn't the strongest hand, but if she could get most of the players to fold before the flop, she might win.

She made a pre-flop raise, and in a display of machismo, the Italian stallion reraised her. All the other players immediately folded, either because they had junk cards or they didn't want to be involved in a hand with him. He had been extremely aggressive and was a "table bully," betting large amounts of money and causing players to fold most of the time.

The first three cards were dealt, and Madison's jacks were over-shadowed by a queen on the board. The stallion, keeping true to his macho ego, made a big bet. Madison put her hand to her forehead, wondering what he might be holding. Deep in thought, the strangest thing happened. It was as if she could see his cards. She saw a four and a jack in her mind's eye. Thinking she was beaten, she called his bet anyway. The turn card was a four of spades just like she pic-tured it. *How weird,* she thought. He made an even bigger bet, and Madison called in hopes her vision was correct. The river card was the jack she had envisioned. Stallion pushed all in for the remainder of his chip stack. There was now six hundred dollars in the pot.

Madison put her head down and closed her eyes, hoping to get a vision of what he might be holding. She had accurately seen the jack and four coming her way but now needed to know if she had the best hand. There were no more visions. She had to rely on gut instinct to call the all in. The pot total was now over nine hundred dollars. He turned over his queen and ten, giving him two pair.

She looked over at him and saw a smirk on his face, to which Madison said, "I put you on two pair." He took this to mean that she had only one pair. "You're right, little lady," and he turned over his two pair, so sure that he was the winner. He started to reach for the pot when the dealer, who had taken a shine to Madison, asked her to turn over her two cards.

The entire time the stallion had been at the table, he had been betting big and pushing players around. The other players had grown tired of his antics and were secretly hoping she would win. She gladly obliged the dealer's request and showed a pair of jacks, giving her three of a kind and the winning hand. The dealer pushed the massive pile of chips in Madison's direction.

To show their disapproval of him, each one congratulated Madison on a nice hand, sending a message to the stallion. He was so mad he went on a rant.

"You put me on two pair and still called me all the way to the river. They should never let women play!" He got up from his seat abruptly, almost knocking the chair to the floor, and left the table. His comments created quite a stir with the rest of the players. The older man on her right said, "Don't mind him, we like having you here," to which she thanked him, and the game continued.

Chapter 14

Madison was up fifteen hundred dollars, and with her initial buy-in, she needed a little more than seven thousand for the entrance fee. Her luck and cards were holding steady. As she played on, the visions of her opponents' cards were becoming crisper in her head, and she used this to her advantage. When she was involved in a hand with a player, she would put her hand to her forehead and quietly ask herself, "Are they red or black?" A voice in her head would respond back. She would then ask, "Both or one?" Again, after a moment of thought, she would see the color of the two cards. Taking her time to decide, her opponent said, "I'm gonna call time."

The dealer let Madison know that she had one minute to act. Then when an image appeared, she looked at the board and again asked a question, "What are the numbers of the cards in his hand?"

She seemed to be accurate more often than not. Not understanding what was happening, she rolled with it, winning almost three thousand dollars total.

Nearing midnight, Madison was getting fatigued. She decided to cash out, catch some shut-eye, and return the next day—hopefully to win the remainder of the money she needed to buy into the tournament. She got up from her seat and addressed the table, "Nice playing with you."

Madison had made quite an impression with her good looks and aggressive playing. Some of the players said "Same here" while others, mainly the ones she took money from, stayed quiet.

Exhausted, Madison blasted her radio to keep her alert for the drive home for fear of falling asleep at the wheel. It had been both a physically and mentally tiring day, and she couldn't wait to get into her comfortable king-size bed with her down-filled duvet. Just the thought of it made her sleepy.

She arrived home safely and made her way into the house. Flipping on the switch to turn on her center hall light, she dropped her keys and her purse on the hall table and headed for the coat closet. Grabbing a hanger for her jacket, she spotted an unfamiliar black coat, a man's. She hung hers up and then took the black one off its hanger and held it in her hands, trying to think whose coat could it be. She searched the pockets and felt something. She pulled it out. It was Frank's business card. "It's Frank's coat. This must have been here a good six months." She clutched the coat in her arms and held it close to her breast. "God, I miss him so much." She almost started crying uncontrollably. Instead, she put on the emotional brakes and kept it together.

She took a whiff of the coat and could still smell the scent of Frank's cologne. It was unmistakably his because it was his favorite, and Madison had given him a bottle for his birthday. As she lingered in the moment, relishing his odor, visions had started to come to her.

They were blurred, like in a fog, and she couldn't make out what she was seeing but felt a lot of pain in her neck.

She could smell a different scent, unlike the masculine cologne that she had been smelling. It had a floral odor and seemed to be feminine. In despair, Madison yelled out, "Frank, what happened to you?" She heard a voice in her head as clear as if someone standing next to her had spoken. "Teen."

"What about teen?" she asked, and then the voice stopped, and the scent faded away.

Madison had no idea what had just happened nor what any of it meant. She wondered if she was missing Frank so much that her imagination was in overdrive. Tired out, she headed to bed to get some sleep and to put the day's events behind her. Madison fell right to sleep, foregoing her usual ritual of watching television.

That night, she had a dream. It was about Frank. Madison was with him in a house that she didn't recognize, but suddenly, the scene changed, and she was in Frank's apartment. He was naked, sitting in bed with a woman who had long brunette hair with waves on the ends. The woman's back was turned toward Madison, so she wasn't able to see the woman's face. Madison's attention then turned to the floor. There was something about the floor, but Madison didn't know what that was about. That was the end of her dream.

Chapter 15

Madison woke up later than usual the next morning. She had twenty-one days to restore the missing funds or face financial ruin and, even worse, the wrath of Nikolai. She wouldn't rule out that he might seek revenge and possibly go so far as to have her killed. Even though she was well-trained in martial arts, she feared for her life and was always on guard. Having to be on the alert all the time was unnerving.

Feeling under the gun, literally, she skipped her morning routine, and instead, dressed and headed straight for the casino to try to win the remainder of the buy in to the tournament. Wishing she would be as successful as she had been the day before, she wondered if she still had her newly acquired ability of seeing her opponent's cards in her mind's eye.

It was midmorning when Madison arrived at the casino. At this hour in the morning, the poker players consisted of those that played all night long—retirees, professional players, and a few who had nothing better to do. Madison got her chips and took a seat. She looked around the table to see whom she would be playing against. Choosing to sit out the first few hands, she wanted to see how people played. She was looking to see who the aggressive players were as well as the submissive ones. She wanted to know if there was a table bully or a slow roller. Two of the nine players had huge stacks in front of them. These were the guys she had to watch out for.

She nicknamed the player with the largest stack Ralph Lauren because he was wearing a V-necked sweater with the RL logo. He was in his late fifties, wore thick black-framed glasses, and was very conservative looking. The second largest stack belonged to a guy who looked like he had been up all night. She didn't have a nickname picked out for him just yet but would come up with one in short order. After playing in a hand with him, whether she lost it or won, she would label his outstanding playing characteristic.

Madison patiently waited for a strong playable hand, knowing that you could sit for hours without getting premium cards or winning a hand. That was how the game of poker went, and it only added to her feelings of being stressed out.

It was well into the second hour, and Madison still wasn't getting very good cards. She decided to take another tack. She dubbed it, "Use what you got." For Madison, that meant if she was dealt only small cards, then she would play them. Madison was dealt a nine and a ten. She decided to go for it, believing that poker was a game of war.

The cards were the artillery, and her chips were her army of men. Given this view and the fact that her "army" chip stack was medium in comparison to the other players, she was going to have to outmaneuver her opponents, at least until she increased the size of her army.

Ralph Lauren raised before the three community cards came out, and from watching him play, she knew he was a tight player, only betting with the best hand. Two players called the raise. It was now up to Madison. She took a second look at her nine and ten and decided to play the hand. The flop was dealt and contained all small-numbered cards. All Madison had was her lonely nine and ten.

RL made a continuation bet. One player folded, and the second player called. Madison was concerned that the caller may have paired the board or was chasing a high card. Regarding RL, she figured he had high cards and was trying to push the two of them out of the hand. Madison made the call. The turn card was a nine, giving Madison top pair. RL had proven that he was aggressive, and she could count on him to bet it, so she checked. On cue, RL made a very large bet, and the other player folded. Madison had a decision to make and quickly. She wondered if she should call his bet or gamble that she may catch another nine or a ten or even maybe raise him.

She chose to call his bet. The last card was a queen. Feeling like she had lost the hand, Madison checked. RL made a final bet. There was a lot of money in the pot, and she hated the thought that he might be bluffing or trying to bully her. She took a deep breath while putting her head down against her fist and closed her eyes. Nothing happened. She didn't get a vision or hear a voice. She told herself, "If he's got it, then he's got it." She was afraid he paired the queen but put her chips in the pot anyway. The two players held their cards in their hand, waiting for the other one to show first. The dealer said, "Show me a winner."

Since Madison called the bet, it was up to RL to show his cards. He still didn't turn them over, so she said to the dealer, "I called his bet." The dealer said, "Sir, please turn over your cards."

Reluctantly, RL turned them over to show an ace and a king. Madison was accurate in her read of RL. He didn't even have a pair; it was a total bluff. Madison turned over her nine and ten and took the pot down. It was a gutsy move on her part and a good read of her opponent.

It was skill and luck that won the hand for Madison. She couldn't understand why images didn't appear when she put her hand to her forehead, but soon realized that it was only when she relaxed and wasn't anxious that the images of her opponents' cards appeared. These visions puzzled her, but she used it to win the remainder of the money she needed to enter the tournament.

With her newfound ability, Madison wanted to continue playing but, on the other hand, didn't want to risk losing her winnings. Besides, it was getting late, and she hadn't eaten all day. She cashed in her chips and went to get a bite to eat, thinking she could always return later and play at another table. Needing a break and some food, she headed to the casino restaurant.

She finished her lunch and leisurely sipped on her coffee and read her emails. To relax some more, she played dominoes on her phone. About an hour or so had passed leaving Madison feeling refreshed and ready to do battle again.

When she returned to the poker room, she decided to register for the tournament now that she had all the money she needed. After paying the entry fee, she counted the money that she had left. It was more than enough to allow her to continue playing. She thought why not try to win some money and get ahead. Walking over to the desk to give her name and garner a seat, she asked to play at a higher stakes game.

There were several available for immediate play. The players in these games were usually more aggressive, which led to more money in the pot. She went to the cage to buy her chips and then headed over to table fifty - one where there were two open seats.

Madison chose one and placed her chips down in front of her as she perused the competition. The other players were checking her out also. Some of the guys said hello to welcome her to the table, and one just nodded. She got the feeling that he was looking at her as if she was shark bait. With her beautiful blonde hair and youthful good looks, not to mention that she was a minority among all these men, he assumed she would be easy pickings. Madison had an uphill battle proving to him and all the other men that she could hold her own with the best of them.

She sat down, and the first hand dealt to her was pocket aces. She raised it to twenty-five dollars and had four callers. Everyone wanted a piece of the action and weren't scared off by her raise. The three community cards came out, and it was nothing special. Five, deuce, and an eight. With five players in the hand, it was likely that someone had made a pair. Three players checked, and the fourth bet sixty dollars to which Madison called. The fifth player was the shark. He raised it to a hundred and twenty. It was now back to the other three players to act. "Too rich for my blood," one of the players said out loud, and two more folded their hand also. The original player, who raised, threw the additional chips into the pot, and Madison did the same.

The turn came out, and it was a second eight. Whoever was holding an eight in their hand had trips and the best hand up to this point. The original bettor checked, and Madison, trying to bluff, bet two hundred. The shark said, "I'm all in," and pushed his mountain of chips out in front of him. There was over two thousand dollars at stake, with one more card to come and a chance to win the pot. Madison knew the odds of hitting an ace on the river was slim. Statistically, it was a bad bet and more of a gamble. Jason, the other player in the hand, called the all in, and it was now up to Madison. Recalling the title of the book that fell off her shelf and causing her to go back to playing poker, Madison talked herself into calling the bet. She looked down at her cards, closed her eyes, and over and over again, said to herself, *Ace, an ace, ace, an ace.*

It was by far the largest pot of the evening. You could feel the tension of the players in the hand and the excitement of the onlookers as the dealer took a little longer to put out the river card. It was nerve-racking for the players who had money riding on the last card. With her eyes still closed, the river card was dealt. She heard a loud holler, like the kind you hear in a sports bar when a favored team scored.

The noise came from Mike, the player Madison nicknamed "the shark eater." He jumped out of his seat with his fist raised in the air and screeched "Yesss!" He must have had the winning hand the way he was yelling and carrying on. It never even occurred to him that he could have been beaten.

Madison opened her eyes and, seeing the ace, took a deep breath. Disgusted, Jason threw his cards in the muck. Madison innocently asked Mike, "Do you have quads?"

He replied, "Hey, girlie, I don't need 'em."

Madison was infuriated at having been called "girlie" and being spoken down to. She dauntlessly said, "I have a full house." Madison turned over her pocket aces, which gave her the winning hand. She was always gracious when she won a pot, but if someone had been rude, like Mike, she liked to put them in their place. "Yep, I'm just a girlie," she said as she reached for the massive pile of chips.

Humbled, he quickly sat back down and muttered, "Nice hand." Madison had established her table image and had gained the esteem of all the men at the table including the shark eater. She continued to play, and when she raised, instead of everyone jumping into the hand with her, she would now get the hard-earned respect that she sought.

In the middle of a hand, her cell phone went off. The caller ID showed it was from Cathy. Mucking her cards, Madison got up from the table and went to the back of the poker room and out onto the porch to take the call. Cathy was calling to ask how she was feeling and if they could get together for a late dinner. Madison didn't want her to know where she was, so she had to come up with an excuse fast.

"I would love to," Madison apologetically responded, "but I'm waiting for my client to come out of the restroom. I've been showing property all day, and we were just on our way to dinner."

Disappointed, Cathy told her she understood. "Duty calls. Lord knows I've been there too." Madison had evaded Cathy's offer.

"I'm so glad you understand. I'll call you later in the week, and we can pick a date for dinner. I owe you that for helping me get home." Cathy said that would be fine, and Madison was relieved not having to explain to her friend why she was at a casino.

By now, three guys were on the porch smoking and making Madison nauseous from the smell. She opened the door and headed back to the table. Settling into her seat, she reached for the back of her chair to put her cell phone in her backpack. Returning her gaze to the front of the table, a player was making his way to claim the remaining empty seat. It was Shep. She was taken by surprise but should have expected it. After all, he was a professional poker player.

Chapter 16

Shep sat down and, looking at Madison, flashed her a broad smile, the kind that goes from ear to ear and makes your insides tingle. "Just like old times, eh, blue eyes?" he said to Madison, unconsciously moistening his lips with his tongue. "Not quite," she snapped back.

She was more focused on making money than his good looks and the sexual vibes he gave off. He was taken aback. It was rare for him to be rebuffed. When he paid attention to a woman, he had a charm about him that made her feel that he was genuinely interested in her and not just out for sex. Madison attributed it to his European upbringing where sex was plentiful and a natural part of life, not the big taboo Americans make it out to be. Sex was freer and easier in his country, so it wasn't his sole objective to get a woman in bed. His past experiences, she believed, were the reason why he was such a good and considerate lover. He cared about a woman's pleasure, not just his own.

Madison got back into poker mode as she sat waiting for a playable hand. Now that Shep was at the table, she definitely had to be on her guard. Only the best cards would do. She wanted to avoid getting in a hand with him, but if she had great cards, then she was going to call the bet.

Madison sat patiently waiting for just the right cards to jump into the action, but it never seemed to come. Shep dominated the table with his playing ability. Twenty minutes into the game, the number of chips in his stack grew while the other stacks dwindled.

He studied the players and was adept at figuring out what they were betting on. As a result, he toyed with them and usually won. He had a commanding appearance and an air of confidence that enabled him to bluff very easily.

The cards were dealt, and it was now up to Madison to call, raise, or discard her hand into the muck pile. It was past midnight, and she had been playing for over twelve hours, and fatigue was setting in. She sat quietly, moving her tongue over her teeth. Then she started to rub her fingers together in a circular motion and stared off into space. The players who still had cards in their hand were wondering if this was a sign that she was going to raise. Thirty seconds went by, and Madison still hadn't acted. Annoyed, one of the players said to the dealer, "I'd like to call time." The dealer politely told Madison that she had one minute to act or her cards would be folded.

It seemed that Madison didn't hear a word of it or didn't care as she continued to stare into space. The minute passed, and the dealer took her cards and put them in the muck pile.

By now, Shep had become concerned. He got up out of his seat and went over to her. "Madison, it's time to leave and get some rest." Still not moving, Shep reached for Madison's backpack.

"I raise," Madison said as she looked down at her empty hand. "Where are my cards?"

"Madison, let's get you home." Shep nudged her.

"No, I want to play a little while longer."

In a drill sergeant voice, Shep told her, "Madison, let's go. Now!" He wasn't going to take no for an answer as he held onto her arm and helped her out of her seat.

"I am really tired. I'm going to go home," Madison said as if she hadn't a clue as to what just happened. Madison and Shep picked up their chips and went to the cage to cash out.

He walked with her out to the parking lot and asked Madison where she parked her car. They headed over to it, and when they had gotten there, Shep asked her for her keys. Madison thought he was trying to put a move on her. He told her that she zoned out and seemed like she was drunk. She denied that she had been drinking and was definitely not drunk. Shep stood waiting while she reached into her backpack to pull out her keys. He grabbed them from her and demanded that she get in the car. "No!" shouted Madison.

"Get in the damn car, or I'll drive off without you." It was an idle threat, but Madison didn't know that.

She got into the car, and he drove her home. When they reached her driveway, Shep's demeanor softened. As they sat there, Shep explained to her that she was acting very strange like the night they met for dinner. He was genuinely concerned about her and felt she shouldn't be left alone.

"You need to get your rest. I'm going to sleep on the sofa and stay overnight to make sure you're okay," he said with a finger pointed at Madison as she was about to say no.

"You know I've always been a gentleman and wouldn't take advantage of you in that way. Now let's go."

True to his word, Shep slept on the sofa that night. In the morning, he made a pot of coffee and took his cup upstairs to check on Madison. She was still asleep. He stood there, coffee in hand, and watched her. She took up the whole king-size bed with her leg crossed over her body and a pillow under it, just as she always did when they were together. He silently reminisced about those days, and a sadness came over him.

Madison started to stir, and as she opened her eyes, she saw him standing there and let out a startled scream, not realizing it was Shep.

"Sorry, I didn't mean to scare you," he said in a calming voice.

"Yeah, I'm not used to seeing someone in my bedroom, especially standing over me."

"Can I get you a cup of coffee?" he asked.

"That would be great," Madison answered.

"Still take it with cream only?"

"Uh-hmmm," came Madison's reply.

Shep returned with Madison's coffee and sat down in the overstuffed armchair located next to her bed. It was an awkward moment for both of them. Quietly, they drank their coffee. After a couple of sips, Madison broke the silence. "I must have been exhausted," she said.

"How are you feeling?" Shep asked.

"Rested. A lot has happened to me in the past few weeks." She almost spilled her guts out to him concerning Frank's murder and the missing money.

"You want to talk about it?" Shep asked.

"Not really," Madison told him. She didn't want to get into it or involve him in any way, so she kept the conversation superficial. "You were doing pretty well at the table last night," she said to him, knowing that once she changed the subject to poker, Shep would go on forever. Madison was right. He talked about the hands he played last night, describing every detail regarding the flop, the turn, the river, and how he bluffed constantly. Because Madison used to be an avid poker player, practically bordering on addiction, she appreciated everything he was describing. She in turn discussed her day at the tables.

Shep asked her if she had been playing all these years apart from him. Madison explained that she had gotten into real estate and had concentrated her efforts on building up her business. To justify her trip to the casino that day, she lied, saying that she was having a slow day at work and thought it might be fun as well as an innocent diversion to hit the slots and play a little poker. Madison stressed that by no means did she have any intention of returning to her former lifestyle of daily poker playing.

Shep had finished his cup of coffee and said he was going to get another one, but after that, he would be on his way. He offered to get her a second cup.

There was a hesitation in her voice and a sound of disappointment when she said, "Sure."

Madison was responding more to his comment about leaving rather than to wanting a second cup.

He then asked her if it was convenient to get a ride to his car. Her voice picked up with enthusiasm, and she said, "I'd be glad to drive you, it's the least I could do." Shep thanked her, and Madison told him that she appreciated his concern for her and the care he took of her. "I guess I was kinda out of it," she continued.

"Guess so," Shep responded then went downstairs to the kitchen.

Madison lay there waiting for Shep's return. She sat straight up in her bed, still in her pajamas, thinking how she was enjoying the conversation she'd been having with him. It was so familiar. The sun began to shine through the curtains, and for the first time in days, Madison felt peaceful.

It wasn't long before Shep returned with two cups of coffee. He handed Madison her cup, and this time, he sat down on the edge of the bed. Madison gripped her cup tightly in her hands and held them to her lips as if protecting them from an unwanted advance.

"Madison." That was all Shep said.

"Yes, that's my name. Was there something you wanted to say?' Madison was intrigued by his opening gambit.

"Yes, there's been something on my mind all these years." He fell silent for a moment, and she could hear him take a deep breath. "I didn't like the way we parted." Not sure what he was going to say next, Madison, who always had the bad habit of interrupting or immediately jumping into the conversation, remained quiet. She wanted to hear his entire thoughts.

"I wanted to apologize for my past actions. The breakup was my fault. I wanted to call you so many times, to be able to see you and hold you in my arms again, but I lost my nerve. I was afraid you'd reject me and rightfully so. I deserved it. I should never have put pressure on you to have an abortion."

Madison was stunned by his confession. When Shep found out that Madison was pregnant in their poker days together, he initially said that they would work around having a baby. But as the days went by, and they continued the all-nighters in the casino, it became glaringly apparent that a child could never fit into that lifestyle. Shep made Madison a promise that if he were to win a big tournament like the World Series of Poker or the WPT, which paid out millions in prize money, he would quit playing and settle down with her and start a family in a traditional manner. Madison loved Shep with all of her heart and had faith in him that he would be true to his word. He was a kind man and had never lied to her before. Madison was at a difficult crossroads. If she had the baby, she would be doing it alone because Shep would never stop playing poker until he realized his dream. Madison faced both a moral and ethical dilemma and the fear that if she sacrificed this life growing inside of her, she might not be able to have children in the future. She worried that the baby could be deformed or have serious health issues. All of these thoughts tore at her heartstrings.

Weeks went by, and in a weakened state of mind and physical being from unrelenting morning sickness, Madison agreed to terminate her pregnancy. She was too weak to give up the man she loved with all her heart and made the ultimate sacrifice for him.

No longer pregnant, Madison was ever so careful not to have that happen again until the time was right for starting a family. Months of poker playing went by, and soon a year had passed since she had the procedure. Madison would never forget the date and the exact time. As the day approached and the clock ticked down to the significant moment, she would stop whatever she had been doing and silently hold a vigil for the child that would never be.

Six months later, the World Series of Poker was starting. Players from all across the United States and the world flocked to Las Vegas for a chance to win millions of dollars in prize money. It would be a grueling seven days of nonstop poker playing in an effort to win one of nine seats at the final table to be held in November.

Living with Shep that week was hell for Madison. They saw very little of each other, and when they did, it was only for a quick dinner. Shep needed to stay focused and not let anything or anyone interfere with his game. Madison stayed home on the last day instead of being present in the tournament room. It was more nerve-racking for her than if she was playing in it herself. Incredibly, Shep had made it to day seven, beating out sixty-seven hundred entrants that year. His luck and skill had held up as well as his nerves. She fell asleep early that evening only to be awakened by a drunk Shep banging around the condo. He had won a seat at the final table and went out to celebrate with his buddies. He had overcome the first hurdle, and it would be several months later before the final tournament was to be played to determine who would emerge victoriously as the first-place winner.

Life returned to the way Madison was used to. They continued playing, drinking, partying, and having the time of their lives. Whenever depressing thoughts of the pregnancy entered Madison's thoughts, she refused to think about it by focusing on the moment at hand.

November rolled around, and Shep took his seat at the final table. Each day, after many long hours of play, one or two players would be knocked out, leaving behind the chance to win the gold WSOP bracelet and millions of dollars.

Day three of the tournament, and it was down to two players, Josh Dummar from Canada and Shep, making them heads up for the first-place prize. The two of them were both excellent players, capable of pulling off incredible moves, and neither player was going to go out without a fight. This was a battle for the most coveted title in poker. After a record seven hours of one-on-one playing, Shep shoved all his chips in one more time, and Josh called.

Shep had pocket aces, and as luck would have it, Josh had pocket kings. Pre-flop, Shep was ahead, but if one of the five cards to come on the board was a king, Shep could lose, and Josh would take first place. The cards were dealt. The flop came, and it was all small cards. Shep was still ahead. The dealer put out the fourth card, and neither a king or an ace hit the board. Shep's aces were still in the lead. The two players sat anxiously awaiting their fate. With only one more card to come, it looked like Shep would realize his dream of being a big-time winner. There were roughly a hundred spectators in the room, and not one of them made a sound, not even a cough or a sneeze when the last card was about to be dealt. The dealer turned over the river card to reveal a king. Josh Dummar won the tournament and five million dollars. Shep took second place, winning two million dollars. This time, instead of celebrating by going out and getting wasted, Shep went home immediately to tell Madison the news.

He woke Madison up by gently kissing her on the cheek. She rolled from her side onto her back and opened her eyes. Madison sensed something was wrong. She could see the disappointment on Shep's face. He was feeling disheartened, having gotten so close to achieving his dream and then, with the turn of one card, have it slip through his fingers. Two million dollars may have seemed like an extraordinary consolation prize for the majority of people, but it was winning the title that mattered most to him. He tried his best to put aside his disappointment as he described the losing hand to Madison. She sat up and kissed him lightly on the cheek to console him. What she really wanted to do was to make love with him. He picked up on her desire, and they indulged in a night of long past due lovemaking.

Later that morning when Madison woke up, she was excited about the prospect of quitting the poker life and starting the family that Shep had promised her. The exhilaration of the win set in for Madison. While she made plans to move, he returned to the casino. Shep returned night after night even though he became a millionaire and could retire for life. Madison questioned him about his promise to give up poker and lead a normal life if he won millions of dollars. He explained that he hadn't realized his dream of winning first place in the World Series of Poker. He felt he needed to keep playing to keep up his skill set so that he would be ready for the next year's tournament and the chance to become number one.

The desire to be number one was so heavily sewn into the fabric of Shep's character. He excelled at everything he did, and it was that quality about him that attracted Madison to him, and now it would undermine their relationship.

Madison felt betrayed and deeply let down. She had sacrificed so much, emotionally and physically for Shep. His return to the casino after the "big win" was the turning point. She knew all too well that no amount of talking to Shep would change his decision. Heartbroken, she packed her things and moved back to LA. She hadn't seen nor heard from him up until this point.

Madison finished her second cup of coffee and placed it on her nightstand. Shep took a last sip from his cup and also placed it down. He continued owning up for his actions.

"I'm sorry for what I put you through, and not a day goes by that I don't regret it." Shep lowered his eyes, ashamed for what he had done and feeling much heartache.

Hearing those two words, "I'm sorry," made Madison melt, and in that split second, all the bad feelings she had for him were erased. Enough time had passed, and the pain of those years had dissolved.

"I accept your apology." That was all she said. She wanted to kiss him so badly, but she restrained herself.

Shep looked up at her, and with sorrow in his voice, he said, "Thank you. I appreciate your kindness and understanding." The two sat silently looking at each other for a moment. The electrical attraction between them could light up ten city blocks. A clammy feeling was beginning to form on the back of Madison's neck, then Shep spoke, "I would like very much to kiss you right now. May I?" he asked her.

Madison was transported back in time five years ago. She was at her hotel door in Las Vegas, fishing for her room key, and a man she had just met hours earlier had walked her to her door and asked her if he could kiss her. And now, once again, he was asking her the same question. The passion she had felt then was as strong, if not stronger at this moment, because she knew the man he was and what he was capable of doing.

Her brain and her heart engaged in a tug-of-war. In the two seconds it took her to answer Shep, ten thousand thoughts rushed through her head.

I want to make love with him, but if I do, I'll be involved with him all over again, and I don't want to be. But he was so apologetic, and I'm feeling good about him, and I haven't had sex in a long time, and no one makes love to me the way he does.

Her emotions won out as she acquiesced and quietly whispered, "Yes."

Chapter 17

Madison and Shep showered together then dressed and went out for breakfast. They talked the entire time during the meal, but the pair never discussed what took place in the bedroom. They had an unspoken understanding that it was a onetime thing that added closure to their past.

When they were done eating, they left to go pick up Shep's car, still parked at the casino from the previous night. Playing her favorite Pandora station and tapping her hands to the music on the steering wheel, Madison's troubles seemed a million miles away.

They arrived at the casino, and Shep told Madison to drop him off at the front door. He was going to do what all professional poker players do when they're at a casino. He asked her if she was going to go home to work. She thought about it for a second and said, "No, I'll come in and play since I'm here." With a smile on her face, she also told him, "I'm going to sit at another table, not with you." He knew what she meant and let out a laugh.

Madison valet parked her car and went inside to get a seat in the poker room. The complexion of the tables had changed. The qualifying tournament was a few days away, and the other professionals and entrants had started to arrive. They were a bloodthirsty group, and it was going to be far from child's play at the tables that day.

Madison felt the excitement she used to feel when playing regularly in Las Vegas. It was partly the afterglow of lovemaking and partly the desire to take money off these guys and mess with their minds. Her competitive nature reared its head.

She placed her chips on the table and promptly took her seat. Madison settled in and looked around the table to see who had the largest chip stack. She was always extra cautious when entering a hand with a player with the most chips because in no-limit hold 'em, a player could bet any amount, forcing his opponent to risk all their money.

Madison preferred to determine how people played before she entered the game unless her cards were spectacular. It wasn't too long before Madison was dealt a great hand to play. There were several players with her in the hand and a lot of betting and posturing going on. Madison stayed in till the last card was dealt. It turned out that she had the best hand and won the pot. It was a good start to her game and table image. She played for several more hours, managing to hold on to her winning chips for the most part. A few of the players tried to bluff her, but that's what poker's all about, and Madison didn't acquiesce easily.

The hours went by quickly, and by early evening, Madison had tripled up her money. She was about to go home when she became involved in a battle with another player. Madison had a good hand, and the thought of one more win sucked her in. It got down to the last card when Tom, the other player, made a huge bet, threatening the loss of all her chips that took her eight hours of playing to win. Tom was a middle-aged man with a beard neatly trimmed, who Madison classified as pretty much a straight shooter. Madison studied the board and tried to figure out what he could have and what her next move should be.

She reasoned that he had been betting the whole time, so he must have at least a pair or better. There was a king on the board and a queen. She had paired the queen. *Could he have the king,* she wondered. Madison was struggling to decide whether to call or give up her hand. If she called his bet and lost, Madison would be risking losing all her money. But on the other hand, she could win a boatload. She closed her eyes for a second and put her hand to her forehead as if to relieve a headache. When her hand touched her head, she saw two cards in her mind's eye. They were a pair of tens, both black. She didn't know what to make of it. Perhaps it was just wishful thinking and reasoned that this straight shooter wouldn't be betting such large amounts of money with just a pair of tens. Feeling pressure to make a choice, she let out a sigh and said, "What the hell, I call," and matched the chips he had bet. Madison waited for him to show his cards, fearing he had a king and the winning hand.

"You won," he said, nonchalantly, and threw his cards away, accidentally flipping over one of them. It was a ten of clubs. Madison couldn't believe her eyes and ears. Those two words meant she had just won three thousand dollars. Even more overwhelming was how accurate her vision was. Stunned, she asked him what the other card was, and surprisingly, he answered her, "Ten of spades." Her vision was spot on. She scooped up the chips and wondered how she could have mentally seen his cards. It was an eerie feeling that sent a chill down her spine. She asked herself if this was a lucky guess or perhaps a case of déjà vu.

After the stressful experience of almost losing her entire winnings, Madison thought it was best to quit while she was ahead. She gathered up her belongings and stood up from her seat to leave. "Nice playing with you all," Madison told the players at the table. She was always polite, win or lose. She looked around the room for Shep to let him know that she was leaving and to say good night, but he was nowhere to be found.

She cashed out her chips and headed out the door to valet parking. The young attendant walked over to her and asked her for her keys. Madison looked at his name tag and read "David" but said, "Thank you, Scott," in a manner of familiarity.

"Wow, how did you know my name's Scott?" he asked.

"Maybe I heard someone say it," Madison replied. Scott ran to get her car, and Madison pondered to herself, *How did I know that?* Without a plausible answer, she said, "Oh well," and shrugged it off.

Madison drove home, looking forward to having dinner and hitting the sheets early. At home, she made herself a cup of soup, and when she finished, she went straight up to her bedroom. She looked forward to climbing into bed and watching TV like she usually did to help her decompress. The day's activities thankfully kept her from thinking about her problems and enabling sleep to come easily.

Before Madison knew it, it was early morning, and she was in REM sleep, dreaming. She woke up and replayed the dream in her mind so that she would remember what it was about. It was a rather disturbing dream, and oddly enough since her return home from the hospital, it was one that she had before. It was about Frank. Once again, she and Frank were at a house that was unfamiliar to Madison.

But this time, Madison knew that they were there to preview it for a client. It was a sunny day. Then the scene switched to night-time, and it was raining heavily. She went home with Frank. He headed into his bedroom as she stood in the doorway, peering in. He was getting completely undressed. Madison felt embarrassed. She scanned the room and saw Frank sitting on the edge of the bed. There was a woman with him, but she could only see her back. More details about the woman began to emerge. Her hair was brunette, and it looked very long and thick with waves on the end. Madison thought how beautiful it was. A pervasive smell of something floral like roses filled the air. It was nauseating. The brunette had her arms around Frank and was kissing him from behind, then he fell over on the bed and was dead. Madison looked away, turning her gaze to the floor. There were rocks on the floor. The dream puzzled her. Could this be her way of dealing with her loss? She got out of bed to put the dream behind her and to start her day instead of dwelling on her grief.

Madison went about her morning routine and felt that she needed to get down to business. She went into her office and proceeded to make a list of things she had to get done that day. She had neglected touching base with her clients, and it was her goal to reach out to them.

She especially needed to contact Frank's clients and let them know what happened and assure everyone that it was business as usual. She sat at her desk sifting through the numerous emails only to stop to answer the phone. It had been ringing nonstop. Some of the calls were inquiries about houses for sale or rent or from telemarketers. A few were from clients who had heard about Frank's death and called to give their condolences and to find out what was going to happen with their real estate dealings.

She spent the entire morning on the phone that she barely got through her emails. About to take a break, the phone rang one more time. It was Nikolai. Without so much as a hello, he started hammering at her. "The closing's been delayed a few weeks, but I want you to bring a cashier's check to my office today. Understand?" A feeling of panic came over Madison since she still hadn't come up with the funds to turn over to him. She thought it best to give him lip service and said that she would go to the bank to withdraw the funds and deliver the check to him by the end of the day.

"Do I need to remind you that I am not a very patient man, or have you forgotten your last visit to my office?" Recalling the vision of the man falling to the ground lifeless, Madison's hand began shaking, and she was speechless. "Don't be late, for your sake," Nikolai menacingly warned Madison.

When the conversation ended, Madison immediately called Cathy for legal advice. Cathy's secretary put the call through, and when Cathy said hello, Madison acted casually calm to avoid Cathy from becoming alarmed. She talked to Cathy about getting together for dinner. Then she went into the other reason for her call. Madison told Cathy that her client was selling his building and would be closing in a couple of weeks. He wanted the escrow deposit funds that she was holding as property manager for his commercial building delivered to him today.

Madison asked if she should give Nikolai a cashier's check. "Does that mean you were able to get the funds?" Cathy asked her. Madison was caught off guard and quickly told her that she was in the process of refinancing her investment property to cover the loss. "I'm so glad to hear that you'll be able to return the money to your client. I can't tell you how sorry I am that I wasn't able to be of any help," Cathy said. She then advised Madison not to hand over the deposits since Madison hadn't a clue as to what the sales agreement called for, and she was ultimately responsible for the money. Cathy warned her that the sales agreement could have easily stated that the escrow funds go with the sale of the building, and if she gave them to the Nikolai, what was to prevent him from absconding with them. Cathy further advised her that she shouldn't comply with Nikolai's wishes until she received closing documents from the attorney, informing her as to how to disperse the funds. Madison thanked her for the legal advice. She had dodged another bullet and was feeling an ounce of relief.

Instead of calling Nikolai and getting into what surely would have been a knocked-down, dragged-out fight, she simply emailed him, politely telling him that her attorney advised her not to disperse the funds until she heard from the closing attorney as she was ultimately responsible for the money. She added that she was looking out for his best interests and that she enjoyed working for him. "Baloney, baloney, baloney," she muttered out loud.

Madison couldn't wait for her relationship with him to be over. She didn't need his business badly enough to put up with his vile behavior and aggravating personality. She only did it because he was Frank's client. Madison took a much-needed break after that harrowing episode. She went to the kitchen to get a snack and something to drink before returning to her office and work.

She opened the refrigerator door and peeked in. The shelves contained coffee creamer, an outdated carton of milk, jars of half-eaten pickles, salsa and jams, and a leftover meal that didn't look very appetizing. She closed the door and grabbed an apple from the kitchen counter. With nothing in the fridge to eat for dinner, she would need to go to the grocery store sooner or later. Madison hopped into her car and went food shopping even though she felt overwhelmed by the amount of unfinished work she had to do. She raced around the store as if she was in a contest to see who could put the most groceries in their cart in the shortest amount of time and returned home in less than an hour.

With a sandwich in hand, Madison went back to her office and picked up where she had left off reading her emails. It was her goal to get through the remaining pile of work that had accumulated on her desk the last few days. Stressed out since her return home from the hospital, she hadn't accomplished much work.

Not even a half hour had passed before the phone started ringing again. It was Detective Malachek. He wanted to know when she'd be coming in. "I'm not sure when I can get away. I've got a lot of work piled up on my desk," Madison told him.

"I can get a warrant for your arrest if I have to," he said in an effort to coerce her to come down to the station and talk. Madison didn't know if he could do that or not, but she wasn't going to bother Cathy again for legal advice. She told Malachek that she would come in the next day and she set a time to meet with him. She put the appointment in her cell phone and continued what she was doing.

After several hours of working, Madison felt worn out. She went into the kitchen to start dinner and fall into the routine she had before Frank's death. Madison reasoned this would be the best course of action. She was biding her time till tournament day, needing to stay calm and focused since there was nothing she could do at this point to repay the money back to Nikolai. All she could do was hope and pray that she would win the tournament.

The next morning, Madison was awakened by her cell phone ringing. It was Cathy wanting to say hello and to see how she was doing. Madison looked at her clock, and since it was still pretty early in the morning, she asked Cathy if she could call her back after she had her coffee. Cathy was getting ready to go into court and then afterward had a business meeting that would take a while. Cathy suggested that they get together for dinner the next evening, and Madison agreed. "Let's meet at The Palm, around seven, okay?" Cathy asked.

"Okay, see you then." She threw her legs over the side of the bed and sat up for a moment. Her dream that she was having just before the phone rang flashed back into her mind. She went over it in her head. It was the same dream as the night before but with slight changes. This time, Madison saw the brunette sitting on the edge of the bed, naked.

There was a small tattoo on her left shoulder. At first, Madison couldn't make it out. She moved closer to the bed and saw that it was a butterfly. That was all Madison could recall before the phone call from Cathy.

Since she didn't have a lot of time before her appointment, Madison immediately showered and grabbed a protein bar to eat on the way. She arrived promptly at the police station and announced her name to the desk sergeant on duty. Malachek came out personally to greet her and took her to a room down the hallway. He shut the door and directed her to sit down and make herself comfortable.

"I want to apologize for threatening to get an arrest warrant, but I needed to speak with you in a timely manner so we would have the best chance to catch the killer or killers. I hope you understand." Intimidated by his authority, Madison submissively said yes. Little did she know that his apology was just an interview technique to put her at ease and to establish rapport so that she would provide him with more information. He paused for a moment to let his apology sink in and to guarantee that Madison would feel relaxed.

"I know you suffered a nasty blow to the head. I hope you're feeling better by now," he said, showing concern for her. Madison didn't say a word, feeling miffed at his bullying tactic to get her to come in. "I just want to get your side of things and find out what you might know. You're free to go at any time," he assured her. A seasoned cop, his method was textbook 101 on how to interview a witness. "Would you like a cup of coffee or water?" he politely asked.

"No, I'm fine, thanks."

"Well then, let's get started, Madison. May I call you by your first name?"

"Yes, that'll be fine."

"You can call me Jim if you like," he said to further establish rapport.

"That's okay," Madison told him. "I'd rather just call you Detective."

With small talk out of the way, he got down to business. He proceeded to ask the usual questions. "How long did you know the deceased, and what was your relationship with him?"

When she disclosed that they were business partners for the last five years, he sympathized with her loss. He took detailed notes, listening to her very intently. He followed up with open-ended questions asking Madison to mentally reconstruct the circumstances surrounding the incident. He was particularly concerned with why she was at the condo at that time and what, if anything, did she hear or see.

Madison didn't want to tell him the real reason for her being there. She thought it might complicate things and give him reason to believe she might have been involved in Frank's murder. Instead, she said she had tried for hours to get a hold of him concerning a mechanical problem in one of the buildings they managed, and when she couldn't, she became worried.

Malachek asked her if she always worried when she couldn't get a hold of someone for hours. She was caught off guard by this question and showed signs of nervousness.

"It depends," she said, buying herself a moment to think of a good answer. "It was his week to be on call for emergencies so when I couldn't get in touch with him, I was concerned that something may have happened to him. He was very responsible, and the fact that he didn't answer his phone under these circumstances was not like Frank." Madison regained her composure, feeling that her answer satisfied the detective's question.

Malachek wanted to know if she had a key to Frank's unit, and if not, how did she get in. "No, I don't have a key. I'm not sure how I got in. You know my memory of that day is kinda foggy for me."

He said he understood and told her to take a moment to see what came to mind. A minute passed, and Madison hadn't said anything. He proceeded questioning her. "Okay, so you don't have a key. Was the door open?" he asked.

The question jarred her memory. "Yes, well, sort of. I remember knocking on his door and no one answering it. So I kept knocking and still no answer. Then I think I rang his doorbell. Then I tried the doorknob, and it was unlocked, so I went in."

"Seems like you were really worried about your friend. Knocking on the door, ringing the bell, trying the knob." Madison didn't respond to his observation.

"Did you notice anything out of the ordinary when you first went in?"

Madison explained that everything seemed in order. "Frank was always very neat," she added. She went off on a tangent about what a neat freak he was and relayed an incident where Frank rearranged a client's house that he was getting ready to show, putting things in drawers because he couldn't stand the mess. Malachek avoided interrupting her and let her continue in this extraneous recollection. When she was finished, Madison caught her breath and relaxed for a moment. Once again, he asked if she would like something to drink. This time, Madison asked for water.

"Would you like to take a break?" Malachek asked. They had been talking for over an hour and a half to this point.

"Are we going to be going on much longer?" Madison asked.

"I've got a few more questions, and then you can go about your day."

"Okay, let's continue and get this over with already." Madison was growing impatient. She felt that she really didn't have anything to add to the detective's investigation.

"How did you come to suffer a hit on the head?" he asked.

"Oh gosh," Madison exclaimed as she put her hand to the top of her head, reliving the moment it happened. "I was in Frank's condo, and nobody was around. I was looking for him. I walked down the hallway to his bedroom." Madison stopped for a moment and closed her eyes to remember. "No, wait," she said. "I'd gone in the kitchen first to see if he was there, but he wasn't. So that's when I walked down the hallway to his bedroom. Then I heard the front door open. I knew I had shut it out of force of habit. We don't live in a barn, my mother used to say." Madison appeared offbeat with her comment. "I went to turn around to see if it was Frank coming home, but I never made it that far."

Madison took a deep breath. Malachek encouraged her to take a moment to collect her thoughts. "Hang in there. I've got two more questions." She nodded yes and took a drink of water.

"Can you think of anyone who might have wanted Frank dead?"

Madison shook her head no. Her hand was covering her mouth, and she became quite pensive.

"Who do you think could have killed him?' he asked.

"I, I don't know. How could anybody kill anybody. They're not enlightened."

D.G. PARTINGTON

Madison believed that anyone who killed another person other than for self-defense was someone who was not in tune with the universe.

"I understand, and it's my job to find those unenlightened souls and bring them to justice," Malachek said. Listening to what he was saying, Madison felt a bond had formed between her and Malachek.

"One last question before you go. Madison, is there anything you can tell me that would further aid me in this investigation? Any little detail, no matter how small or insignificant it may appear to you?"

"No, not really," she said. But then, feeling that newfound connection with him, she paused a moment and then spoke, "You're probably going to think I'm crazy, but I keep having this recurring dream since I got home from the hospital."

"Oh, "Malachek said with intrigue in his voice. He paused to allow Madison to speak and possibly provide him with information that might lead to the killer's arrest.

Responding more like a friend than a professional, Malachek said, "I'm all ears." He purposely did this to make her feel comfortable in telling the dream without editing parts that may be uncomfortable.

"I'm with Frank. We are somewhere looking at a house together. Not for us but for a client. We used to do that quite often because we worked as a team. So we're at the house, but then the scene switches to his condo. Frank went into his bedroom and started to get undressed. I was embarrassed because we didn't have that kind of relationship, and I hadn't seen him naked before. Then he was joined on the bed by a woman who had thick dark hair. I remember that because I was thinking how beautiful it was. That was the end of that dream. Then I had a second dream. It was pretty much the same, but no, wait. In the first dream, she was kissing him, and then he fell dead. I remember thinking in the dream how strange that was since I didn't see any blood or anything, and I didn't get the sense he'd died of natural causes. In the second dream, I saw him lying on the bed and his head was twisted, and it was on backward, and there were all these rocks on the floor." Madison stopped speaking while Malachek

100

waited to see if there was more to the dream. "What do you think of my dream?" she asked.

Malachek was noncommittal in his response for several reasons. He was not a professional therapist, so he didn't feel he should comment specifically on it, and secondly, he couldn't say what significance, if any, her dream had. "I think dreams have a way of expressing unresolved feelings. You've been through a lot lately. And on that note, I'd like to thank you for your time and cooperation. I also want to instruct you not to discuss anything you've told me with anyone while the investigation is ongoing, and a killer is on the loose."

"Not a problem," Madison reassured him.

"Would you mind if I gave you some advice?" Malachek asked.

Curious, Madison said, "Go ahead."

"If you don't mind my saying, you're a very attractive young woman who should look out for her safety. Do you own or carry a gun?"

Madison answered him freely, "No"

She wasn't worried that she might be a suspect.

"I hope you at least carry Mace."

"No, I don't. You needn't worry about me. I'm actually working toward the fifth-level black belt in martial arts. Well, I was. I've just been so busy lately that I haven't had time, but I'll get back to it."

"I'm glad to hear that you're not totally vulnerable. Okay, I may need to contact you again. Meanwhile, enjoy the rest of your day."

Madison was glad the interview was over with and that it turned out better than she thought it would. Without further delay, she left the police station.

Chapter 18

It was early afternoon by the time Madison was done with the interview. Drained from the experience of having to relive the murder scene and answering uncomfortable questions, she didn't feel like going back to work. Since the police station was halfway between her home and the casino, Madison opted to go play poker. Playing poker was the ultimate diversion, and that was just what she felt she needed right then. But first, she wanted to get some breakfast in her if she was going to be able to concentrate. Madison kept an eye out for a diner, reasoning that "You have to work hard to get a bad meal at one."

When she arrived at the poker room, she was hoping to run into Shep. While waiting to be seated at a game, Madison looked around to see if he was playing. She didn't see him, probably because it was still too early in the day for him to be there.

Madison played for quite a while before taking a break to go to the tournament counter to find out how many players had registered. She was told there were 1,046 entries so far. The tournament was two days away, and the number could grow considerably due to the many players that wait till the last minute to enter. Madison returned to her seat and played continuously, only to stop to take business calls. She was not unlike the other players in this regard.

It was an amazing sight to see. Some players had been playing twelve to sixteen hours straight, only stopping to relieve themselves. They ordered food from the cocktail waitresses and ate in their seats.

There was a player at a table behind Madison who was asleep at the table. He sat upright by resting his chin on a Coke bottle turned upside down. A player at her table told her that the sleeping player had been at that table for twenty-four hours straight.

By late evening, Madison was still grinding it out. She had been playing for eight hours nonstop except for the brief trip to the bathroom or to stretch her legs.

There were more seasoned players at Madison's table that day, making it difficult to win. That was bad enough, but in addition, the cards were not coming her way. She had lost some money, but overall, was still ahead from her previous day of playing.

Madison hadn't been getting good cards for hours on end, so she decided it was time to call it a night. She grabbed her jacket and chips and headed to the cage to cash out. While standing in line, a familiar face headed over to get chips. It was Shep. He walked up to her. "Hey, blue eyes," Shep said with that famous smile of his. But this time, he had a twinkle in his eye and feeling in his voice. Madison lit up, glad to see him.

"Hi" was all she said, not knowing if she should kiss him on the cheek or what to say. She felt nervous talking to him.

"I was about to get my chips and play. How'd you do at the tables?" he asked.

"Not good. I lost a little. It wasn't my day."

"How well I know," he said, empathizing with her. "Have you had dinner yet?'

"No, I was cashing out and getting ready to go home," Madison replied.

"Let me at least buy you dinner."

She accepted his offer, wanting to be with him even though she wasn't thrilled at the prospect of eating casino food. They took a seat inside the deli and placed their order. Shep made small talk, but within minutes, brought the subject around to their lovemaking.

"You probably want what happened the other morning to be a onetime occurrence, and I will respect that. It brought back a lot of memories for me, and I still feel the same way about you now as I did in the past."

"It doesn't have to be," Madison said, referring to the onetime occurrence. As the words popped out of her mouth, she thought to herself, *Did I really just say that?* Making love with Shep was addictive, and she was under the influence. Shep had no problem understanding what she meant.

"Should I cancel our meal?" Shep asked. Madison nodded yes.

They drove separately to Madison's house. She arrived home first and turned the porch light on. Shep pulled into the driveway a few moments later. Hearing his car, she opened the door for him. He didn't waste any time doing what he had been wanting to do. He cupped her face in his hands and kissed her with intensity. After a minute of standing in her foyer, kissing, he took her hand and led her to the bedroom.

Completely satisfied, Madison rolled off Shep and onto her back, content and not able to move a muscle. Her orgasm was more gratifying to him than his own; he felt a deep satisfaction in knowing that he had brought her great pleasure. Shep got up and went into the bathroom to wash up. When he returned, he sat on the bed next to a half-sleeping Madison. He leaned over and gently kissed her several times. Aroused once again, Madison wanted to make love, but her body said no. "I'm going to go so you can get some sleep. Good night, Mademoiselle." With that, Shep got dressed and left Madison to fall into a peaceful slumber. It had been years since she had been called "Mademoiselle." It brought back a flood of feelings for him. Drifting off to sleep, she fought hard not to become romantically involved.

When morning came, Madison woke up at her usual time despite having gone to sleep later than usual. She immediately showered and dressed in an effort to have a more productive workday than yesterday. She wanted to clear her desk of all the paperwork once and for all so that she was free to enjoy dinner that evening with Cathy. The threat of Nikolai and the loss of the money was still looming over her head, but she was determined to put it out of her mind and get on with her day.

Madison worked diligently, and it paid off. Her desk was free of papers, and she was one step closer to getting her real estate business back on track. She turned her office lights off and went upstairs to get ready for dinner.

The Palm was an excellent steak house and always filled with well-dressed businessmen and women. Madison put on her go-to little black dress and heels. It had been a while since she had dressed in anything but jeans. She freshened up her makeup and hair and raced out the door to meet Cathy. The rush-hour traffic had subsided, making the drive possible for Madison to arrive on time. Even though it was a weeknight, the place was packed, and a reservation was necessary if you wanted to be guaranteed a table. Cathy had arrived early and was standing at the hostess desk, giving her name. Madison walked up to her and gave her a big hug.

"It's so nice to see you. Been too long," Madison told her.

"Yeah, girlfriend, I was beginning to worry about you."

"Me?" Madison queried. "Worried about what?"

"Just things. You know." That was all Cathy said.

"Well, I'm fine," Madison reassured her. "We have a lot of catching up to do."

The hostess led them to a booth located in the center of the restaurant. They ordered martinis and started chatting away, interrupting each other excitedly. Cathy told her about her law practice picking up and an interesting case she was working on. They ordered a second drink and continued jabbering. By the last drop of their drink, they were both feeling tipsy.

"You need to find time to devote to your love life," Madison admonished her. "You know when you're old and gray, all that money you're earning won't keep you warm or feed you applesauce." A reference to the aging process, they laughed so hard they almost peed their pants.

"Okay, we need to eat something and stop drinking. Otherwise, we'll have to Uber home," Cathy said in her most authoritative voice.

"I'm glad one of us is responsible," Madison said. Again, they both broke out laughing.

They ordered dinner and slowed their drinking down. During dinner, a good-looking man approached the table and said hello to Cathy. She introduced him to Madison, who picked up on the fact that he was a lawyer when he proceeded to talk about his long day in court. When he left, Madison wasted no time asking who he was.

"He works in the law firm on the ninth floor of my building. Sometimes we ride up together in the elevator."

"He's good-looking. Is he married?" Madison asked her.

"I hope not. We went out a couple of times," Cathy replied.

"So there may be someone in your future to feed you after all," Madison joked, and the two of them, still feeling the effect of the martinis, cracked up laughing.

"I don't hear you telling me about anybody in your life," Cathy said teasingly.

"Probably because there is no one."

Madison took a bite out of her food to avoid having to elaborate. But the legal eagle sensed there was more to the story than she was telling.

"And there is no one because..." Cathy asked as if leading a witness to give a more detailed answer. Madison became very serious and defensive in her response. "Because there isn't. And given the death of Frank, it's not been a priority."

"I'm sorry I pushed you, honey," Cathy said apologetically. Madison wanted to share the news about Shep but didn't want Cathy to get the wrong idea.

"Shep's back in town. But before you can say anything,"— Madison put her hand out in the air, motioning Cathy to refrain from saying anything—"I'm not getting involved with him again, so don't give me the lecture, Mother."

Cathy grimaced but remained silent.

"I don't have to be psychic to know what you're thinking." When she heard herself say those words, Madison stopped for a second and thought to herself, *Yes, lately it seems as if I am psychic.* She shook off the thought and chalked up knowing what Cathy was thinking to the fact that they knew each other so well.

"Yes, I slept with him. Twice," Madison told her.

"Oh, Madison, you're headed for trouble," Cathy warned her.

"I wasn't planning on it. He called me and said he was in town for a while. I could care less and was planning to avoid him. But you know how persuasive and charming he is."

"Yes, he is all that," came the response.

"Cathy, he apologized for all his actions in the past, and he told me he missed me and loves me just as much now as he did then. My heart melted. How could I not? You would have done the same." Cathy nodded her head in agreement.

The waiter came by and asked the ladies if they were finished with their plates and if they wanted anything more. It was getting late, and Madison wanted to get home at a reasonable hour to get enough sleep for tomorrow's tournament. They got the check and left the restaurant, promising to get together sooner than later.

On the drive home, Madison replayed the fun she had seeing her friend and the laughs they shared together.

Despite having a good time during dinner, Madison nevertheless could feel the stress in the pit of her stomach. It was always present just beneath the surface. She tried to enjoy herself as much as she could since there was nothing more at this point she could do to resolve her problems. Whether she worried or not, her fate would be sealed in a matter of weeks.

Madison learned a long time ago to compartmentalize her problems in order to keep on going. It happened months after the breakup with Shep. Madison became dysfunctional, not eating or sleeping, and almost got fired from her job. Her friends couldn't help her no matter how much they tried. One day, her landlord posted an eviction notice on her door. That's when reality hit Madison and set in. She realized she either had to make a change or just give up living. Her will to survive was stronger than her will to shrivel up and fade away.

She pulled herself together, and the next day, she dressed in a business suit, put on some makeup, and went to work. At work, she promptly went to her boss and confided in him what was going on in her personal life, and that going forward, she would be more reliable. He took her at her word and gave her a second chance. The result was that Madison became stronger than before her relationship with Shep ended and was able to deal with whatever crisis came her way.

But this time, things were different. She was feeling a little older and not as resilient as before. Shep's presence didn't help matters either. Not only was she up against Nikolai Gusev, but she was having to fight demons that she thought had been extinguished years earlier. Once again, her entire life was on the line. To think about it was overwhelming. Instead, she chose to focus on the joy of the moment.

She pulled into her driveway and saw that she had forgotten to turn the porch light on. Using the flashlight app on her cell phone to light the way, Madison put her key in the door and turned the lock. There wasn't any resistance as if it had been left unlocked. *Did I forget to lock the door also?* Madison wondered. She cautiously walked in and turned the center hall light on.

Perhaps the door was locked, after all, she thought and proceeded to hang up her coat. There on the floor in front of the closet door was a slip of yellow paper. She recognized that it came from a legal pad, and since Madison didn't use yellow legal pads, she became suspicious that someone might be in her house. Her adrenaline kicked in, and her heart raced. She was full of fear as she stood frozen, listening for the sound of any movement. Hearing nothing, she picked up the note and read it. The number 5573 was the only thing written on it. That was her house address. "Did someone purposely come to my house? What could they want?" she asked herself.

Nikolai's name came to mind. He was the only person she knew who was revengeful and sick enough to want to cause her harm. Could it be that he was so displeased that she didn't cooperate and bring him the check that he hired someone to shake her up? She wasn't sure of the answer, nor was she going to take any chances.

Her fear turned into anger, and she went into combat mode, quietly going from room to room, checking to see if someone was in the house. Madison then carefully went upstairs to scope out the second floor. She returned downstairs and went into the kitchen and noticed the back door ajar. Whoever was in the house was gone now. Concerned, Madison locked up and decided that the first chance she got, she was going to install a security system. She turned the outside lights on and went to bed, locking her bedroom door behind her.

Chapter 19

Madison was able to fall and stay asleep till morning time in spite of the scare she experienced. She had set her phone alarm to ensure that she would wake up in time to get ready to play the qualifying tournament. It was scheduled to start at nine that morning and would go on all day. It would be one of many days that she would have to play if she made it all the way to the end.

With each passing day since her release from the hospital, she felt better and better, and her energy level returned to normal, just as it was before her injury. She made sure she ate a good breakfast and packed snacks in her backpack as well as her headphones. A tournament of this size would be long and tedious, and listening to music would make the hours go by nicely for Madison.

Remembering the events of last night, she wished there was time to purchase a security system, but there wasn't any. She had more important dragons to slay. She also wanted to call Nikolai and ask if he had anything to do with the person in her house but knew it would be futile. He would just deny knowing or having anything to do with the incident. She dismissed the thought and concentrated on getting ready to leave for the casino.

When Madison arrived, she went straight to the registration desk to sign in and find out how many players had registered at that point. While waiting in the long line of registrants, she overheard a group of guys, several places behind her. They were talking about their friends who had registered and mentioning that there were more "girls" than usual. Oblivious to Madison's presence, one guy joked that they didn't need to worry about them because "girls never make it to the final table and probably wouldn't even last the first day." He was about thirty years old, nice-looking, and dressed in blue jeans and a striped shirt. Madison thought to herself what a jerk he was. She shook her head and hoped she wouldn't have to play against him.

By the time Madison reached the registration desk, she was told there were twenty-seven hundred entries and growing. She got her entry ticket and had to walk past the group of guys who made the disparaging remarks. Their utterances angered Madison that she wanted to say to them, "See you at the final table, boys," but refrained from doing so. She looked for her table and put her backpack on her seat then went to the restroom. When she came out, she scanned the room, hoping to find Shep. Spotting Madison first from across the room, Shep waved and headed toward her.

"Good morning, blue eyes," he said and leaned toward her and gave her a kiss. "For good luck," he said. Madison tried to fend him off. "It's business as usual," she told him. "I have to treat you like any other player. No offense."

"None taken. May the best man or *woman* win." He put the emphasis on woman, then flashed a big smile. Madison put up an invisible wall so as not to crumble. She returned to her seat just as the tournament was about to get underway.

The tournament director grabbed a microphone and asked everyone to please be seated so that they can start. He rattled off the rules then gave the proverbial shout to begin. "Shuffle up and deal" was the call to action.

The tournament had begun. Madison, as well as many of the other players, was anxious. It was an initial reaction, but she would soon settle into a groove and play her best.

She was going to play only the best cards to start with until she got a feel for how people played. She sat in her seat watching all the action, like an eagle watching and waiting to swoop down upon its prey. Madison played very few hands that first hour, choosing to be extremely cautious. During the next half of the tournament, she chose to make a move and played more hands.

When she wasn't playing, Madison listened to soothing music to help her focus and stay calm. In a meditative state, she practiced the power of positive thinking and envisioned getting dealt an ace and a king. She then saw the three community cards as jack, ten, and a four. She didn't see beyond that but did see herself reaching out to scoop up an enormous amount of chips.

If only that were true, Madison thought to herself. She practiced patience by watching all the action at her table and sucking on a lollipop to satisfy her sweet tooth.

Occasionally, she would get up from her seat and walk around the table for a moment or two to get the blood flowing in her legs. Madison didn't want to be out of her seat longer than necessary in case she was dealt a playable hand.

The first official break was several hours after the start, and the next one wouldn't be till much later. Madison had lots of stamina to stay the course. At times, her mind wandered to Shep. She was wondering how he was doing and planned on hooking up with him at lunch. Hand after hand was dealt, and a player named Roger emerged as the big stack. He dominated the table, with a chip lead three times the amount of the others. Flipping through the Pandora stations on her cell phone, Madison stopped to look at her cards. She had been dealt an ace and a king. "Fantastic," Madison said to herself.

When it was her turn to act, she took her headphones off and put on her poker face, staring at her cards and taking her time before making a move. She did this to keep the other players guessing whether her cards were good or bad. Madison made a bet, signaling her cards were good and hoping only one player would call and not several. Instead, she was called by the player on her right, Steve, and the big stack, Roger. The dealer put out the flop containing a jack, ten, and a four. It was déjà vu. Madison stared at the flop, struggling hard to conceal her astonishment that her vision came true. It was up to Roger to act first. He made a bet two-thirds the size of the pot. Madison was thinking that he had a winning hand, or maybe he was just trying to get her and Steve to fold.

Steve sat still for a moment, leaving Madison to wonder what he was going to do. Unexpectedly, he raised big stack's bet, and now the heat was on Madison. With a bet and a re-raise, Madison was apprehensive that she might not have the best hand after all, but her gut was telling her to look at one more card. She called the bet. The fourth card was a six, which didn't improve her hand and probably didn't help Steve's either. The big stack, in a deep, authoritative voice said, "I put you all in." When he spoke those words, he looked directly at Madison, ignoring the fact that there was still another player in the hand.

Steve folded immediately. Roger's bet was forcing Madison to risk all her chips and possibly be eliminated. The way he said, "I put you all in," brought back bad memories of her father and his controlling ways. She always felt threatened by him, never sure what he might do. Once, when she was a teenager, he slapped her face for disobeying him, and it strongly reinforced her vow to never to let a man control her—until Shep came along. He was an entirely different story.

Madison couldn't let her past history dictate her actions in light of Roger's show of dominance. She struggled to overcome her pathology of competing with men and wanting to one-up them. She could fold her cards with her tail between her legs or put all her chips in, risking being eliminated. Recalling the words of the jerk in line, "Girls never make the final table," made acquiescing that much harder. Instead, Madison weighed the odds of calling his all-in bet, reasoning it was a strategy to force her out of the hand. With her tournament life on the line, Madison bravely made the decision to call.

She looked down at the floor while waiting for the last card to be dealt. It was unbearable not knowing if calling was the right move to make, but she would find out in short order.

Hoping positive thoughts would help, she quietly repeated to herself, "Queen, queen, queen." She held her breath and waited for the dealer to turn over the last card and reveal her fate. It seemed as if five minutes had passed, but only five seconds went by. Madison's heart was beating so fast she almost fainted. It was a queen. Her opponent turned over his pocket queens to reveal that he had three of a kind. Madison turned over her ace and king showing a straight. It was the winning hand. Roger shook his head, and everyone could see the look of defeat on his face. He still had chips left, but his stack size had been decimated and was nowhere near what he had started with.

Madison pulled her winnings toward her, and the dealer started dealing a new hand. She barely had time to stack her winning chips when she stopped to look at her two new cards. They were garbage, so she readily discarded them.

She bided her time till the lunch break, and as the chip leader, she had the luxury of being choosy regarding what cards to play. Madison felt that she didn't have to play every hand, she just had to win big in the ones she did play in order to win the tournament.

Five hours later, the tournament director announced the lunch break and advised everyone to return to their seats in an hour. The noise level in the room rose considerably from the tumultuous crowd. Players sought out their friends to brag about their wins and minimize their defeats.

Madison grabbed her backpack and headed over to Shep. He was talking to an attractive female who was dressed like she was out to attract a husband rather than win a tournament. Madison stopped short of reaching them and was about to turn around and leave when Shep saw her. "Hey, Madison, come over," he shouted. Madison had no choice but to walk over and say hello. She made her way past the other players, and when she reached Shep, he introduced the woman to her. "Madison, this is Alannah. Alannah meet Madison." Both women smiled cordially and said it was nice meeting each other. Madison got a definite vibe that Alannah was interested in Shep. Who wouldn't be? Alannah smiled at Shep continuously and touched his arm several times while talking. If Madison was still interested in Shep, Alannah posed a threat to her.

Shep had always been faithful to Madison in their earlier relationship, and now that he professed his continued love for her, perhaps another woman couldn't come between them. "Madison, let's go grab some lunch," Shep told her.

Madison's claim on Shep had been staked. "Good luck in the tournament," Madison said to Alannah as she put her arm through Shep's and walked away with him.

They ate lunch at the sandwich shop because it was quick. While waiting for their sandwiches, and well into their meal, the tournament monopolized their conversation. They discussed the hands they had played and dissected their overall performance. The conversation made the lunch hour fly by, and with ten minutes left before the tournament resumed, they wished each other good luck and left for the poker room.

The bell rang, signaling the second half of the game had begun in full swing. It would continue with ten-minute breaks every two hours until early evening. Stamina was the word of the day. Players tried to solidify their position by becoming more aggressive and taking on more risk. Madison had the ability to endure, guarding her winning chips like a mother tigress watching over her cubs. At times, she would put her hand to the middle of her forehead and clear her thoughts in an effort to relax or get a chair massage from the therapists offering their services.

Sometimes when in a hand, she pressed her fingers against her head and would see cards. She took them to mean they belonged to her opponents and acted on her visions. More than 70 percent of the time, she was right and began to think this was more than coincidence.

The tournament had been going on for ten hours, and the playing field had been thinned out when the director made the announcement that day one was over. Madison had survived. This was just the beginning, for it would take two more days of playing to determine who the final ten would be in the upcoming tournament for the eight million dollars.

Chapter 20

It was evening time, and Madison was worn out. She didn't bother looking for Shep and left before he could find her. Feeling hungry and too tired to cook, Madison headed to Rosie's Pub for one of their nourishing hot dinners. It was her favorite bar and grill restaurant located close to her home and known for their homemade meals and friendly atmosphere. The bar was equally popular with the locals who loved to hang out and partake of the huge selection of craft beers.

Once inside, Madison chose a booth in the far corner away from the bar to catch a little peace and quiet. She ordered a club soda and the dinner special. While eating her meal and hoping to wind down from the days' activity, she couldn't stop thinking about the next tournament day to come. It would be another grinding day at the tables, and she prayed she would be as successful as she had been today.

Madison rushed through her meal in anticipation of climbing into her cozy bed and falling asleep. She signaled the waitress to bring her check and without delay, paid her bill. Madison was getting ready to leave when she saw Dr. Chandler, the neurosurgeon who took care of her in the hospital, walking in. She slid back into the booth and waited for him to be seated before she went over to say hello. She had wanted very much to talk to him about her accident. Madison waited a moment for him to settle in his seat, then walked over to his table with her coat and backpack in hand.

"Dr. Chandler. Hi, I'm Madison Mitchell. You took care of me in the hospital recently."

He looked at her for a few seconds, trying to recall which patient she was. "Oh, yes. You came into the ER with a nasty blow to the head. How are you doing?"

"Good. My head is hurting less every day, and I'm getting back to normal," Madison told him.

"Please, won't you have a seat?" Dr. Chandler asked.

Unsure that she should have even said hello, she stumbled her response. "No. No thank you. I don't want to interrupt your dinner."

"You're not. Besides, I'd enjoy the company. Please, take a seat." He stood up and pulled out a chair for Madison to sit in. She had no choice but to put her belongings down and take a seat. "Do you come here often?" he asked her. She felt intimidated being in his presence. To overcome her feeling of awe, Madison pretended he was some man she just met in the restaurant empowering her to answer him.

"Once in a while," she replied. "Rosie makes the best lasagna. I don't even bother to make one myself." She started to feel more comfortable being around him and went so far as to ask him a question. "And you? Do you come here often?"

"Only when I get off work late, and I don't feel like cooking. You can't beat the food," Dr. Chandler replied. By then, the waitress came over to take his order. Madison offered her opinion and said, "I recommend the dinner special. It was excellent."

"The dinner special it is and a Blue Moon," he told the waitress. "Would you like anything?" Dr. Chandler asked Madison. She politely said no and thanked him. The waitress walked away, pen in hand, writing down his dinner order. He shifted gears and asked Madison, "How long have you been out of the hospital?"

"About two weeks," came her reply. Always the eternal doctor, he informed Madison that she still needed to see him in his office for a follow-up visit.

"Okay, I'll make one," Madison said in a dismissive manner. She knew that she wouldn't be following through anytime soon because she was too preoccupied with playing the tournament. Madison quickly changed the focus away from her and onto Dr. Chandler. "Have you always wanted to be a neurosurgeon?" she asked.

"Not initially," came the response. He then elaborated. "I grew up on a pig farm in Idaho, and when I was young, I used to help my dad slaughter the pigs. I always thought I'd take over the family hog business. I don't want to gross you out, but I became fascinated seeing their brains, and from that point on, I wanted to study the brain, so I chose to become a neurosurgeon." Sensing Madison might be queasy after his explanation, he asked her what she did for a living. He was correct in his observation, and Madison was relieved he quit talking about pig brains.

"Nothing as exciting as brain surgery. I'm in real estate. If you ever want to buy a house or sell one, I can do that."

"A very important business nonetheless." He paused for a moment and looked away. Then he glanced at her and brought the conversation back to Madison's health. "You know, you suffered a really bad contusion. Any strange things happening?"

Curious about his question, Madison asked, "Like what?" Before Dr. Chandler could answer her, the waitress returned to the table with his beer.

He waited for her to leave before he continued, in an effort to keep his conversation private. "Do you have any periods of time you can't account for? Or have people said you were out of it for a time while they were talking to you?"

Slightly troubled, she immediately responded to his question. "No, not that I'm aware of. If I did, what would that mean?" she asked.

"Given where your contusion was, you could be having partial complex seizures."

Madison was taken aback. "What's that?" she promptly asked.

"In layman's terms, epilepsy," Dr. Chandler replied.

Madison became defensive and quickly told him, "If I was having a seizure, I think I'd know it."

"Actually, no, you might not," he said. Madison didn't want to deal with the thought that she might have epilepsy and pushed aside his comment.

"There is one thing that's different," she began, and rapidly added, "but it's a good thing." Madison thought this might be the perfect time to discuss the bizarre visions she was having. His curiosity piqued, Dr. Chandler moved from leaning over the table to sitting up straight in his chair. Madison definitely had his attention and could tell he was eager to hear what she had to say.

"I like to play poker. I used to play a lot a long time ago, and now, occasionally, I play." Before she explained about her visions, she wanted to be sure that he could follow along. "Have you ever played the game?" she asked.

"I played in college when I had free time. Ever since medical school, free time doesn't exist anymore," he said.

"Sorry to hear that," Madison empathized. "But anyway, you understand how the game is played." Dr. Chandler nodded yes while Madison stopped to catch her breath before continuing.

"So I'll be in a hand with one or two players. One of them makes a big bet, and while I'm deciding whether to call or not, I can see their cards. Not in reality, but in my mind." Hearing herself say "not in reality," Madison looked down while putting her finger to her mouth, wondering if she should continue for fear that Dr. Chandler would think she was crazy.

"Their cards flash by. I can see if they're red or black, and sometimes I can see the numbers. A couple of times, I'll see a hand playing out in my head, and then, several hands later, it happens for real, or I'll know what someone is going to say before they say it. It happens all too frequently to be a coincidence. It's almost as if I'm psychic." By now, Madison was nervous and feeling foolish for revealing her thoughts.

Madison quit talking, hoping Dr. Chandler would say something to the effect that she was perfectly normal. She gazed at him while he sat stone-faced, causing her to become anxious by the minute. He took a swig of his beer and set the bottle back down on the table. Much to her relief, he finally spoke. "Funny you should say that," he said to her. Madison unconsciously had been holding her breath and let out a big sigh. "I just returned from a neurosurgical conference with several guest speakers. One of them presented a paper on temporal lobe injuries and side effects. That's where your injury was. One of the side effects is seizures, which can occasionally lead to acquired psychic ability. The phenomena is thought to be caused by disinhibition in the brain's activity."

Madison, astounded by what she was hearing, just about fell off her seat. Instantly, she interrupted him. "I don't understand what you're saying, and I definitely don't understand what disinhibition is. Can you explain it to me?" Madison asked.

The waitress arrived with Dr. Chandler's dinner and set it down before him. Madison had to wait to get the answer to her question while the waitress asked if there was anything else he needed. She went on and on about how fresh the ingredients were and that they came from the owner's garden.

Patience was not Madison's strong suit, and she had to restrain herself from telling the waitress to leave. Dr. Chandler told the server he was good, and finally, she left. He took a bite of his food, and putting his fork down, he began his explanation.

"Okay, so you're driving down a busy avenue like Wilshire Boulevard, typical weekday, on your way to the art museum. Now pretend that there aren't any traffic signals or stop signs in any direction. Scary, isn't it? I'd hate to think how many accidents there'd be." Madison didn't utter a sound.

"Our brain has a mechanism to deal with all this activity or excitation in medical terms. If our excitation neurons were firing all the time, we'd be in sensory overload. Our brain has to make sure that the stimuli slows down or even stops when necessary. This is known as inhibition. Madison couldn't contain herself any longer and asked him about inhibition.

"So how does inhibition make someone with a head injury psychic?" Madison asked.

"As I pointed out before, a temporal lobe injury such as the one you sustained can cause epileptic seizures, which is associated with a decrease in frontal lobe function called disinhibition. Basically, the brain has the ability to shut down external stimuli and allows other source information to be processed, which we label psychic phenomena."

Dr. Chandler stopped for a moment to take a bite of his food. Madison held her hand to her mouth and shook her head back and forth in disbelief as she tried very hard to process the information. She was concerned that she had already taken up too much of his time but needed further clarification to help her overcome her feeling of despair.

"So what you're saying is that it's possible that I've become psychic, but I may have epilepsy? Right?"

"Not necessarily," Dr. Chandler proclaimed. "Some people can alter the neural pathways and awaken psychic abilities through meditation. It doesn't always have to be associated with seizure activity. I really don't like making armchair diagnoses. I urge you to make that appointment with me rather sooner than later. Also, until you come back for your checkup, I would strongly advise you not to get overly tired and stay away from alcohol as those factors can trigger seizures." Madison was appreciative of his time, and his final words offered some consolation.

"Thank you so much for taking the time to explain things to me. You truly are a very special doctor for caring so much about your patients. I'll see you soon," Madison told him and then interjected a little humor. "And that's not a psychic prediction."

Dr. Chandler laughed and said good night. Madison was more tired than ever, having stayed so long talking with him. She sped home, pushing the speed limits, but not exceeding them, in anticipation of going to sleep.

Chapter 21

Madison wanted to get up early the next morning to get some office work done but mostly to prepare for the tournament. She set her alarm to ensure she didn't oversleep, and at 6:00 a.m. sharp, it went off. Madison felt like only two hours had passed since she first laid her head on the pillow. She dragged herself out of bed and took a hot shower to help her to wake up.

With the start of the tournament a couple of hours away, Madison made herself an extra strong cup of coffee and went directly to her office. Too early to make business calls, she did paperwork and read her emails. When she finished, she set about getting ready for the tournament.

However, thoughts of her conversation with Dr. Chandler from the previous evening filled her head. She replayed it in her mind, and what stood out was what he said about the possibility of her being psychic. She also recalled him saying that through meditation an individual could achieve the state of mind or disinhibition, as he called it, that enables someone to be psychic.

She Googled how to meditate and printed the instructions. It seemed easy enough. She moved to the leather chair in the corner of her office and got comfortable. Her mind was going its usual million miles a minute when she started the mediation process. She repeated a mantra over and over according to the instructions, and slowly, her mind began to quiet down. The meditation process had begun to work, and next, she focused on her breathing.

A calm came over her, and she felt a deep sense of peaceful-
ness. Madison stayed in this meditative state until her phone rang,
breaking the silence. She answered it only to find out it was a wrong
number. Looking at her watch, she saw that it was time to get ready
to leave anyway.

She made herself some snacks to take for the day's work ahead
and packed her backpack. Her thoughts turned to Shep, and she
wondered how he had done on day one. She also wondered if he had
been thinking about her.

Speaking out loud, she admonished herself, "Stop, Madison. I
can't be thinking about him now. I have to concentrate on this tournament, and I do *not* want to get involved with him again," empha-
sizing the word *not*. "Change your thoughts. Think about winning
the tournament and how that will feel." She pictured herself winning
a seat to the final table and coming in number one. She saw herself
standing next to the tournament director, who was holding one end
of a large cardboard check for eight million dollars, like the kind you
see for lottery winners, and herself holding the other end.

Imagining her financial troubles were behind her, she felt
euphoric, if only for the moment. She gathered up her belongings
and headed out the door ready to do battle at the poker table.

The rush-hour traffic had subsided, giving Madison plenty of
time to get to her destination. To maintain her feeling of tranquility,
Madison played relaxation music on the drive to the casino.

It was an exceptionally clear sunny day compared to the usual
smog in Los Angeles, and the sky was filled with large white clouds
that took on the appearance of animals as she drove along. Madison
was feeling empowered.

But then, images started to flash rapidly in her mind one after
the other, jolting her out of her blissfulness. It was too fast to make
them out. *Click, click, click,* like the shutter of an old Kodak camera.
She saw arms around a man's chest. Rocks flying through the air. She
almost hit the car in front of her when it suddenly came to a complete halt on the freeway. She was now stuck in traffic, and instead
of seeing flashing images, she saw cars backed up in front of her and
behind her for what looked like miles. She was thrown into a panic,

worried that the backup might cause her to be late for the start of the tournament.

Adding to the strain of sitting in a line of stopped traffic, the visions continued. Talking out loud to herself, she asked, "What does it mean? Arms around a man's chest like in my dreams. I know it's Frank, but why do I keep having these visions? It doesn't make any sense." Madison was frustrated in her attempt to figure out the meaning behind the apparitions. "Is he trying to tell me something? And rocks, they were flying in the air. What's that supposed to signify? In my dreams I didn't see the stones flying, they were on the floor. Wait a minute, I said stones instead of rocks." Madison paused for a moment to reflect on her choice of words she used to describe the dream. "That's it. I saw a blue stone on the floor in my dream." She'd had an epiphany. "It was a ring."

Madison pulled her cell phone out from her purse and started dialing. "Precinct 5, homicide division. Sargent Lopez on duty. How can I direct your call?"

"I'd like to speak with Detective Malachek please."

"Your name?"

"Madison Mitchell."

"I'll see if he's in his office. Just a minute."

"This is Detective Malachek, Madison."

"Oh, good morning." She was surprised that he answered her call right away. "I'm stuck in traffic, and I was going over my dream. The one I told you about." Thinking Madison was bizarre for calling him about a dream, he humored her. "Uh-huh." Malachek said. "Do you remember that I told you I saw rocks on the floor?" Halfheartedly listening to her, he said, "Uh-huh."

"Well, when I was thinking about the dream and talking it out, I said stones. And then I recalled that I saw a stone on the bedroom floor, and it dawned on me that it was a ring."

He began to treat her like a child and asked her, "And what was the color of the stone? Was it a diamond or was it green?"

"It was blue," Madison stated.

"What shade of blue was it? Blue like turquoise or dark blue like sapphire?"

"It was dark blue with flecks of gold like a lapis."

"I see," Malachek said, once again, indulging her. Then in a dismisssive attitude, he asked her if there was anything else on her mind.

"No, that's it." she replied.

"Well, if that's all, I'll get back to work. Thank you for your call, and have a nice day." He struck Madison as being insincere. Instead of being offended, she chose to chalk it up to the off chance that he was extremely busy.

Madison hung up her phone, and by now, traffic was moving. She passed the point of the slow-down and saw a brown Jeep and two state troopers on the side of the road. It was just plain old rubber necking that caused the cars to pile up and stop traffic. "How annoying," Madison said and continued on her way.

The rest of the ride to the casino was uneventful, and Madison got there with plenty of time to spare. She went to the registration desk and got her bag of chips she had placed with them the day before as required by the tournament rules. She then headed to her seat to put her jacket down before going to the restroom. While walking to the ladies room, she ran into Shep. Madison was in a much better mood having meditated, and its effects were still resonating with her. She leaned over and gave him a kiss on the cheek. Shep was caught off guard by her friendliness. Surprised, he said to her, "Nice to see you too, blue eyes. I looked for you yesterday, but you bolted out of here so fast." He then asked her, "How'd you do?"

"I won a huge pot from the big stack at my table, and I became the chip leader. I was very careful not to give them back."

"That's great. One can only hope I'll see you at the final table." He gave her a kiss on the cheek and said, "Let's take our seats."

The tournament was going to begin shortly; Madison settled into her seat and looked around her table. None of the nine players were from her table the day before. There was one familiar face. It was the guy who was in line behind Madison talking like a male chauvinist and putting women down. She would have to start all over again to determine how they played.

Her work was cut out for her, but Madison was confident that she would figure it out in no time at all. The players took their chips out of the bags and set them up by values in front of them. Some players liked to put them in short stacks, and others liked to pile each color as high as they could go in a show of dominance. When everyone was done, she checked out their stack size, but oddly enough, all eyes were on her as she had the most chips in front of her. She overheard the male chauvinist's friend call him Todd. He never once looked at Madison.

The call to the dealers to "shuffle up and deal" had been made, and the clock had started running. Starting play was always a little stressful, and Madison hoped the technique of meditation would help her stay serene throughout the day. Each playing level would last twenty minutes, and there would be two breaks before lunch. If Madison was one of the lucky ones to make it to day three, she could expect to be there late into the evening.

Playing poker for hours on end was fatiguing, and a player had to have stamina and the ability to concentrate for long periods of time. Fortunately, that was one of Madison's strong points. She had been used to playing poker for twelve to sixteen hours a day in her past. With so much riding on this prequalifying tournament, she had to be prepared for the challenge.

The first hand dealt to her was not playable, and the next hundred seemed to be the same way. She waited patiently for the right hand like a cat waiting in the bushes. Then unexpectedly, along comes a mouse, and the cat pounces on his unsuspecting victim who now becomes dinner.

An hour and a half passed before that prey came Madison's way in the form of two aces. She raised the pot, and only one player chose to enter the arena with her. The amount of chips Madison had in front of her was a threat, and all the players had noticed she hadn't been playing a hand until now. They figured that she must have had a monster of a hand and would only call if they also had a giant of a hand.

The first three cards came out, and they were all of a low denomination. Madison's cards could conceivably be the best. One way she could tell would be to make a bet and see if her opponent called her or not. On the other hand, if he raises her, she might not have the best hand.

Madison looked over at her opponent in an effort to get a read on him, but his blank stare revealed nothing. Poker players will say it's a game of skill, but right now, Madison felt that it was more of a guessing game with dire consequences. She made a very large bet and he called it. Madison hadn't gained any information. Quietly, she fretted deep inside and thought to herself, "If I am psychic, where's my power now that I need it?" The fourth card was about to come out, and the cat and mouse game would continue. It was a queen, and Madison checked in preparation for trapping her prey. Assuming Madison had nothing, he took the bait and said, "I'm all in." Madison snapped her response. "I call," she blurted out confidently.

The dealer told them to turn over their cards as required in a tournament. He showed two kings against Madison's two aces. A sinking feeling came over his face with the realization that his tournament life might be coming to an end. Her cards were not a guaranteed winner; they could be easily "cracked" as they say in poker lingo if another king came out, giving him three of a kind and the winning hand.

The two players were standing by their seats, anxiously awaiting their fate. The anxiety was too much for Madison to bear. She walked away not wanting to see the last card. She heard one of the other male players say to her opponent, "Sorry, bro," signaling that she had won the hand. Madison took a breath of air, and taking her hands off her stomach, she took her seat and sorted her chips.

The other players eyed them with envy except for Todd. She overheard him whisper to the player on his right, "She was just lucky." Madison couldn't wait to be in a hand with him and take all his chips to prove that women can play poker as well as any man, and maybe even better. She was used to hitting the glass ceiling either because so many men looked down on women or she chose to be in arenas usually reserved for men. If a man had won, Todd would have readily congratulated him and said, "Nice hand."

With her stack size even bigger than before, Madison was proving she was a force to be reckoned with and should be taken seriously.

She relaxed a little as her chip stack had gone from the biggest at the table to even bigger. If things kept going her way, she could easily make it to the last day.

The two bottles of water Madison had consumed while at the table were starting to kick in. With break time a few minutes away, Madison made a dash to the bathroom to get a head start and avoid the bottleneck in the room. There was no one in the bathroom when she entered, so she unbuttoned her pants while running into the nearest stall.

Preparing to exit the toilet, she could hear voices from several ladies entering the bathroom. She zipped up her pants and opened the stall door. Two women had come in and were standing with their backs to Madison. She walked over to the sink to wash up and noticed the woman standing in front of the mirror primping had long chestnut-brown hair with waves on the end. That sparked a memory of Madison's dream. *Could this be the woman?*

Madison rinsed her hands and reached for the paper towels, stealing a look at the woman's face. She was an African American, and Madison instantly knew that she wasn't the woman she had seen in her dreams.

When she headed back to the tournament room, the players were still on break. Madison looked around and happened to see Shep in the back of the room talking to someone. Wondering if she should go over, he caught a glimpse of her and motioned with one finger in the air to get her attention and let her know that he would be over. Madison put her backpack down and waited patiently by her seat. A couple of minutes passed, and Madison was about to sit down when Shep appeared.

"Hey, how's it going?" he asked.

"Good, but I don't want to jinx myself. How are you doing?"

"I got down real low in one hand and thought I was going to be eliminated for sure, and then I guess the poker gods felt sorry for me, and I came back even stronger. It's a wild ride at my table."

"I'm glad to hear you're doing well. My table's a mixed bag. We had one player who was always trying to make a move and bluff the crap out of his hand. He did it one too many times and got called and lost big. I can't say I was sorry for him."

A buzzer rang, and the director shouted out, "Players, take your seat. The break is about to be over."

Shep gave Madison a kiss on the cheek, taking her by surprise and causing her to become momentarily distracted. She took her seat and told herself to focus. To further ensure success at the table, she put on her headphones and listened to relaxation music. It worked as she settled down into the zone.

Having maintained her chip lead, Madison felt it was time to change up her strategy so she wouldn't be predictable. Shep used to say that poker wasn't just a card game, but a game of people played with cards. Recalling his words, Madison devoted more attention to playing mind games. She became more aggressive, taking advantage of her chip lead to intimidate and dominate her opponents.

Day two of the tournament was half over, and the action heated up. Players were eliminated at a faster pace than the previous day, and there were roughly a thousand players remaining. At one point, Madison was moved to another table, and the mind games began all over again as she sought to psych out her opponents and keep her chip lead. She started bluffing more and showing the bluffs to throw off her opponents when they folded the would-be winning hands. Keeping her lead was no easy task as there were two other players with larger stacks who seemed to be getting all the best cards. She hesitated to get in a hand with them unless she had really great cards, and even then, she thought twice about it. For Madison, the end of the day couldn't come soon enough. The long hours were beginning to take its toll on her.

She watched the action of the players at her table and continued listening to music to pass the time. Her phone rang, and she reached into her pocket to answer it.

She stood up and walked away from the table to take the call. It was Detective Malachek wanting to talk to her. Madison asked him if she could call him back later, pretending to be in a business meeting instead of in a casino. He told her that would be okay.

Five hours later, the tournament clock showed that the last hand being played at all the tables would be it for the day. She was glad to have survived and done so well. She packed up her chips and placed them in the tournament bag, labeling it with her name and chip count. Then she took it over to the tournament desk and decided that this time, she would wait to see Shep. He showed up ten minutes later with his bag of chips filled to capacity. He obviously had done very well.

"Thanks for waiting. I was hoping to catch up with you," he said then he kissed her. "I thought we could go and get a bite to eat together. How about it?" Shep asked, unsure of what Madison might answer. Feeling elated that she had made it to the third day, Madison said yes to Shep's offer of dinner. "I'm going to run to the powder room to freshen up, and I'll be right back," she said. It would be her chance to speak with Detective Malachek privately.

Madison got Malachek on the phone, and out of character, he apologized for being short with her in their last conversation. She said it was no problem and hadn't taken offense even though she did feel slighted.

"I was busy working on another case and didn't mean to appear disinterested," he said.

"You're fine," Madison assured him.

"There's another reason I called. I wanted to know if Frank had been planning any trips or vacations?" Malachek asked.

"No, not that I'm aware of. He did say he was very much in need of one as we both were."

"Oh," Malachek said casually. "Did you take vacations together?" he inquired.

"No, not really," she said nonchalantly.

"Not really like in never?"

Madison bristled at his question. "Well, once in a while, we would go away. We were friends, you know, not just business partners."

"Yes, I could tell you were friends. I saw a picture in Frank's nightstand of you and the deceased together in the mountains. Why do you think he kept it there instead of out in the open?" Searching for an answer, you could hear how flustered Madison was from her response to him. "I don't know, and I guess we'll never know now, will we?"

"Were you lovers also?" Malachek asked very bluntly.

"That's pretty personal and none of your business." Madison was becoming irritated by Malachek's line of questioning.

"Madison, do I need to remind you that this is a murder investigation, and any information you can provide might lead us to the killer, no matter how irrelevant it may seem to you." Malachek pressed on. "So were you on intimate terms?"

Madison hesitated for a minute. Her mind wandered to Shep, who was waiting in the casino, probably wondering what's keeping her. "Yes, we were intimate, but that ended a long time ago."

Madison realized that she'd been caught in a lie when she confessed to being lovers with Frank. It didn't take a rocket scientist to figure out that she had to have seen him naked even though she said she never did in her initial interview with Malachek. Feeling uncomfortable in this revelation, she couldn't get off the phone soon enough.

"I'm standing in a bathroom, and I need to use it. May I go now?"

She was the master of telling half-truths; she didn't really need to relieve herself, but after all, she was standing in the bathroom. That way, she could justify to herself that she wasn't lying again.

"Yes, go before your bladder breaks," Malachek told her, and they hung up.

Madison exited the bathroom and walked over to Shep, who was talking on his cellphone. His call ended by the time Madison had reached his side.

"I thought you skipped out on me," he said somewhat concerned. "So what are you in the mood for?" he asked—in such a way that it could have a double meaning.

Madison easily switched gears from business with Malachek to pleasure. "I know a great Italian restaurant that's halfway between here and my house. That way, after dinner, you won't have a long drive back to your hotel." That was Madison's way of making it crystal clear that she had no intention of going home with Shep. He obligingly went along for now when he said, "Sounds like a plan. I'll follow you in my car."

Shep was always polite, given his European upbringing, but he was still a man—and an aggressive one at that. When he saw something he wanted, he went after it and was usually successful at getting his way.

They arrived at Salvatore's Italian Ristorante and met in the parking lot. Madison waited for Shep to escort her inside.

"Looks like a nice restaurant. You can even smell the garlic out here," he commented.

"I know you're going to like it," Madison assured him.

Salvatore's was a family-run restaurant that had been operating for ninety-five years. The current owner, Salvatore, aged eighty-seven and named after his great-grandfather, the original Salvatore, ran the restaurant. He greeted them at the door and welcomed them in. The waiter had finished cleaning several tables, and the pair was immediately seated. When asked what they would like to drink, Madison and Shep spoke in unison, "Sparkling water."

They looked at each other and smiled; after all the years apart, their preferences were still the same. Abstaining from drinking, they sipped their water as if it was wine and placed their dinner orders with the waiter. It was late enough that most of the dinner crowd was gone and the room had a romantic feel to it. Burned out from playing, Shep kept the conversation off the tournament.

"Believe it or not, Switzerland has the best Italian restaurants outside of Italy," he proclaimed with expertise, especially since Switzerland was his native country.

"Really? I would never have guessed that," Madison said, eager to hear more about it.

"Well, when you think about it, they share a border. In fact, back in the late nineteenth century, there was a huge migration from Italy into Switzerland. At one point, the Italians numbered three million; but that number has dwindled down over the years. Still, their influence in food and music has remained."

"I never would have known that," Madison said.

Aside from being drop-dead gorgeous, Shep was extremely intelligent, making him even more desirable to Madison. He had gone to private school for most of his education with children of diplomats from around the world. His father had been a military attaché assigned to the minister of defense for Switzerland. As a result, the family got to travel a great deal, and Shep, through his education and experiences, was fluent in five languages.

She took a sip of water and then asked him if he had ever been to Italy. Oddly enough, this topic of conversation had never come up in all the time they had lived together. He told her that he had been to Italy many times as a young man and recounted story after story of his trips there and the teenage trouble he had gotten into. Madison talked about her trips to European countries, but they were nowhere near as exciting when compared to Shep's experiences. They continued talking about their favorite places and things they had done while traveling. It was like they were getting to know each other all over again, and the attraction grew with each story told.

Their dinners arrived, and the conversation and laughter continued. It was not difficult for the staff to notice the magnetism these two had for each other. One such person was Salvatore himself. He walked out of the kitchen, a violin cradled on his shoulder like he was carrying a baby, and began to play a slow, mesmerizing melody right at their table.

Shep and Madison put their forks down and turned their attention to Salvatore and his music. Occasionally, Shep looked over at Madison. She couldn't help picking up on the vibe he was sending her way. Somewhat embarrassed, Madison put her hand to her mouth to hide any feelings she might be having then quickly turned her head to keep her eyes focused on Salvatore.

When he finished playing, Shep, Madison, and the few remaining diners clapped vigorously. Salvatore continued playing as he made his way over to the other tables. He played festive and less romantic music for his next medley.

While Madison enjoyed the serenade, she was glad that Salvatore moved away, taking the limelight off her and Shep. She hurried to finish her meal, feeling it was getting late and not wanting Shep's not-so-subtle intentions to go any further. He paid the bill, and they walked out of the restaurant. Shep showed Madison to her car, and she tried with all her might to avoid any physical contact. She kept her back turned to him and grabbed the car door to open it herself. In a low, enticing voice, Shep called out, "Madison." She turned around to address him, and before she could move away, his hands were stretched out and cupping her face. He gave her a kiss that sent an exhilarating sensation down her spine. She didn't try to resist but kept on kissing him for several minutes more, becoming further aroused. Then she put up her hands and pushed against him.

"We can't," she said, almost pleading with him. "I have the tournament tomorrow." She corrected herself, "*We* have the tournament tomorrow, and we can't let anything distract us."

She acted like a teenager with her first boyfriend in the heat of the moment and came to her senses.

Instead of being a dog like some males and saying something like, "You'll feel so much better in the morning," he acted like the gentleman he was and told her that he would respect her wishes.

He held the door open for Madison and went to his car feeling disappointed. It was not because they didn't make love, but because he still had deep feelings for her and wanted to show her.

The drive home was painful for Madison. She repeatedly played his kisses in her mind and was so turned on that she wondered if it would have been better to make love with him and satisfy herself than endure this feeling of frustration.

Chapter 22

The morning sun signaled it was day three of the tournament. The playing field had been thinned out, and today's tournament would determine the final ten to play in the eight-million-dollar tournament winner takes all.

Madison awoke to the sound of her alarm going off and immediately showered and ate breakfast. Too early to leave, she chose to make good use of the time by cleaning house and doing some paperwork. She was so efficient at getting her work done that she utilized the remaining time to meditate.

Feeling relaxed, Madison looked at the clock sitting on her desk and decided now was a good time to leave. Traffic on the expressway was light, and Madison reached her destination earlier than she expected. Instead of hanging around the casino, she chose to get a cup of coffee and Googled to see where the nearest Starbucks was located. There were two within a short distance of the casino. She picked the one with a drive-through window for the sake of time. When she reached the Starbucks, she headed for the drive-through only to find an orange traffic cone blocking off the lane.

Madison looked at the time and saw that there would be enough to go inside and order. She parked her car and went in. There were only two customers ahead of her, giving Madison time to decide between a caramel macchiato and something less fattening. When it was her turn to order, she opted for the macchiato and gave the barista her name. Having placed her order, Madison walked over to the bags of coffee for sale, hoping to find a bargain and to wait for her coffee.

"Travis, egg and cheddar breakfast sandwich, mocha Frappuccino!" the barista shouted.

Madison thought to herself that the egg sandwich sounded good, but if she ate one, it would go right to her belly. She continued looking through the various blends of coffee for sale, killing time waiting for her order.

"Christine, double vanilla latte expresso." There was something about the way the barista had said Christine that sounded familiar to Madison. She repeated the name quietly under her breath, "Christine, Christine."

Madison peeked her head around the corner to see a tall, slender woman with long, thick brunette hair at the pickup counter. With her order in hand, she turned around and breezed past Madison on her way out the door. The smell of the woman's perfume wafted in the air, canceling out the strong coffee odors coming from the freshly poured drinks. Madison caught a whiff. It was strangely familiar. Madison had a revelation!

"Christine, not teen. That's what Frank was trying to tell me the night I found his coat in my closet. That's the woman I saw in my dreams. Oh my God!" Madison proclaimed to herself in disbelief.

"Now what am I supposed to do?"

"Madison, low-fat caramel macchiato, no whipped cream," the barista called out.

Madison grabbed her coffee and, practically knocking down a man standing next to her, sped out the door and into her car.

Her mind was racing, figuring out what to do as she sat in her vehicle. Madison looked at the clock on her dashboard and saw that she had very little time left before the start of the tournament. *Okay,* she thought to herself. *I've got to think about this rationally. I just saw the woman I believe to be Frank's killer. But I don't know for sure, and the tournament is starting really soon. That I know for a fact.*

Madison started up the car and drove out of the parking lot talking to herself all the while. "I can't do anything about that woman right now, I have a more immediate problem. The tournament is about to start, and if I don't play in it, I can't win, and I desperately need to win 'cause my life and my career is at stake."

Madison began to feel overwhelmed, and a feeling of fear crept into her thoughts.

"I don't want to be another murder-for-hire victim. I wouldn't put anything past that ruthless Nikolai." She took a sip of her coffee and let out a deep breath. She would have to set priorities, making it very clear to Madison what her next move would be.

She drove to the casino and turned her attention to the upcoming mission. Madison parked her car, grabbed her belongings, and ran inside to the tournament room. Her stomach was in knots. Never before had she felt such a level of anxiety and trepidation before a tournament. A lot was riding on it, possibly even her life.

She went to the cage to get her chips and seat assignment, then walked over to her table to take her seat. Madison was hoping to see Shep, but he was nowhere to be found. She placed her backpack down and began sorting out her chips along with the few players that were already at the table.

It was getting close to starting time, and when Madison was done, she closed her eyes and cleared her mind. She imagined herself winning a seat to the final table and feeling ecstatic as if she had already won. Her vision was broken by the voice of the director making some announcements.

By now, the remainder of the players had arrived at her table and were in their seats. Madison looked around to scope them out. She saw an attractive woman who was wearing a low-cut T-shirt with the words "Hold 'Em" across her chest. It was either referring to the poker game or her ample breasts that were exposed.

Madison wasn't threatened by her good looks or bra size but was more concerned with the fact that she was a female. Getting a read from a woman was more difficult for Madison. They had a way of masking their vibrations unlike male players. It was a strange phenomenon, and Madison explained it to herself in metaphysical terms. She chalked it up to estrogen against estrogen canceling each other out. It was akin to the workings of a flashlight. You need a positive and a negative charge to make it work. This explanation made sense to Madison and caused her to be extremely cautious when going up against a female player.

Without the ability to rely on gut instinct when involved in a hand with this woman, Madison would have to determine how she played poker by watching Liz's every move.

Madison had learned the woman's name when a guy next to her introduced himself, and she said hello back. Madison was all ears and eager to learn anything she could about her adversary.

It was the third and final day, and the natives were getting restless. Players were taking more risks and making moves to increase their chip count. The tournament had been going on for less than fifteen minutes when a player went all in and lost, causing him to be eliminated.

Madison sat quietly watching the action and waiting for the right opportunity to play a hand. She had a good chip lead and didn't need to take risks like the others.

Shortly thereafter, Madison was up at bat. She had been dealt a pair of queens; an excellent hand to raise with. She made a sizable bet with the potential that another player could reraise her, and put more of her chips at risk.

Madison had to make the size of the bet large enough to prevent everyone from calling. Making it too expensive to play the hand was an excellent strategy. Madison only wanted one caller, and that's what she got. Her game plan worked.

The community cards came out, and it was looking like a potential straight in the making. With just one pair, it was a dangerous board for Madison's hand. Her opponent made a huge bet, and with one minute to respond, Madison put her hand to her forehead and closed her eyes to help her think about what to do.

Madison called the bet, hoping the next card would be a queen and she would have a chance to win the pot. It was another card leading to a straight. Her opponent bet making the next call for Madison even riskier than this last one. Madison refused to give up the fight. She put her chips in.

The last card came out, and it was the coveted queen. With a set of queens, Madison made a large bet. The other player called it, and as luck would have it, he made a straight and won the hand. Madison had lost a third of her chips in that one hand. She chided herself for being so stupid and stubborn for the way she played.

The winning player scooped up his chips while Madison privately berated herself and went over in her head how she could have played the hand differently. She would have to work even harder now at not losing her chance for the final table. Losing a pot as big as that one felt like someone had stabbed her in the heart with a knife. She feared her chance of making it to the final ten players had gone down the drain.

There was a great deal of chatter going on inside her head, and Madison told herself that the hand was over and done with. She feared going on tilt and making another stupid mistake to compensate for the loss. She reminded herself that the game wasn't over as long as she had a chip and a chair and that she needed to concentrate on the remainder of her game.

She took a deep cleansing breath as the meditation book had told her to do, and once again, she regained her focus. Madison came to the conclusion that she had been too aggressive in her play and that, in the future, she would let the other player do the betting unless she had a sure winner.

She took her headphones off to pay closer attention to each player involved in a hand, especially the player she had just lost her chips to. Out of the blue, Nikolai's name and face popped into her head. Spooked, Madison thought to herself, "No, I can't be thinking about him right now." A feeling of angst came over her. She had been able to put him out of her mind, up until now. She heard Nikolai's voice call out, "Madison. The closing." The voice was so clear that she looked over both shoulders expecting to see him standing right behind her. Of course, no one was there. "Lord, have I got an imagination, but I don't need one right now," Madison said and returned her attention to the poker game.

The more she tried to push any thought of Nikolai out of her mind, the more he appeared in her thoughts.

A cocktail waitress came over to the table carrying a tray with bottles of water, asking if anyone wanted a drink. "I'll take a bottle of water please," Madison said and immediately opened it and took a gulp. Stressed out, she took a another and another, concentrating on the sensation of water rolling down her throat instead of thinking about Nikolai. She heard his voice again, bringing him back into her consciousness. 'The closing date's been set." Madison put the empty bottle under her chair. She was determined to cast aside any thoughts of him.

Two new cards were dealt to her. Madison grabbed them, bringing her attention back to the game. She was thinking that they were decent cards but waited to see if anyone was going to raise and how many would be in the hand. It would determine if she played or not. No one raised, and there was only one caller in addition to the big blind. The action came around to Madison, and it was up to her to play, raise, or fold. She wanted to play them and forget about Nikolai.

Madison was about to put her chips out when her cell phone went off. The rule at the poker table was that you couldn't be on your phone when you were in a hand. She threw her cards in the muck and answered the call, rationalizing that her cards were not that great anyway.

In a soft voice so as not to disturb the other players, Madison said hello. The voice on the other end was unmistakably that of Nikolai's. Madison's psychic ability had not abandoned her.

Panic-stricken upon hearing his voice, Madison's first thought was "If only my psychic ability would kick in when I'm playing a hand." She got up from her seat and took a few steps away from the table.

"The closing date's been set," he said, just like she had involuntarily predicted.

Scattered thoughts continued to flash in her mind, acting as a protective diversion to keep her from flipping out. "Why can't I predict whether or not I'm going to win this tournament?"

She was anxious anticipating Nikolai's next words. Was he going to tell her that the closing was going to take place tomorrow?

The final tournament was weeks away, and if the closing was before that, she might as well kiss her chance to make restitution of Nikolai's money goodbye and prepare her epitaph.

Nikolai repeated, "The closing date's been set." Then there was silence. The tension in Madison's stomach ratcheted up a notch. The pause was unusual coming from the loquacious Russian. "Tentatively."

The word *tentatively* was a game changer. It could mean that Madison would have time to raise the money she needed to pay him back or it could mean that it was going to happen any day now. With overwhelming trepidation, Madison would have to face her fear and pose the question. "Tentatively?"

She was feeling a tightness in her chest, and the thought that she was having a heart attack crossed Madison's mind. She took a deep breath to release the pressure, and it seemed to help. "The inspection report showed some problems with the building!" Nikolai shouted. "I've got to do some repair work before we can close." Madison was hoping that would mean that time was on her side.

"It could take two weeks, two months, two years!" Nikolai yelled. He was furious, especially since Nikolai was used to having things go his way and was not a very patient person. And if they didn't go his way, he manipulated situations to make them.

"We'll see. I'll notify you," he said. Madison was trying hard to keep her emotions in check and not let anyone around her know what was happening. She was sure that players in her vicinity could hear the shouting on the phone. "Meanwhile, it's business as usual. Just keep collecting the rents, and you better have the deposits for closing or there'll be hell to pay." True to form, Nikolai had to throw in a threat and take his anger out on Madison. Then he abruptly hung up.

The pain in Madison's stomach lessened a little, but the strain of winning the qualifying tournament wouldn't fade. She had been away from the table, missing several rounds of play. For all she knew, she might have been dealt a winning hand. Madison took her seat, and with Nikolai temporarily out of the way, she put on her poker face and dove headfirst back into the game.

Between hands, Madison tried to figure out how it was that she could know that Nikolai was going to call. She wondered, was it really her head injury causing her to be psychic?

She thought about what she was doing and thinking at the time Nikolai came into her thoughts. "I was paying attention to the players in the hand, and I felt I was tuned into the action and not really having any thoughts of my own," she told herself. "My mind was a blank slate, and I had the same feeling I get when I'm drifting off to sleep, half conscious, half unconscious."

She then recalled Dr. Alex's explanation of disinhibition and how the brain normally shuts out stimuli, but in her case, she has the potential to let in other information from another source. She told herself that when she has these psychic experiences, she sees a strange light. "If only I could bottle this," she thought to herself, "then maybe I could win the main event."

Chapter 23

Break time couldn't come soon enough for Madison. Her day had been one crisis after another, leaving her feeling helpless. She ran into the woman in her dreams who might be Frank's killer, she lost a large portion of her chips, and she was threatened by Nikolai. It was a challenge for her to stay calm and keep her eye on the prize.

She looked for Shep, who was also coming to find her. She wrapped her arms around him tightly, seeking comfort in his embrace. She followed with a deep, long kiss. It was definitely the stress reliever she needed. Shep whispered in her ear, "I want you too, baby, but not right here."

Madison took a step back. "Sorry," she told him. "I've had a hell of day, and it's only halfway over."

"You don't need to apologize," he countered back in his most sincere voice. "What's going on?"

Not wanting to go into details about Christine and Nikolai, she blamed her actions on the loss of her chips. "I lost a big pot, and you know how that goes." She let out a big sigh.

"Blue eyes, you need to remember, each hand is a new hand and a chance to double up or even triple." His words were meant to encourage the obviously discouraged Madison. She loved it when he called her blue eyes. He had a way of lifting her up and removing her feelings of hopelessness. She crossed her arms and gained her composure.

"You're right," she said. "You're always right. Thank you."

"After the tournament, win or lose, let's get together," he requested.

"That would be nice. Here's hoping we both make it to the final ten," Madison added. She felt revitalized and capable of returning to the table and playing her best. Shep and Madison headed back to their respective seats when the call to shuffle up and deal was made, signaling the break was over. The playing field had dwindled down considerably from the morning start, and the closer it got to the final ten players, the crazier the playing became. At times, there was shouting, cards being flung across the table, and F-bombs dropped. In these instances, the tournament director was called over to settle the dispute, and players had to be warned that if they kept up their behavior, they would be thrown out of the tournament. Whenever money was involved, it brought out the worst in players.

The blinds were going up, making it more expensive to play a hand and assuring that the tournament would end by early evening. Madison had to play smarter and not just wait for the best cards to be dealt to her if she was going to be one of the finalists. She was under the gun. If she waited too long, there was the possibility that she could lose without playing a hand just by having to pay the blinds. Bluffing was definitely going to escalate, and the playing of any two cards was going to happen a great deal more.

Madison witnessed players win hands with the two worst cards in the deck. It was enough to make her want to quit, but quitting was not an option.

She had put away her headphones and put on her sunglasses. It was down to serious business. She played many more hands than she had in days one and two. As the tournament finale was getting closer, her stress level increased, and accepting losses were getting harder to swallow when so much was riding on winning.

To relieve the pressure, Madison meditated in between hands while some of the players rolled their chips between their fingers in a rhythmical manner over and over. The noise from the chips rubbing together grew louder, acting as a distraction to the other players and themselves.

While meditating, a thought spontaneously popped into her head. Madison perceived that poker was a random game, much like most of life. She began to understand that the only real control she had was whether she chose to play or not to play the two cards dealt to her. The size of her chip stack and the number of hands she had won gave her a false sense of control.

She had no power over what the other players would do or what cards would come out. Only by betting aggressively could she exert some influence over her opponents' actions, but ultimately, she was at the mercy of the cards and the other players' decisions.

Given this insight, Madison chose to change her approach and be less controlling. Instead of trying to exert her power, which only led to constantly feeling tension, she was going to take a leap of faith and let go, to replace strain with well-being. By allowing good feelings in, she opened up her mind, and her psychic powers increased. She couldn't change her reality, only the way she thought and dealt with it. Going forward, when playing, she would put her hand to her forehead and concentrate on relaxing. Oddly, images would flow into her psyche. The more she relaxed, the more she was able to make predictions and to know what to do. The process of disinhibition was working at its best. Whether it was sheer luck or by design, Madison emerged as one of the final ten to win a seat at the winner-takes-all eight-million-dollar tournament. Numb with disbelief and mentally fatigued, Madison was simultaneously feeling overjoyed.

She got up out of her seat and looked around the room to see Shep. It was next to impossible to see through the crowd of spectators who had surrounded the tables and boisterous players high-fiving and hugging each other.

Then slowly, a hush came over the room, and everyone stopped dead in their tracks. The director was announcing the names of the ten finalists. "Evan Murphy, Jose Perez, Madison Mitchell, Omar Petroski, Ben Shepherd, Dan Lacosta, Gunner Adams, Skip Turner, Scotty Murrin, and Jamal Brooks." Madison stopped listening when she heard Ben's name called. He too had emerged victoriously. With the announcement made, players headed for the exits while the director wished the winners good luck in the upcoming main event.

Madison remained by her seat, knowing Shep would make his way through the crowd and over to her.

With the room half empty, Shep easily spotted her and pushed his way through the remaining crowd. When he reached Madison, he hugged her and kissed her ardently.

"We did it, blue eyes, we did it." He kissed her again. When their lips released, he had tears in his eyes and said, "This brings back a lot of memories of you and me."

He kissed her a third time, and Madison melted in his arms. The first leg of the battle had been fought and won; and if only for a moment, she was going to relish the feeling. Madison was overcome with excitement, causing her to forget about the morning's chance meeting of the woman in her dreams.

"Let's celebrate," an exuberant Shep said. "Anything you want, lobster, filet mignon, and, of course, Cristal," referring to Madison's favorite champagne.

"That would be fabulous," Madison said with a huge smile on her face and her eyes shining.

"Let's go someplace close to here," she requested. Madison had it in the back of her mind that she was going to make love with Shep at the end of the evening. She wanted to be close to his hotel. This time, she wasn't going to let anything get in the way. Madison reached for her belongings, and the two hurried out the door to Shep's car. Madison Googled five-star restaurants while Shep drove. Living in Los Angeles, it wasn't going to be difficult to find, but they were farther away than Madison had wanted to be.

"The one that looks the best is an hour away. There's a steak house nearby that I've eaten at, and the truffle mac and cheese was the best I'd ever had. Can we go there instead?" Madison asked, manipulating the situation.

"Anywhere is fine, as long as I'm with you," Shep told her. He could have any woman he desired, and what he desired was to be with Madison. She couldn't help but fall in love with him all over again.

They headed to Chops Steakhouse, and instead of anticipating the delicious mac and cheese, Madison's thoughts were on Shep.

The food was as outstanding as Madison had said it would be, and instead of champagne, they had a very expensive bottle of red wine to go with their steaks. Madison rushed through dinner. When Shep commented how hungry she must have been, she went along with his explanation for why she gobbled down her dinner. She didn't want to be so obvious about her desire to head back and make love with him. He too had thoughts of being romantic with Madison and didn't delay asking for the check.

They left the restaurant and walked to his car. Shep walked Madison to her side, but instead of opening the door, he said, "I'm going to kiss you, and this time, you're not getting away." They kissed for several long minutes when Madison gently pulled away and said, "I'm ready to leave." Shep knew exactly what she wanted.

They got in the car and immediately drove back to the casino hotel. Their lovemaking was as explosive as the very first time they had ever had sex. That evening, they stayed up all night making love several times over. They couldn't get enough of each other.

Chapter 24

"Good morning, maid service," the female voice from the other side of the door called out. She knocked again and repeated, "Maid service." It was enough noise to cause Shep and Madison to be awakened.

"Come back later!" Shep yelled out in a groggy voice, annoyed that he hadn't put out the "do not disturb" sign. He had been preoccupied with making love to Madison the night before that it hadn't crossed his mind. He looked over at Madison, who had her eyes opened and was just lying there, not moving a muscle. He leaned over and gave her a good morning kiss, then rolled onto his back.

Shep looked over at the clock on the nightstand and announced, "It's ten o'clock. I'm not going to be able to get back to sleep. We might as well get up." Madison lay there quietly. She was either very exhausted or perhaps she was hoping to make love with him again.

"Come on, I'll buy you a wonderful breakfast and the strongest cup of coffee they serve," he urged Madison.

"All right," she reluctantly responded. "I need to get home anyway to change my clothes and get some work done."

All during breakfast, the conversation centered on yesterday's tournament with Shep doing all the talking. He discussed some of his opponents' style of playing and his wins, giving a turn-by-turn description of the action.

Madison was getting bored with it all, glad the tournament was over. Unlike Shep, Madison was playing poker to win enough money to save her career and put an end to Nikolai's very real threats.

Madison had vowed to never set foot again in a casino when the final tournament ended. To Shep, on the other hand, poker was his life; and just like he couldn't get enough of Madison, he couldn't get enough of poker. He informed Madison that after breakfast, he was heading straight to the poker tables. Many of the professionals and the wannabes who played in the tournament would be hanging around, and that meant there'd be easy money.

They finished breakfast and walked out to the casino floor. Shep kissed Madison on the lips and said, "I'd like to see you tonight."

Madison knew that Shep would be playing all night long, and then maybe around three in the morning, he would make time for her.

"We'll see" was all she said. Madison didn't want to relive the lifestyle she once shared with him. She had carved out a different kind of life for herself although she had never gotten over him. It had been her decision to leave Shep long ago, but she had no idea what she was giving up.

Every relationship she had in the ensuing years held promise, but one thing or another would cause it to end. When she was proposed to, the heartache from missing Shep would interfere, and she would break it off. While she had chosen to give up the life she led with him, she could never forget him.

It was the best decision at the time, given the circumstances, but she had no way of knowing just how deeply it would affect her future.

As the years passed, Madison philosophized about her life, saying you get the experience first and the lesson later. It was this backward way of life that often frustrated her.

Chapter 25

Madison bathed and changed her clothes. Her desk was piled with unopened snail mail in addition to an inbox full of emails and voice-mails to return. It was time for Madison to get to the work she had been putting off. She worked all day, only stopping for coffee. At times, her mind drifted on to Shep, wondering how he was doing at the tables and if he was missing her. She would stop what she was doing for a brief moment and daydream about him. She wished that Shep was a businessman and they were happily married, not in the "white picket fence, two kids, and a dog" sense, but working regular jobs that didn't involve gambling. Madison would shake her head, ending the daydream and forcing her to get back to work.

By late afternoon, she was burned out and hungry. She called Cathy to say hello and to see if she was available for dinner. Cathy was glad to hear from her best friend but was unable to dine with her on such short notice. Instead, they talked for quite a while, catching up. Madison never disclosed to Cathy that she had been playing a tour-nament. When asked what she'd been doing the past week, Madison told Cathy that with Frank's passing, she had double the work load. It was a plausible excuse for Madison's lack of communication with her friend, and once again, Cathy gave her condolences. Their call ended when another call beeped in for Madison. It was Shep.

"Hey, gorgeous, what are you doing?"

"I finished work and was talking to Cathy. I wanted to see if she could go to dinner," Madison told him.

"So, you going?" he asked in such a way that you could tell he was hopeful that Madison wasn't going with her.

A disappointed Madison told him that Cathy couldn't make it tonight.

"Well, how about having dinner with me?" he sheepishly asked her.

Madison let out a sigh, followed by a cough to disguise her hesitation. "Just a minute, I need a drink of water," she told him. She put the phone down and headed into the kitchen to get a glass of water and to give herself a minute to think about his offer.

"If I have dinner with him, I'll probably end up playing poker, and then we'll end up in bed." Madison disliked that she was vulnerable when it came to Shep. Conflicted, she poured a glass of water and walked back to her desk.

"Okay, I'll have dinner with you," she said in such a way that made him feel second-best.

"Don't sound so excited," Shep admonished her. Madison chose to ignore his comment and told him that she would pick him up in front of the casino in about an hour, giving her a sense of being in control of the situation. Shep agreed to her plan and said, "See you in an hour."

Madison took time to freshen up before going out. She put on a blue shirt that made her eyes look turquoise, and a pair of black skinny jeans that showed off her curves. She sprayed her hair with perfume to make the scent last and put on a shade of soft pink lipstick that made her eyes look even bluer. Ready to hit the town, she grabbed her purse and headed out the door.

When she arrived at the casino, Shep was outside obediently waiting for Madison. He hopped in the car, and they drove away.

"Hi, hope you weren't waiting long," Madison said in a very friendly voice. Her tone and attitude were a one-eighty from earlier.

Not sure how Madison would react, Shep jokingly asked, "Where we going for dinner, boss?"

"I don't care. I'll drive, and you look out the window, your choice," Madison told him.

"Okay. You're not going to get mad if I pick some greasy spoon?' Shep asked, testing her.

"Nope, I really don't care. I'm glad to be out and about."

"Ouch!" Shep exclaimed. "So you could be out with Jack the Ripper, and you'd be happy just to be out of the house?"

"Sorry," Madison said with a laugh. "I didn't mean it like that. It did sound really bad though, didn't it?" Shep saw the humor in her words and laughed along with her. They drove several miles before Shep spotted a restaurant on the other side of the esplanade.

"Hey, make a U-turn. There's a place across the road called Benny's."

Madison drove to the nearest intersection so she could turn around.

"Phil told me about it. Did I tell you I ran into Phil the Greek at the tables? You remember Phil, don't you?"

"Yeah, I remember him. Still playing professionally?' Madison asked.

"Not really. He lives in Orange County and heard about the tournament. Decided to come out of retirement and play. He's married now, has four kids. Can you imagine?"

"Yes, I can imagine," Madison said with hostility. The ice in her voice sent a shiver down Shep's spine. He shut right up, realizing he struck a nerve with her. The conversation ended abruptly, and a deafening silence filled the interior of the car. Madison drove around the block looking for a parking spot, and on the third time around, a car was pulling out.

"Wow, right in front. Perfect timing," she said pleasantly, and Shep could tell that the awkward moment had passed. Once inside, Shep looked around. There were booths and tables and an inviting bar with high-back chairs that looked comfortable enough to sit in all night long.

"You want to sit at the bar, or would you prefer a table?" Shep politely asked Madison. She walked over to the next room to see what was there. There were pool tables and guys playing and drinking. She walked back over to Shep.

"The bar's fine," she replied.

"Welcome to Benny's," the bartender said. "You know what you want to drink?" he asked.

"What do you have on tap?" Shep asked.

"We've got so many. I'll get you the list." The bartender reached behind the bar and grabbed a menu. Shep looked it over while asking Madison what she would like to drink.

"White wine," she said. He looked up from his menu and turned his head to face her.

"White wine?" he asked. "That's not the Madison I know." It sounded like a put-down to her, and Madison was very competitive. Before Madison could strike back, Shep called the bartender over.

"Blue eyes here will have a French kiss, and I'll have a Paulaner."

"Coming right up," the bartender said. He wasted no time making Madison's martini and serving it to her followed by Shep's beer. Raising his bottle, Shep made a toast. "To good health," to which Madison repeated, "To good health," and their drinks bumped together. Three martinis and two dozen chicken wings later, Madison had loosened up and, for the first time in weeks, was having fun.

"Let's shoot some pool," she suggested. Madison was a reasonably good pool player having played in college, and Shep was better at it than she was. He excelled at everything he engaged in. They played several matches, and of course, Shep won three out of five. Madison called it quits and, surprisingly, suggested they play some poker. She didn't have to convince Shep, but he said they would leave on one condition. He told her that since she'd been drinking, he would have to do the driving. Madison handed over her keys without an argument.

"Fine," she said, feeling tipsy. "You can drive, but you won't find me sitting at the poker table with you," Madison said, shaking her index finger at him.

Curious as to the reason why she wasn't going to sit with him, Shep asked her.

"One beating is enough per evening. Besides, I don't want your head to get swelled if you beat me at poker," she answered.

He let out a laugh and replied, "Okay, blue eyes, have it your way."

By the time they arrived at the casino, the poker room was full, and it would be a wait to get a seat. Madison didn't mind that she wasn't seated right away because she needed to sober up a bit before sitting down to play.

To pass the time, Shep suggested they play blackjack. He liked the change of pace from poker since it didn't take as much concentration, and there was money to be made. Madison enjoyed it also. Her knowledge of the game had improved greatly since that night in Las Vegas when she played blackjack for the very first time and her chance meeting with Shep.

They sat down and started to play. Madison knew the rules of the game, but when she would get a funny feeling in her stomach, she ignored the rules. Madison would lower her head and put her hand to her forehead, quietly asking herself, "Should I take a card or not?"

Sometimes she got a premonition about what the next card to come out was going to be, and based on that, she would make her decision, defying all the rules.

She was right more often than not. In fact, Madison began to feel that she might like blackjack more than poker. She didn't have to put on a poker face and be serious all the time.

She was playing against a dealer who could care less if she won or lost. The end result was that she was having fun as well as all the other players at the table. Everyone was joking around and laughing continuously. She enjoyed seeing the lighter side of Shep.

Madison's phone beeped. She was getting a text from the poker room that a table opened up. She went to the cage and purchased her chips, taking them with her to her seat. She had sobered up by now and told herself to get into poker mode. Playing poker was a big change from the blackjack table for her. She sat quietly concentrating on the game and people's method of play. In the old days, Madison enjoyed the challenge, and that was what had kept her coming back. Now the watching and waiting for hours was tedious and more like a job than fun.

Madison got up from her chair to take a break from playing and to check on Shep, who had been seated shortly after Madison. He was in a hand when she approached him.

"I'll catch up with you later," he hurriedly told her.

That "later" could be the wee hours of the morning. Madison returned to her chair, and a new player was seated next to her.

Out of sheer boredom, she began talking to him. It turned out that he was fascinating. He introduced himself as Michael and told her that he was a writer. That got her attention.

They talked incessantly about the kinds of stories he wrote and how he got started writing. All the while, Madison's chip stack went up and down in size, but at least she was having a good time. At one point, she looked at her watch and was surprised to see that it was two in the morning. They had talked nonstop for hours. She told him that she enjoyed "playing" with him and excused herself to go home and get sleep. "I hate going to bed so late because I'm always dragging in the morning," she told Michael.

Madison got up from the table and looked over at Shep, who seemed to be so engrossed in the game that she decided not to disturb him. She went over to the cashier to turn her chips back into money then headed to the front door to the parking lot. The casino floor was still packed with gamblers and was just as loud and frenetic as it was earlier in the evening.

Madison reached into her purse to get her keys. Shep had considerately returned them to her earlier, figuring she would be sober enough to drive home when the time came. She walked out to find her car, remembering that Shep had to park on the side from the main entrance due to the lot being packed.

At two in the morning, there were just as many cars in the parking lot as there were at 7:00 p.m. She walked down the aisles and saw row M, recalling that was where her car was parked.

She approached the side of her car and was about to press her fob to unlock the door when she felt someone grab her from behind. She jabbed her elbow into their gut and called on her knowledge of martial arts to defend herself. Madison knew she had to get out from between the cars so that she was better able to protect herself using kicks and punches. She made her way to the driving lane followed by her attacker, who was dressed in ninja clothing. He was wearing all black and had a head mask covering his face so that Madison couldn't see who was attacking her. They sparred right there in the open parking lot. Madison held her own until her assailant got her in a neck lock. It's a very difficult move to put someone in and more difficult to get out of. A move of this type is fatal, and very few martial artists are capable of executing it. She was then slammed against the hood of her car and felt something hard pressed into her side.

She thought, *This is it. I'm going to be killed.* At that very moment, she heard a male voice shout, "Freeze! Put your arms up in the air."

Madison worried that she was going to be shot by her attacker before she could be saved. Unable to move, she could hear the sound of metal clanking together.

Her attacker had been handcuffed. Someone helped Madison to stand up. It was Detective Malachek. Shocked and relieved all at once, Madison asked him what he was doing there.

"Never mind that," Malachek said without giving further details, while a second officer read her attacker his Miranda rights. Malachek then instructed the officer to take the perpetrator down and book him. Shep, after not finding Madison in the casino, had arrived on the scene just in time to see the attacker hauled away.

"What's going on here? Are you all right, Madison?" He put his arms around her, deeply concerned that fatal harm could have come to her.

"Yeah, I'm okay physically but shaken up a bit. The officer arrived just in time," she explained.

In a stern voice without any regard for what just happened to Madison, Detective Malachek said to her that he would want to get a statement. Malachek commanded, "Madison, come down to the station later this morning and make a statement," and then he walked away.

"He called you Madison. Do you know him?" Shep asked, surprised that the officer had called her by her first name.

"Yes," Madison replied, not offering any other information.

"Baby, are you in trouble?" Shep questioned her.

In a fog-like manner, Madison replied, "No, he was the detective that…" She hesitated for a moment. "The detective that interviewed me about Frank's death, my business partner."

"You never breathed a word about it. Look, it's late, and you've been through hell. We'll talk in the morning. Meanwhile, you're going to stay here with me—that's an order, not an option." Madison took hold of his hand, allowing Shep to lead her back to his hotel room.

Chapter 26

Too tired to undress, Madison climbed into bed. Shep got in on the other side, and Madison naturally laid her head on his chest. He wrapped his arm around her and held her tightly, relieved that she hadn't been visibly harmed.

This time around, Shep remembered to put out the "do not disturb" sign. His only concern was for Madison's comfort and well-being and didn't want her sleep to be disturbed.

Madison fell asleep instantly from all the exhaustion and stress she was feeling. It was a fitful sleep; she was constantly awakened from all the tossing and turning she did throughout the night. She kept Shep up most of the time, so he moved over to the sofa to try to catch some sleep.

It was one in the afternoon before Madison woke up. Shep had been up for some time, quietly waiting for her to awaken. A puzzled Madison looked over at him, confused as to where she was and why he was sitting on the sofa. She looked down at herself to see she was still dressed in the clothes she wore from last night. Dazed, Madison asked him where she was.

Shep got up from the couch, walked over to the bed, and sat down on the edge. "Don't you remember?" he asked. Still clueless, she told him no and asked him what was there to remember.

"You were attacked in the parking lot last night. I didn't know you'd left the poker room or I would never have let you walk outside alone."

Shep gave her a big hug and followed it with a kiss. Unaffected by his show of affection, Madison sat up, and the memory of the attack came back to her.

"Oh yeah, I remember it like a bad dream. I got him out in the open where I could defend myself, but he overpowered me, and just then, Detective Malachek came along at the right time. I don't know what he was doing there, but, boy, was I was glad he was there." She returned the hug and then leaned back against the headboard. Several strands of Madison's blonde hair fell across her face. Shep gently stroked them to the side and looked in her eyes, just staring at her. The two of them didn't say a word, nor did they need to. They were communicating to each other just fine without the words.

After a minute, Shep broke the silence when he said that he was thankful Malachek was there and that they caught the attacker. With that, Madison was reminded that she needed to go to the station to make a statement. Shep told her that he was going to go with her and not leave her on her own. Madison felt that wouldn't be necessary and pointed out that if she couldn't be safe in a police station, then she wasn't safe anywhere. He didn't argue with her reasoning and agreed to let her go alone but on the condition that she called him when she was finished talking with the detective.

"Not a problem," Madison promised.

"At least have a bite to eat with me, and then I'll let you leave," Shep requested, afraid to let her go for fear of something more happening to her.

"I'm not hungry right now, and I'm anxious to find out who attacked me. I'll call you later, I promise," she said. To further reassure him, she added, "I'll be okay."

Madison skipped eating and headed straight over to the police station to see Malachek. Arriving to the front desk, she knew the drill and immediately gave the officer on duty her name and who she was there to see. He called Malachek's office and was told that it would be a while before Malachek could see her.

"How long is a little while?" Madison asked innocently. The officer took offense at her question and seized the opportunity to exert his authority.

"Could be ten minutes, could be ten hours," he said smugly, treating her as if she was a criminal. Pointing to some chairs in a corner, he instructed Madison to sit down and wait.

"You can take a seat over there. I'll let you know when he's available," the officer commanded.

Madison did as he said and sat down in the hard brown uncomfortable chairs in the waiting area. She read the outdated magazines on a table next to her. Having thumbed through all of them and with nothing left to read, Madison grew impatient. She took a chance on getting an update and went up to the officer to ask him if he could call Malachek to see how much longer he would be.

"He'll be out when he's out," the officer rudely told her.

Madison had no recourse but to once again take a seat and wait. By now, she was getting hungry and thirsty, and the lack of sleep from the past two nights was catching up to her. Madison yawned uncontrollably. She pulled out her cellphone to surf the web and to make the time pass by more easily. If Malachek didn't come out soon, Madison had made up her mind that her statement would have to wait till another day. She wasn't going to wait around indefinitely.

She went to a website she had bookmarked in the past and read one article after another. By the time she got to the next article, her phone dropped from her hands, and Madison started shaking uncontrollably. She fell to the floor with a huge thud, getting the attention of the officer sitting at his desk. He jumped up from his seat and bolted through the locked double doors to her rescue, yelling for someone to call for an ambulance.

Madison was unconscious, and all four of her limbs were shaking. Fortunately for her, the officer was experienced with people having seizures and knew just what to do. He rolled her on her side so she wouldn't aspirate. He knew he couldn't stop her seizure, but he could prevent her from injuring herself until she stopped shaking. The violent contractions subsided after a minute, and Madison lay there limp as a rag doll.

Several minutes later, the ambulance arrived and the medics burst through the door. The officer yelled out "Over here!" and they immediately attended to her. "She's had a grand mal seizure," he told them, having seen it before in his own family.

The female medic placed an oxygen mask on Madison while the other medic started an IV. They asked if anyone was with her and what her name was. The officer was able to provide them with her name, but that was all. He gathered up her phone and her backpack while the medics placed her on a gurney to be taken to the hospital. He followed them outside, and once she was in the ambulance, the officer gave the female medic Madison's belongings.

The ambulance arrived at the emergency room door in a very short time, and Madison was rushed inside. She had started to come to, opening her eyes as the medics wheeled her into a room. An ER doctor came in and introduced himself to Madison followed by a nurse who immediately started taking her blood pressure. Dr. Phillips needed to determine how alert Madison was.

"Do you know where you are?" he asked. Madison looked around and saw the two medics in their jackets with the name of the ambulance company boldly displayed on their backs as they exited her room. Madison replied that she must be in the hospital.

"What is your name?" the doctor asked.

"Madison," she said in slow motion, still dazed and in a fog.

"Do you know your last name?" the doctor pressed on.

"Mitchell. Madison Mitchell," she said as she was becoming more lucid. Before she finished repeating "Mitchell," the curtain to the room opened, and a fellow doctor walked in.

"Bob, I'll take it from here. I know this patient," he said. "Okay, thanks for the help," Dr. Phillips said. He then took his colleague aside to fill him in about Madison's condition. Dr. Phillips turned toward Madison before leaving the room and assured her that she would be well taken care of. "You're in good hands," he told her.

Madison recognized Dr. Chandler without any difficulty. "Dr. Alex, we meet again," Madison exclaimed.

"Hello, Madison, wish it were better circumstances for our running into each other," Dr. Alex commented.

"Yes, to say the least," Madison countered.

"It's pretty serious," Dr. Alex said as he paused to collect his thoughts. "Dr. Phillips informed me that you were brought in after suffering a generalized seizure. Did you have any warning as to what happened?" he asked her. Madison turned her head to one side and looked down, trying hard to remember. Her memory was vague regarding her actions prior to the seizure. She tried her best to recount the experience.

"I was sitting in the police station waiting to talk to...uh, talk to a detective," she said, unable to remember Malachek's name. "I'd been attacked the evening before, and he needed me to make a statement—"

When Dr. Alex heard the word *attack*, he instantly interrupted her. "Did you suffer any injuries, especially to the head?" he asked her, concerned now more than ever.

"Just some bruising, but no head injury. I was more shaken up than hurt. Not because I was attacked but because I was overpowered by a maneuver the attacker used that I had no way of getting out of." She stopped for a moment to catch her breath, replaying the attack in her mind.

"You see, I have a black belt in martial arts, and I was on my way to the next higher level way back before I met you the first time in the emergency room, as usual," Madison said. Even after experiencing a seizure, she hadn't lost her sense of irony.

"I should have been able to defend myself, but I couldn't. That's what's so scary." Madison was feeling a sense of defeat relaying the incident to him.

"Okay, so you were in the police station, what happened next?" Dr. Alex asked.

"I was feeling nauseous, and I dropped my phone. That's all I remember."

"Did you have any alcohol today?" Dr. Alex questioned, to which Madison replied, "No."

"Were you overly tired?" was his next question.

"Well, I haven't had much sleep these last couple of days. Life gets in the way, you know." Madison was referring to her all-night lovemaking two nights ago but wasn't about to share that with him.

With a genuine concern for Madison's well-being, Dr. Alex admonished her, "I thought I warned you, when we met at Rosie's, not to get overly tired."

"I did my best," Madison said defending herself.

Dr. Alex let up on the medical inquisition but told her that given what had happened, he wanted to run some tests on her.

"I'm going to need to admit you to the hospital and observe you overnight," he advised Madison.

She raised her voice and protested very loudly, "No way am I staying in this hospital. You can't keep me here."

"No, I can't keep you here against your will," he said. He crossed his arms and shook his head in dismay. He absolutely felt the need for Madison to be hospitalized. "Let me just tell you this, your next seizure may be your last one."

That got Madison's attention. "What do you mean?" she asked him, scared of the answer he was going to give her.

"Just that you could have another grand mal seizure and die." Dr. Alex said the words *and die* very matter-of-fact without any inflection in his voice. Frightened by the thought of dying, Madison reluctantly acquiesced, saying she would stay the night.

Dr. Alex unfolded his arms, relaxing them momentarily. "Good," he said. Then he asked, "Is there anyone I need to notify to tell them you've been hospitalized?"

Aside from Cathy, Shep's name came to mind along with an image of him sitting at the poker table. He was the one person nearest to her heart and the only one that really mattered to her. Not wanting to upset Shep, she thought it would be best if she called him herself once she was admitted. Madison told him that she would handle it and thanked Dr. Alex for his kindness and compassion. Feeling a little embarrassed, he shrugged the compliment aside and told her that he wished all of his patients felt that way about him.

"The nurse will be in to fill out the paperwork and get you situated in the neuro ICU. I'll have her hurry along. You need your sleep."

Madison was rolled up to the neurosurgical intensive care unit and transferred to a bed where she settled in. A nurse took her vital signs and connected her IV to a bag of fluids that would deliver anti-convulsant medicine. She then asked if there was anything Madison needed before she left the room. Madison asked for her cell phone and thanked her. She needed to call Shep as promised so he wouldn't worry where she was.

"Hi. I left the station and did some shopping, but now I'm headed home. How you doing at the tables?" she asked him, worried that he might press her for details.

"I'm up big time. There's a lot of fish at my table, and I'm loving it. When can I see you?" Shep asked.

"It won't be tonight," she said. She needed to come up with a plausible excuse for not being able to see him. "I'm going to be tied up the next few days. I've been neglecting my real estate business, and I've got to get back on track. I've got a lot of work, and I can't let my business go to hell in a handbasket. You understand, don't you?"

"Sure, blue eyes," a disappointed Shep told her. "I'll miss you."

"Yeah, miss you too. Keep up the good work," Madison told him, referring to his poker playing. She ended their conversation with a simple "'Bye." It sounded so permanent.

"'Bye," Shep responded back.

When the call was disconnected, Madison took a deep breath and was glad that was over with. She shut her phone off for the evening, put her bed in the down position to sleep, and closed her eyes, falling easily into a deep and much needed sleep.

An hour later, she was awakened by the nurse on duty walking into her room and turning on a light. Half awake and not feeling her usual friendly self, Madison snapped, "How am I supposed to get my rest if you keep waking me up!"

"Sorry, hon, I have to check your vitals every hour. Common procedure for someone who's had a seizure." Trying to sound sympathetic, she added that she understood that it's never fun being a patient in a hospital. She worked quickly to check out Madison and let her get back to sleep. Unable to fall back asleep, Madison turned on the TV in her room and flipped through the channels looking for something to watch. It helped. She closed her eyes and dozed off.

Chapter 27

"Call Dr. Chandler and tell him to get up here STAT," the nurse in charge of Madison's care instructed the charge nurse. She ran into Madison's room after hearing Madison's alarm going off. Madison's arms and legs were uncontrollably shaking. She was having another grand mal seizure. The nurse rolled Madison on her side and said a prayer for her well-being while she waited for the shaking to subside.

Dr. Alex was still in the hospital seeing patients in the ER when he received the call to come up to the floor. He hurriedly entered Madison's room as she convulsed one last time. He felt for her pulse, fearful she might have passed away. Thankfully, her pulse was still beating. He instructed the nurse to push another five hundred milligrams of her anticonvulsant drug. Dr. Alex and the nurse stood watch over her, waiting for her to regain consciousness. Slowly, Madison came to.

"You had us worried there for a moment," Dr. Alex told her. "But you're going to be all right," he added so as not to frighten her.

Still groggy, Madison asked the nurse, "Can I have a drink of water?" She took a drink, becoming more alert as the minutes passed.

"Madison," Dr. Alex began in his most serious voice, "we're going to have to hook you up to an EEG monitor and watch you very closely over the next few days."

Feeling her feisty self again, she reminded Dr. Alex that it was supposed to be for one night only. "I agreed to stay overnight, that was it," she adamantly said.

In a very stern voice, Dr. Alex said, "Madison, we've had this conversation before, and now it's more imperative for your health and safety that you be monitored."

Madison pleaded, "Isn't there any other way? Can't I come back another day?"

Dr. Alex softened his voice and proceeded to answer her question, "I don't want to sound morbid, but I'm going to remind you that you take the risk of there not being another day."

Madison lay there, tears forming in her eyes. The nurse held her hand. "It'll be okay, honey," she said. The tears made their way down to Madison's chin. The nurse took a tissue from the box on the nightstand and wiped them away.

"Do I have your cooperation?" Dr. Alex asked.

In a very quiet, almost inaudible voice, Madison said "Yes." Dr. Alex proceeded to tell the nurse to call the EEG lab to get a technician to come to Madison to hook her up to an EEG monitor and video feed.

It wasn't long before the technician arrived with his cart to begin setting up the monitoring of Madison. He went to shut the door, but Madison instructed him to leave it open so she wouldn't feel so closed off from the world. To further calm her nerves, she made small talk with him and learned that his name was Edward. He finished his job and explained to Madison how the monitor would be charting her brain waves and the video would enable the nurses to see her.

He packed up his equipment and was on his way out the door when Madison began to shake violently. Edward stood at Madison's open door, and not wanting to leave her alone, he yelled out for a nurse to come immediately. There was a nurse attending a patient in the next room who quickly came out and rushed into the room to see Madison in the midst of another seizure. The nurse told Edward to roll Madison on her side while she went to place a call to the doctor. Three minutes later, Madison's seizure was over, but Dr. Alex hadn't arrived in the unit at that point. The nurse put in a second call for him. Dr. Alex was tied up with a trauma patient in the ER and couldn't come to Madison's side. He instructed the nurse to give her another thousand milligrams of the anticonvulsant medicine and would come to the unit as soon as possible.

Throughout the rest of the evening and into the early morning, Madison was seizure-free. It was 6:00 a.m. before Dr. Alex came into Madison's room on his morning rounds. She was awake and eating breakfast. Dr. Alex told her that he wanted to get another diagnostic test on her to see exactly what was going on. Tired from a lack of sleep, Madison didn't put up a fight and went along with Dr. Alex's recommendation. He ordered the nurse to have Madison scheduled immediately for an MRI scan of her brain and that when it was finished, he would return.

Madison was motivated to find out what was causing her seizures and get treatment so that she could deal with her problems. The final tournament was a few weeks away, and Nikolai's closing might be even sooner. Madison was sitting on a time bomb. Her blood pressure was through the roof, and the nurses taking care of her constantly reassured Madison that she would be all right. Their words didn't help her to calm down but served as a reminder of just how sick Madison was, and had the opposite effect on her. To complicate matters, Madison knew that the more she became stressed, the greater the possibility of another seizure.

It would be several hours later before Madison was wheeled down to radiology for her scan and another hour before it was finished. The scan completed, Madison was brought back to her room around lunchtime. Edward, the EEG technician, had just arrived to reconnect Madison to the monitor. The duty nurse came in to take her vitals and offered her lunch.

Madison was more tired than hungry, so she skipped eating and chose to catch some sleep.

She fell easily into a deep sleep only to experience another grand mal seizure. The alarms went off, and the nurse came running in following the same protocol as the other seizures. This time, Dr. Alex was by Madison's bedside as fast as the elevator could take him to the neuro intensive care unit. He told the nurse to give Madison phenobarbital to try and suppress this latest seizure.

Madison came out of it within five minutes. Dr. Alex remained by her bedside, and when she was fully with the program, he told her that she had another seizure. He also explained to Madison that he gave her a medicine that should help stop further seizures and left it at that. He didn't want to worry her or cause added tension. "Just get as much rest as possible in this hotel," he joked, "and I'll be back later to check on you."

"Thank you" was all Madison could eke out.

The phenobarbital was helping to stop Madison's seizure activity. She made it through the night and, in the morning, was optimistic that they had permanently stopped. It seemed that was the case until around three in the afternoon when Madison had another grand mal seizure. The nurses' notes showed that the time between each seizure took Madison longer and longer to come around. At this point, Dr. Alex had only one solution at his disposal. He went to Madison's room to discuss it with her. The solution was to intubate Madison and put her under general anesthesia in an effort to calm the brain. Since she was in a very weakened state, she readily gave him permission to try the anesthesia.

Two days had passed when Dr. Alex decided that he needed to take Madison out from under the anesthesia. He was going to discuss her EEG and the MRI results that he wasn't able to share with her on the day the scan was done due to her having another seizure. When she was fully extubated and had some time to adjust, Dr. Alex returned to her room.

"Hello," he said. "I hope you're feeling more rested."

Madison said that she felt like Sleeping Beauty and humorously added that Dr. Alex was her prince in shining armor ready to take her away. "I wish that were true," Dr. Alex said in a very serious tone. He proceeded to discuss her test results. "Your MRI scan shows focal dense scarring in the right temporal lobe from your original head injury, but more disturbing is that your EEGs showed continuous seizure spiking in the same lobe despite being under general anesthesia."

Madison's sense of humor had been put on hold. "That doesn't sound good," she said.

His tone of voice was very somber when he apologetically replied to Madison's comment, "I'm sorry to say you're right. I can't suppress your seizures. I've tried all the nonsurgical options available."

"So am I just going to keep on having seizures till I die?" Madison asked. She was scared out of her wits anticipating his answer.

"There is one last solution," he told her. Madison, who had the habit of interrupting, sat up a little straighter and quietly listened to every word he spoke. "There's an excellent probability that I can cure your seizures with surgery," Dr. Alex told her.

Madison remained silent while she mulled over in her head what he had just said. "What if I don't have the surgery?" she asked.

Dr. Alex didn't rush his response. Surgery was a big step, and it had to be Madison's decision. "People can die from persistent seizures," he told her.

Still thinking it over, Madison asked, "What's the downside?"

Dr. Alex began to rattle off the litany of possible side effects, sounding like an ad on television for pharmaceutical drugs. "There's the risk of paralysis to the left side of your body, a risk of damaging your short-term memory and a change to your personality." He stopped for a brief moment, saving the worst for last. "There's a risk of death," he said.

There's that word again, Madison thought to herself. To help Madison cope with the devastating news, her sense of humor had returned. "I'll take all three of them and hurry."

Dr. Alex understood where her response was coming from and didn't say a word. Madison returned to a serious mood and asked him a question, "About the possible change to my personality, do you mean I might lose my psychic ability?"

"Better to lose your psychic ability than to lose your life" was his reply. "I'll give you some time to think about it," he said and then left the room.

Madison lay back in her bed thinking about all that transpired. This was the hardest dilemma she would face in her lifetime, and it wasn't going to be an easy decision to make. She would have to weigh the risk of losing her psychic power along with the possibility of death or doing nothing—and still face the prospect of death.

Madison's world was falling apart. She was losing her health, possibly her life, and the threat of Nikolai wasn't going away anytime soon. Even if she had the surgery and was cured, she still wasn't home free. There was the potential of losing her business if she defaulted on delivering the escrow money, and worse, the possibility of going to jail as what could be seen as embezzlement. It was enough to send her over the edge.

Despondent, Madison wanted to disconnect herself from all the machines and walk out of the hospital. That's when she knew she needed help in deciding whether to have the surgery or not. She texted Cathy and asked her to come to the hospital after work to see her. This was the first time that Cathy had learned Madison was in the hospital. Worried, she told Madison she would be there the minute she was out of court.

Cathy arrived at the hospital early evening and went directly to Madison's room. She walked in expecting to give her friend a comforting hug but was shocked to see wires coming out of Madison's scalp and cardiac monitoring leads protruding from her hospital gown. Her index finger was hooked up to a device that looked like a clothespin but was obviously measuring some bodily function. Cathy just stood there, afraid of disconnecting some important piece of equipment if she touched her.

"Hi, honey," Cathy said, not knowing where to begin the conversation.

"Yeah, don't I look gorgeous?" Madison joked. Cathy was anxious to find out what happened and why she was hospitalized. Madison filled Cathy in on the details. She told her about the grand mal seizure that had her brought to the hospital and how the seizures were getting more frequent and worse in nature.

"Oh my God," Cathy blurted out. "What are we going to do?" she said, taking on the problem as if it were her own.

"That's one of the reasons I called you here tonight," Madison replied. "But first, I want you to do me a favor."

"Anything, just name it, you got it. If I could trade places with you, I would," Cathy volunteered.

"I need you to cover for me," Madison told her.

Cathy was surprised. She was thinking that it was going to be a more mundane request like get her mail or check on her house. "Cover for you?" The lawyer in Cathy was coming through. "Are you in some kind of trouble?"

"Nothing like that. I've been seeing Shep."

Madison could see the words forming on Cathy's lips, but before she could get one syllable out, Madison beat her to the punch and blurted out, "Don't lecture me, now's not the time."

Cathy got the message and let her friend continue on without chastising her. "I'm not getting back with him. Look, he's only in town for a short while, and then he'll be gone." Feeling resigned, Madison added, "You know he's my Achilles' heel."

Cathy nodded her head yes repeatedly. She knew that Shep was the love of Madison's life. Cathy and Madison had been friends since high school and went through many of life's ordeals together, including Shep. It was Cathy who helped Madison get through the pain and heartache that she suffered when Madison left him five years ago. That's the reason they considered themselves more like sisters than girlfriends.

"I was supposed to see him, and I haven't been in touch in days. I don't want him to worry or to try to contact me while I'm here."

"I understand," Cathy said, in support of her friend's wishes.

"Tell him that I asked you to call to let him know that my sister called and asked me to help her move into her new cabin in the mountains in Colorado. Then tell him that I don't have cell phone reception and that I didn't want him to wonder where I was and that's where I've been."

Cathy assured her that she would do as requested. "You've got it."

Shep knew Madison had a sister but didn't know much about her, so this story would easily fly. Madison had an uncanny knack for making up completely credible excuses when necessary.

Her ability to be cunning and manipulative was probably why she was so good at poker even before she developed her psychic ability. The mind games involved in poker were the reason why it had been such a thrill playing the game. Madison would often say, "I play the player, my cards are secondary."

"Other than the obvious, you said there was another reason you wanted to see me," Cathy said.

"Yes, I was going to get around to that. It's about my grand mal seizures, and—" Madison stopped talking in the middle of her sentence and puckered her lips nervously.

"Take a minute if you need to," Cathy said, almost treating Madison like a defendant who had just broken down while testifying on the witness stand.

A few seconds later, Madison picked back up. "It's about the seizures. Dr. Alex, my neurosurgeon, has tried several different drugs to stop them, but they only work temporarily. He even induced a coma by putting me under general anesthesia for several days to try and calm my brain. But that didn't work either. When he took me out of the coma, I still had a seizure."

Cathy was aghast at Madison's revelation. "My Lord, Madison. What you've been going through and all alone. You should have called me sooner. I would have dropped everything to get here," Cathy sympathetically told her without sounding like she was admonishing her.

Madison acknowledged her concern, saying she shouldn't have kept her friend in the dark and continued explaining her situation. "Dr. Alex tried just about everything he could."

Cathy, hoping the answer was yes, asked her, "Isn't there a drug you can take or some other cure?"

"No," Madison flatly told her. "I have a different type of epilepsy. It's called intractable epilepsy. My seizures can't be controlled with drugs or nonsurgical treatment."

Cathy became extremely worried upon hearing that and had to struggle to act naturally so as not to upset Madison. "Can't be controlled with *nonsurgical* treatment. Then does that mean surgery is an option?" Cathy asked optimistically.

Madison hesitated before giving her an answer. "Surgery's a possibility, but it's not that simple. That's why I asked you to come. I need help in making this decision." Cathy told her that she would do her best to help her and asked her what her reservations were. Madison proceeded to tell her.

"Well, let's see. I could become paralyzed on the left side of my body. Not too bad, I could adapt. My short-term memory could go to hell in a handbasket. I could end up like Drew Barrymore in the movie *50 First Dates*. Just imagine that I'm talking business with an important client and then asking 'Who are you?' That'll go over big for my business."

Cathy was saddened to hear about the possible side effects. "Madison, please, tell me there's alternatives," Cathy implored.

"Wait, it gets better. There's the risk of death. That wouldn't be so bad because I wouldn't be around to know the difference."

Cathy had heard enough and told Madison to stop talking that way and making light of the situation. "Get a hold of yourself. I know you like to make jokes as a way of relieving your stress, but this is really serious. We need to look at this rationally," Cathy advised, speaking like the lawyer she was. "And if you don't have surgery, what's the downside?"

Madison knew Cathy was right and became serious. "Risk of death," Madison answered, sounding gloomy. "Each time I have a seizure, they get worse and worse, and one time, I might not recover."

Cathy stared at Madison in disbelief, tears welling up in her eyes. Not wanting Madison to see her crying and cause her friend to get more upset, Cathy turned her gaze to the side.

Madison was scared and wanted Cathy's input. "I don't know what to do. I'm damned if I do and damned if I don't." Madison begged her friend for an answer. "What do you think I should do?"

Cathy struggled to regain her composure and help her best friend in a very dark hour of need. With a heavy heart, she said, "Madison, as much as I want to help you, I don't know what to say." Cathy felt helpless and as though she was letting Madison down. "But whatever you decide, you know I'm here for you a thousand percent. I love you." By now, tears were streaming down Cathy's and Madison's face. She leaned over the bed to hug Madison, dodging the wires coming out of her head, and kissed her on the cheek.

Chapter 28

Three weeks had passed since Madison had signed herself out of the hospital. The big day arrived that could change Madison's life forever. She would always remember that it was a Tuesday. There was a lot riding on it, causing Madison to feel extremely uneasy, not knowing what the outcome would be. She gathered up her things and placed them neatly into her bag and headed out the door to catch her Uber ride.

It was the start of the eight-million-dollar tournament, winner takes all, and Madison was headed to the casino. She was one of the last players to arrive and check in. Madison was the only female at the final table and was going to have to defend herself against nine male opponents, who were overflowing with testosterone and huge egos.

The tournament table was located in a designated room. It was roped off, allowing spectators to look on. She took her seat to the left of the dealer, seat number one, across from Shep, who was in seat five. He looked over at her and gave a nod, acknowledging her presence. But she could tell, he was all about winning no matter whom he ran over. That was the case with all the players, including Madison. She nodded back and went about counting her chips. Each player would start with the same amount, and the tournament would last a minimum of three days, possibly four.

The tension in the room was high. Gone was the laughter and camaraderie of the players from the qualifying tournament. Everyone was fighting for their poker life and the desire to win the money to spend on anything from a fancy car to paying off debts.

Madison's needs were more unique. She had debt like most of them, but she was the only one whose life and career was on the line, having been overtly threatened by an unpredictable Nikolai.

The call to shuffle up and deal had been made, and not a moment was wasted before the betting had begun. This final group were all seasoned players and very aggressive. Madison was not in this first hand but watched the action like a hawk. Of course, it was Shep who had started the action with a huge raise. He played hard, betting big and establishing himself as an alpha male, instantly becoming the chip leader. It was going to be interesting when Madison had to be in a hand with him. They both understood that they were going to treat each other as aggressively as they would any of the other players, maybe even more so.

The structure of the tournament allowed for a ten-minute break every two hours, and a one-hour lunch break midway through the day. The tournament would end by 6:00 p.m. and continue a second and third day, and if necessary, a fourth day, until there was only one man standing—or woman. Madison was getting big cards and when involved in a hand, for the most part, she was victorious, with one exception. She raised five times the blind, a huge raise by tournament standards, and was called by Dan and, of course, Shep. It seemed Shep was involved in any hand that was raised before the three community cards came out.

Madison had pocket aces and felt like a shoo-in. The community cards came out, and there was an ace, giving Madison a set and the winning hand at this point. She bet it big. Dan readily acquiesced and folded, but Shep called. The other two cards were a three and a six, making the board look like a potential straight, but Madison reasoned that no one in their right mind would call a pre-flop raise that big with small cards. The turn was a king, and Madison continued to bet big figuring Shep probably had an ace and a king, which would make sense for someone to call her pre-flop raise. If this was the case, she was still winning. The last card was a five, but it was highly unlikely a player would call all her bets with an 8-percent chance of getting the winning card, so Madison made another large bet. She was always careful about choosing when to bet all her chips just in case the other player had done something stupid and chased the winning card. Shep called her bet. Sure enough, he was the one. His cards were a deuce and a four to make a straight and "crack" her aces as it is called in the poker world. Madison was furious but never showed it; that would be poor sportsmanship. It would also be admitting to her opponent that he had gotten under her skin, something she never would want to admit, and especially to Shep.

The tournament clock showed it was time for lunch, and all the players were required to leave their seats for security purposes with the dealer remaining to watch over the chips. Only one player had been eliminated up to this point. For the most part, the players were playing solid poker. They chose their cards wisely and made calculated risks. Bluffing was equally a strategy in play.

The players got up from the table to take their break, scattering in all directions. Shep walked over to Madison. His demeanor shifted from fierce competitor to friendly, and he asked her to go to lunch with him. The ability to do an about-face with an opponent and leave your emotions at the door was a sign of a good poker player. Madison, who had been beaten badly by Shep, did exactly that and went to the café with him, forgetting that she had lost big time to him.

This was the first time Shep had seen Madison since her hospitalization. For the first few minutes at lunch, he talked about the tournament. Shortly thereafter, he turned the conversation to Madison's sister.

"How was your visit with your sister?" he innocently asked, believing that Colorado was where she had been all this time.

Madison replied "Fine" and didn't say anything more. "Fine?" Shep asked. "Is that all you're going to say?" He paused to give her a chance to respond.

When she didn't answer immediately, Shep revealed his real reason for asking. "You couldn't call me to say hello or that you were back in town? Forget about maybe you missed me a little." Madison wanted to divulge the details of her hospitalization these past weeks, but now was not the right time and definitely not the right place.

"I'm sorry," she told him. "I did miss you, and I'll tell you all about it when I win the tournament and make it up to you." Madison winked and gave him a big smile, reverting to her old flirtatious self. This was her way of turning a difficult conversation into something more lighthearted.

He relaxed and sat back in his chair, his body language softening. Shep couldn't stay mad at Madison for very long and accepted her apology, preferring to avoid an argument. "Oh, so you think you're going to win this, do you? I guess you haven't been counting my stack or you'd know that I was the chip leader," he said playfully but with an ounce of arrogance thrown in.

"It's still anybody's game. One big hand, and that can all change," she warned him.

Shep agreed with her and turned the conversation to the dynamics of the other players at the table. Madison munched on her sandwich, listening intently to Shep's take on them. She was eager to gain another perspective, especially from someone who was as experienced as Shep. He began talking about Jose. Since she lost a couple of times to him, Madison was extremely curious about what Shep had to say about him.

Madison had a feeling that Jose bluffed most of the time he was in a hand with her, but she didn't want to take a chance and call his oversized bets. She folded her cards to him on several occasions and was left wondering if he really had the best hand.

Shep began mentioning one of Jose's idiosyncrasies he picked up on when Jose had a good hand. Madison put her sandwich down to pay closer attention to what Shep was saying. Madison's phone rang the moment Shep was about to reveal Jose's tell.

It had been turned off during the tournament in accordance with the rules, and now she was able to take calls. It was Nikolai. "Excuse me a minute, it's business," Madison said to Shep and got up from the table and walked over to a quiet corner to take the call. She took a deep breath, expecting to be harassed and threatened by him as usual. Instead, he immediately informed her that the closing date had been set for this Friday at three in the afternoon. Madison didn't know what to think.

If she won the tournament and it was over by the third day, Thursday, she'd be saved. If it went to Friday and she won, that would be cutting it close. And if Friday rolled around and she didn't win, well, she didn't know what she would do.

Madison had to struggle to keep her emotions in check and prevent herself from falling apart. "All right, have your closing attorney email me his address along with the proper name I should make the check out to," Madison said.

Then, true to form, Nikolai started harassing her. "My secretary will give you the information, and you can tell your attorney to go fuck himself. I want you to bring the check directly to me on Friday."

Madison wasn't about to argue with Nikolai. If she didn't have the money, she wasn't going to be able to bring him a check anyway. Madison told him that he would have the check by Friday and not to worry.

"I'm not the one who needs to worry, little lady," Nikolai said to intimidate Madison. "Poof," he said. "That's how I'll deal with you." Madison knew what "poof" meant. She wondered why he was always threatening and if his threats really did turn into action. Madison went back to Shep, who reminded her that the tournament was about to begin again. Unnerved by Nikolai's call, she needed to put his threats behind her. She told Shep she'd see him at the table, and went to recompose herself.

She made a stop at the restroom to wash up and put on a fresh coat of lipstick to make herself feel better. Madison returned to the poker room just in time to hear the starting bell ring. No sooner had she taken her seat when the cards were dealt. When it came around to Madison, she discarded them instantly, not even thinking about it twice. Three players chose to play the hand while the others sat and watched intently, hoping someone would be eliminated.

There would be about five more hours of play left in today's session. She was willing to wait and be patient, a very necessary quality to have if you were going to survive to the end. The battle raged on, and Madison had only entered into a few hands. At one point, she almost ran out of chips playing two hands and losing both of them, dashing her hopes of becoming the winner. Miraculously, she did a one-eighty and, in one hand, tripled up her number of chips, emerging as the leader by the end of the day. Shep trailed her ever so slightly in the number of chips he had. The bell signaling the end of the day rang, and a total of two players had been eliminated this first day.

An exhausted Madison got up from the table and stretched her arms up in the air. Shep approached her side of the table. "Well played, blue eyes," he said.

Madison was very coy and returned the compliment. "I could say the same thing about you."

"Day one done, down and dirty," Shep said, thinking he was cool in his use of alliteration.

Madison agreed with Shep's comment then swung her backpack over her shoulder and said, "Yep, that it is."

"Will you join me for dinner or is that verboten?" Shep asked, recalling that she had refused his offer once before during the qualifying tournament.

"Thanks for asking, but I have to get home. I have a lot of things to get done." It was just an excuse. Madison didn't want to have to explain why she didn't have her car with her. If she went to dinner with him, he would surely escort her to the parking lot, and then she would be obliged to explain why she didn't drive to the casino.

"Besides, you don't need the distraction," she added, being flirtatious.

Shep was quick with a comeback, "That's a risk I'd take any day." She resisted his snappy return and told him that she would see him tomorrow. "Don't work too hard," he said in a disappointed tone while giving her a hug.

Madison made sure to stay out of sight while she waited for her Uber ride, just in case Shep was still around. She couldn't risk seeing him. Finally, the driver sent a text saying he was outside, sending Madison out the door to head home and relax.

She was fatigued, and remembering Dr. Alex's words, "You need to avoid becoming overtired," she made herself a cup of tea, put on her pajamas, and climbed into bed to watch TV and go to sleep early.

While she fell asleep easily, it was interrupted several times throughout the night for one reason or another. The first time was to go to the bathroom, and the other time was because she had a booming headache and needed to take some aspirin. Madison stayed awake for hours waiting for the medicine to kick in, but mostly for her mind to stop tormenting her about Friday's deadline, or D-day, as she referred to it in her futile attempt to fall back to sleep. It was around three thirty in the morning when Madison finally returned to a much-needed slumber and didn't wake again until eight thirty that morning.

Chapter 29

Day two of the tournament, Wednesday, was going to start promptly at 10:00 a.m., and the drive there could be as long as an hour depending upon traffic conditions. Madison hastily showered, ate breakfast, and packed her backpack. Her phone rang, and she was tempted not to answer it for fear it would delay an already rushed Madison. Thinking it could be a tenant needing immediate attention, she answered the call.

It was Detective Malachek. He had wanted to talk with her and was wondering why she hadn't been to see him. Madison explained that she had been hospitalized and was under the care of a doctor. Malachek told her that it was urgent and that she had to come to the station to clear up some details regarding Frank's murder. He also had some critical case information to share, as well as additional questions to ask her regarding the night of the attack.

Madison agreed to come down to the station but added that she wouldn't be able to get there till much later, possibly by seven or eight in the evening. She needed to be able to stay for the entire day two of the tournament in the event that she made it to the end of the day. Madison laid it on thick about her health, hoping Malachek wouldn't give her a hard time. It worked. He'd heard about her being taken away by ambulance on her last visit to see him and must have been feeling sympathetic. He didn't hassle her or threaten to get a subpoena like he had done in the past, but said it would be all right.

Madison hung up and looked at the clock. She was alarmed to see that she had less than thirty minutes to get to the casino. There was no time to call for an Uber ride, let alone wait for them to get to her house.

The words of Dr. Alex, admonishing Madison upon her release from the hospital not to drive, blasted through her mind all too loudly. "You can't drive a car for safety's sake," he told her. But Madison couldn't be late for the tournament; missing even a few hands of play could make all the difference in the world in terms of winning or losing. Rattled, Madison told herself that she would have to drive there, and to further justify this potentially bad decision, she felt it would also be more convenient getting to the police station later that evening.

Madison drove fifteen miles over the speed limit, risking a ticket in her need to get to the casino before the start of the tournament. Traffic was light, and she made it there with minutes to spare. Getting her chips from the cashier, she hurried to her seat and settled in. All the other players had been there awhile and were kibitzing with one another. Shep looked over at Madison and joked, "Nice of you to show up."

It might have been an attempt to put her on tilt, but it wasn't going to work. Madison shot back, "Heavy date last night."

That put Shep in his place and reversed the tables. The corners of his mouth turned down, and Madison knew she had won that round of mind games.

The starting bell rang, and it appeared that it was going to be choppy waters here on out. There were eight players seated and seven to knock out to become the winner. Madison had made an effort yesterday to learn all the players' names. Putting a name to her opponents' faces helped her to remember how they played. She looked over the table to see who the weakest links were. She noted that it was Jamal and Evan who had the smallest stacks and were the players most at risk of being knocked out early. Madison was as much of a target for the opposite reason. If a player took her out, he would assume the lead with her stack size.

The action was fierce and tense. Every hand played had been raised before the three community cards came out, and to make matters worse, Madison wasn't getting good cards. There was one player, nicknamed the Gunner, whose strategy was to be as obnoxious as possible. Whenever he was in a hand, he would talk incessantly, trying to make his opponents go on tilt and make a wrong move. His nonstop chatter was incredibly annoying for everyone at the table. There was one episode in particular when an opponent had to call the director over regarding his behavior and how he delayed the game. Gunner had received a warning, and when he did it again, he was penalized and had to sit out one round before he could return to the table. It was a very costly penalty, and no one had sympathy for him.

Two hours had passed before Madison chose to play her cards. It would have been easy for her to lose her patience and play any two cards, but with each new hand dealt, she told herself to "Stay the course." At one point, she was dealt a nine and a ten of spades. For some odd reason, these two cards were Madison's favorites, so she made the decision to play the hand. They were not the best cards but could become a winner with the right five community cards.

There were two spades on the flop, but they were face cards, and the betting was big! She was playing against Skip and Scotty, two very aggressive players. There was a great deal of posturing going on, like two peacocks fighting over a female. Skip would make a bet, then Scotty would reraise it.

Having called Skip's bet, she felt compelled to call Scotty's because there was so much money in the pot. Madison made her flush on the fourth card to come out. The betting between Skip and Scotty continued on furiously.

Madison was caught in the middle of a pissing contest. She had too many chips committed, forcing her to go along for the ride. If she lost the hand, she would still have chips left but would be seriously wounded. Scotty went all in. The amount of stress Madison was feeling jumped five levels on a scale of one to five while she wondered if one of them had a bigger flush.

They were both good players who respected the board, and a move like that must have signaled that Scotty also had a flush, maybe an even bigger one. Madison was uncertain about calling the all in.

She put her hand to her forehead and let out a sigh, feeling that her chance of winning the tournament was about to end. Her intellect was in a battle with her gut instinct. She reasoned that if Scotty risked all his chips, he must have the winning hand, and the fact that Skip called the bet surely meant that one of them had the flush. Yet her instincts were telling her to call the bet.

So much was riding on this decision. If she called and lost, she was at risk of losing the tournament; and if she won the hand, she would have an even bigger lead over the other players. She took her time making her decision. Skip was just about to call clock on her when she blurted out, "I call" and put her chips out in front of her. Skip still had chips left, but when the last card came, he checked it, and Madison was willing to do the same, not sure if she had the winning hand.

They all turned over their cards, and sure enough, Scotty had a flush. Surprisingly, it was smaller than Madison's, and Skip had three of a kind. It was a miracle that Madison won the hand. To her relief, she had tripled up and remained the chip leader.

Scotty was eliminated, and Skip was on poker life support with very few chips left in his stack.

Madison reached for her winnings when a nauseous feeling began rising in her throat. It was the same kind she had a month ago when she experienced a seizure. She chalked it up to low blood pressure and, after stacking her chips, left to take a break from the table and eat her snack. She could well afford to miss several hands without jeopardizing her lead. In fact, it was a good strategy because other players may enter a hand knowing the big stack wasn't going to be in it, thereby increasing the odds that someone might bust out.

Madison went to the café and ordered a bottle of water to wash down her protein bar. She was planning to stay long enough to feel better. While eating her snack, she checked her emails on her phone. Her phone fell onto the table and her arms followed, outstretched. Next, her head fell onto them. She lay there motionless, the protein bar half eaten, the bottle of water untouched. An older gentleman who had been seated nearby had noticed her.

A minute later, he approached Madison wondering if she was all right. He stood over her and called out, "Ma'am?" Madison didn't respond. He called out again, this time a little louder. "Ma'am, are you okay? Ma'am?" Still she didn't answer. By now a crowd had formed around her table to see what was the matter.

The man, deeply concerned, put his hand on her shoulder and shook her lightly, all the while asking, "Are you all right?" He shook her again and again, and by the third shake, Madison lifted her head and in a dazed voice asked, "What are you doing?"

The bystanders stepped back once she spoke, and the man began to explain his actions. He said that he thought she was ill or even dead, and out of concern for her, he came over. Madison, feeling miffed at his melodramatic description of her, told him, "I'm not dead, as you can see. I'm fine." Madison softened her tone and added, "Thank you for your concern." He walked away embarrassed but feeling if she had a real medical emergency, he would have been justified in shaking her.

The nausea subsided, and Madison returned to the tournament room. She was surprised to see that two more players had been eliminated in the short time she was away, but glad at the same time. There were now five players left, including herself. She studied the table to see who had won Evan's and Jamal's chips, the busted-out players. She saw that Shep's stack and Jose's had increased significantly. Of all the players at the table, Madison secretly hoped Jose would be the first to be eliminated. Not only was he an excellent player, but extremely difficult to play against; you never knew what cards were in his hand. Jose would play two low cards, or rags as they are called in poker lingo, as if they were pocket aces, and then show that he was bluffing all along when he won the hand.

He would play this psychological game to tick off his opponents and possibly causing them to make a stupid move the next time they were playing against him.

As for Shep, she wasn't going to worry about him. He had coached Madison in their early days together, and having played with him for years, she felt she could handle being up against him, but would keep a watchful eye just in case he had changed his style.

The lunch break was just around the corner, and Madison made a strategic decision not to play many hands, only enough to keep her lead, or unless she was dealt two great cards that begged to be played.

The action at the table remained as aggressive, if not more so, since Madison's self-imposed break. She just sat back waiting for the lunch break, and with each new hand dealt, she wished another player would get knocked out.

Shep asked Madison to join him for lunch, but this time, she passed on the offer. Instead, she went outside to catch some rays and to meditate as best she could in the parking lot. She had packed a sandwich from home and ate while trying to relax and keep a cool head about her. Playing a tournament for a prize of this magnitude, let alone playing for one's life, was extremely stressful. In her meditation, she imagined that she had paid off Nikolai and was totally debt-free and had left the real estate business altogether to pursue writing, a lifelong passion of hers.

Madison finished her sandwich and looked at her watch to see what time it was. She still had twenty minutes left on her lunch break. Feeling refreshed, she headed back inside to the battleground. That's what Madison privately called the poker table. She was hoping to catch up with Shep to chat with him before the tournament started back up. Madison felt Shep was the only player she could talk to and still maintain enough distance as his opponent. Nowhere to be found, she went to the café for a cup of coffee since players were not allowed to take their seats this early. She spotted Shep sitting by himself and went over to him. "May I sit down?" she asked.

"But of course, you're always welcome. Where did you disappear to?" He was curious and eager to know why she hadn't joined him for lunch.

"I went outside to get some fresh air and what little peace and quiet the parking lot can offer."

"Did you get your peace and quiet?" he volleyed back.

"Enough to whip your butt at this game," Madison responded back, adding levity and flirting with him. Shep gulped down the remainder of his coffee and suggested they get back to the table, leaving no time for Madison to get a cup.

The other players had assembled in their seats when the two of them arrived. One of the players made a comment, "It's come to Jesus time," and everyone laughed.

The starting bell rang, and the action immediately started with pre-flop raises and re-raises. It seemed the closer to the end of the tournament, the players became wilder, making moves they saved for this moment.

Seated at the table were Madison, the chip leader; Shep, in second place; Skip, who had made a comeback and was third; and Jose in fourth place. Gunner was still in and remained as obnoxious as ever but had skirted being penalized again. He kept up the incessant chatter to throw players off their game, but it didn't seem to work this time around. As the players were nearing the end of day two, their concentration was that much more intense, and there seemed to be an unspoken consensus to take the Gunner out. Madison was hoping she would be the one to do it, but eventually, it was Jose. In the decisive hand that ended the Gunner's bid for first place, Jose exposed his hand and showed a straight. He was now in second place, and from that moment on, he started showing his winning hands. This was a new strategy that he used to keep the other players off guard. Every now and then, he wouldn't show the winning hand, and the players were left wondering if he was bluffing or if he really had the best hand.

Madison hadn't played a hand in what seemed like forever, for fear she would lose her lead. But when she did play, she minimized her losses and remained on top.

She anxiously awaited the end of day two, hoping to survive and go onto the next level. Thankfully, the ending bell sounded, signaling the tournament was over for that day. There were four remaining players who would be going on to compete in day three.

Madison voluntarily went over to Shep to wish him good luck tomorrow. She explained that she had things to do and would see him then. "Get some rest," he shouted out.

"Sure thing," Madison replied and left to go see Detective Malachek.

She arrived at the police station and went directly to the officer on duty, announcing her name and telling him she had an appointment to see Malachek. The officer was polite compared to the nasty one she encountered on her last visit to the station. "I'm sorry, ma'am, he was called away. Don't know when he'll be back. Could be after midnight, so I'd advise you to come back in the morning."

Madison was upset at having wasted her time but didn't show it. She was eager to know who attacked her and if her life was still in danger. Without answers to her questions, she would have to work that much harder to remain focused and not let the unknown be a cause of distraction during the tournament tomorrow. She was also annoyed at having to return the next day, but politely asked the officer, "What time would be best to catch him?"

The desk sergeant was very accommodating and said that he would check the schedule. "Looks like he's on the late shift this week. I'd give him a call after three to be sure he's here. Don't want you to make a trip for nothing." Madison thanked him for his help and scooted out the door.

Chapter 30

It was Thursday, day three of the tournament, and Madison was hoping it would be the final day. Having gotten a good night's sleep for a change, Madison jumped out of bed and pulled back the covers to tidy up. It was reasonably early, and she wouldn't have to rush getting ready with plenty of time to get to the tournament. Her morning was running smoothly while she went about her routine to get ready to leave. She left at nine in the morning, leaving her time to grab a cup of coffee at the casino café and to chill.

Madison arrived at the casino promptly, and when she stepped out of the car, she was surprised to see a small group of people standing outside the front door. She walked up to someone and asked what was going on.

"The air-conditioning is broke. The sign says as soon as it's fixed, they'll open up," the woman said.

"Did it say anything about a tournament?" Madison asked, worried it might be delayed a day.

"Yeah, there was something 'bout that, but I only play slots," the woman replied.

Madison made her way to the front door to read the sign for herself. It said, "To all tournament finalists, we apologize for the delay, but as soon as the HVAC is fixed, the tournament will start. Thank you for your patience," signed, "The Management." Knowing that it would take place sometime that day didn't calm Madison's nerves. She was worried about the starting time.

Concerned that it could run late into the evening, she feared that she might become fatigued, affecting her ability to concentrate and play well. She took a deep breath to prevent herself from becoming panicked and reasoned that the starting time was out of her control. All she could do at this point was to sit on the flower bed wall and wait.

By now, the crowd had grown even larger. Madison was able to see that the other tournament players had arrived, with the exception of Shep. Jose walked up to Madison and asked why she wasn't inside. She explained what was going on.

"Man," he said, frustrated. "If I could fight a war in a hundred and twenty degree weather in a desert, I can play poker without air-conditioning."

Madison nodded her head in agreement. She was at a loss for words, never having experienced a war or the extreme heat of a desert.

Shep arrived shortly thereafter and walked over to Madison and Jose. He shook Jose's hand and said, "Good morning, bro." Then he inquired about the crowd outside. Madison, the designated bearer of the news, told him the air-conditioning was broken. Unfazed by the low-down, Shep responded, "I guess we just have to stick around in case it starts at any time."

"Yeah, I guess we're stuck here," Jose said. Skip came over to join the threesome and wait it out. He had read the sign and was aware of the situation.

Two HVAC company trucks arrived on the scene, and the workmen went in through a side door.

"We could be sitting here for hours," Madison complained.

"Come on, guys," Shep said to the three of them. "The hotel next door where I'm staying has AC, we could hang there."

They left to go over to the hotel lobby while other people headed to do likewise or go to their cars and leave altogether.

The group spread out in a corner of the lobby while Shep grabbed a complimentary cup of coffee and returned to take a chair. Skip and Jose wasted no time in engaging in conversation about tournaments they'd previously played. Shep joined in, and the three of them exchanged their experiences. They were having a good laugh describing the people they played with and their idiosyncrasies.

Madison preferred to lay her head against the overstuffed chair and close her eyes to chill. Once upon a time, she would have been a part of the conversation, but now she had no interest. She reluctantly was forced to play this tournament as a means to an end. When it was over, she vowed she was never going to set foot in a casino again.

An hour and a half passed, and Madison was getting antsy. She excused herself to go to the casino door connected to the hotel lobby and get an update. A few minutes later, she returned, shaking her head as she approached the guys. It was obvious that she was aggravated.

Madison announced that the contractors were still working on the AC and that she was given a standard answer. "They're working as fast as possible, and as soon as it was fixed, the casino would open," she repeated, mocking the person who told her that. It was close to noon, and from sheer boredom, Madison told Shep she was going to the hotel's restaurant to get something to eat.

"I'm going to stay here," Shep told her "And if things change, I'll come and get you." Madison said okay and hoped he'd have good news soon.

She ordered lunch to kill some time, and when she finished eating, she stayed in the restaurant instead of going back to the group. All the talk about poker was sensory overload, and Madison wanted to keep her head as clear as possible. It didn't help that the waiting was nerve-racking, and Madison felt she'd go out of her mind from the delay.

While she was on a phone call, Shep came bounding over to her to let her know the casino was finally open and the tournament was going to start. Madison exclaimed "Thank heavens!" and ended the call instantly. It was one thirty in the afternoon. That meant the tournament could go on as late as ten or eleven in the evening.

The four players got their chips and hustled to the table to get underway as fast as possible. The director apologized for the delay and explained that this would be the final day regardless of the time.

Madison had mixed emotions about the tournament ending that day. As much as she was anxious to get it over with, the flip side was that her fate would be sealed right then and there. Either way, she was caught between a rock and a hard place. She chose to be optimistic and look on the bright side by telling herself that had the tournament gone into Friday, it would be cutting it close to pay off Nikolai.

The players wasted little time getting down to business. These were the final four, and a winner was going to be decided that night. Skip and Jose started the action by going at each other, betting fiercely. Neither one of them would acquiesce to the other's bets, and it was a race to control the table. Jose made a large bet on the fifth and final card to come out. Skip finally yielded, and Jose took down the hand. Meanwhile, Madison and Shep watched the action, secretly hoping one of the two players would be eliminated.

After a few hands were played, the action settled down. Madison studied each player, waiting for the right opportunity to jump in and play a hand. It would have to be the right cards and the right betting position at the table. Shep had gotten involved in a hand with Jose and almost lost the tournament early on. They were both excellent players and equally capable of pulling off a bluff. Shep bet big on the last card, and Jose, true to his aggressive style, raised it. Shep pondered what to do as he studied Jose's face and demeanor. Unable to get a good read on Jose, he decided to call the bet and lost a huge amount. This time, Jose had the goods. Shep was now the short stack and at risk of busting out. Madison's heart dropped in sympathy for him.

Jose was now the chip leader, but all of that could change instantly. One moment a player is in the lead, and in the next, he could be knocked out. Unlike early on in the tournament, players tossed their cards more often into the muck, resulting in less hands being played by two players.

To an onlooker, the players involved in a hand looked more like corpses than human beings. The player who bet first would sit completely still, barely breathing, gazing down at the table so as not to give away any information while his opponent figured out what move to make.

Madison's strategy was to take a back seat and let the other players fight it out. She would be able to do this for only a short while until the obligatory blinds got so large she would have to play a hand, or lose just from putting in her blinds.

Many hours had passed before there was an all-in hand. It was Skip against Shep. All of Skip's chips were in the center of the table and so were Shep's. Skip turned over a pair of kings. It was a very strong hand. Shep got out of his seat and stood up, preparing for the worst. He turned over his cards to reveal a pair of tens. He was the underdog and was at a serious disadvantage. If neither one of their cards came on the board, the highest hand, the kings, would win. The noise in the room came to a hush; all eyes were on the felt. The dealer burned the first card and turned over the three community cards to expose a four, a queen, and a king. The disappointment and pain showed immediately in Shep's eyes. The bystanders clapped, and Skip didn't resist smiling, feeling he had won the hand.

There were two more cards to come. Shep would need two more tens to be the winner of the hand. The chances of that happening were slim to none but not totally impossible.

Shep wasted no time in giving Skip a congratulatory handshake. Then he picked up his pack back while the dealer put out the turn card. It was a ten. The audience let out a gasp, but Skip was still the winner. Shep walked over to Madison to wish her good luck. He was feeling numb and defeated. He gave her a hug and kissed her on the cheek. The last card had been dealt. The crowd went wild, cheering loudly, forcing Shep to turn around and look at the cards on the table. Unbelievable. It was a miracle. Shep had made quads, beating Skip's three of a kind. Shep just about fell over in disbelief. The tables had been turned, and now it was Skip giving Shep the congratulating handshake.

It was down to three players, and the closer to the end, the more difficult and agonizing the game would become. The players opted for a thirty-minute dinner break instead of an hour due to the late start. Madison rushed outside, leaving Shep and Jose behind. She gobbled down her sandwich she brought from home then quickly returned to the tournament room. Shep and Jose were standing around the table waiting to sit down. With the arrival of Madison, the players were allowed to take their seats.

Madison looked at her watch and saw that it was only eight thirty in the evening. The tournament could easily go into the wee hours of the morning, and Madison was already feeling fatigued. Needing a boost of energy, she reached into her backpack and took out the chocolate-covered espresso beans she brought from home. While the other players drank Red Bull, Madison preferred to eat coffee beans. They had the same effect on her as the energy drink but tasted better. She popped two in her mouth and was good to go.

The director welcomed the players back and explained that the blinds had been raised.

Madison strategized that she was going to fold every time she didn't have to ante up the blinds and enter a hand only when her cards were good enough to play. The starting buzzer sounded, and Madison's stomach was starting to hurt from being on edge all day long. She was on the home stretch and still had two more opponents to knock out in order to win. With each hand dealt, her stomach ached more and more, and her anxiety level grew proportionately, although anyone watching her wouldn't have a clue of what she was going through. Madison was a true poker player and made it look easy.

Everyone was playing very cautiously, avoiding going all in. That made it difficult to get a player knocked out. There was a great deal of posturing going on, and the player's stacks size went from high to low and then back again. Just when the players thought one of them was going to bust out, the opponent in the hand would survive, much to their dismay.

Around 10:00 p.m., Madison and Jose were in a hand together. Shep had folded, letting the two of them duke it out, and hopefully, one of them would bust out. Madison was sucking on a Tootsie Roll lollipop to satisfy her sweet tooth. Instead of putting it down while playing in the hand, she decided to keep it in her mouth and use it as a ruse. Jose did a pre-flop raise, and Madison took a lick of her pop and nonchalantly called him. Jose glanced over at Madison, lollipop and all. She had pushed the Tootsie pop to the side of her mouth and looked at her cards in her hand.

Shep was wearing a Mona Lisa smile; he knew just what Madison was up to. She called Jose's bet, and the two of them waited to see the three community cards. When they were exposed, Jose looked at them, rolling his chips rhythmically between his fingers. Madison had taken the lollipop out of her mouth and began licking it. Her intention was to distract Jose and throw him off while he was thinking. He showed hesitation, putting the chips out in front to make a bet.

Madison continued to suck on her pop. Was Jose's bet a maneuver to try and get her to fold or did he make a pair, she wondered. While Madison badly wanted Jose to be eliminated and to be the one to do it as payback, she couldn't let her emotions interfere with her decision-making.

She set the lollipop down on its wrapper and put her hand to her forehead, quietly asking herself, "What should I do?" Her gut was screaming out as if it had developed a human voice. It said, "Call." Was this psychic ability or intuition? Whatever it was, it had gotten her this far. She listened and put in her chips while planning her next move. Should Jose make another bet, she would triple it whether or not she made a pair. The turn card came, and just as she predicted, Jose made another bet. It was larger than the last one.

Madison raised according to her strategy, hoping he would fold. It didn't happen. Feeling he must have hit the board, she said to herself, "I need a wing and a prayer." Jose was putting out a vibe like he had the best hand. The last card came out, and Jose pushed all in.

Madison didn't even make one pair. All she had was an ace and a second card that didn't help her hand. It would take a mountain of courage to call an all-in bet with just an ace. Internally, Madison felt as if she was dying and that her life was over. Without a good option in sight, she mentally surrendered and turned her fate over to the universe. She was worn down and told herself, "If he has it, then he has it" and went all in. The dealer requested, "Show me a winner."

Madison turned over her two cards and apologetically said, "All I have is ace high."

"That's good enough," Jose said and threw his hand in the muck. He added, "Good hand." Jose had been bluffing all the way to the end. Completely stunned, Madison didn't know if she should smile or cry. She went over to Jose and gave him a big hug. And then there were two.

Chapter 31

The tournament director congratulated both Madison and Shep and told them they could have a ten-minute break. Nearly losing everything, Madison needed it now more than ever to regroup and collect herself. She emerged the chip leader and was going to go head to head with Shep. This presented a set of problems in itself. Madison would have to put aside any personal feelings toward him and view him as the threat that he was. She played mind games with herself to keep in battle mode, like the speaker who pictures the audience naked so as not to freeze up while giving his talk.

She thought about losing and what that would mean by playing out ways Nikolai might snuff her out. While these thoughts and possible reality were frightening, she utilized them to see Shep as a villain and to help her muster the drive to overpower him at the poker table and not think about him as her lover.

Ten minutes turned into zero, and Madison and Shep took their seats. Madison put on the sunglasses she had packed away for such a moment. Surprised by this, Shep made a comment, "You're still just as beautiful as ever." His suave and magnetic self wasn't going to penetrate the steel wall Madison had defensively set up.

The call to shuffle up and deal was made, and the game began. The majority of the hands were raised pre-flop, making the cost of playing a hand expensive. Since it was just the two of them, they played each hand instead of folding and giving their opponent the edge. This meant that Madison and Shep would play any two cards dealt to them regardless of how bad they were. It was a totally different strategy playing heads up. There were a lot more mind games in an effort to psych out each other.

At one point, Shep raised an enormous amount of chips, and when Madison folded, he turned over his cards to show that he had a seven and a deuce, the two worst starting cards in "hold 'em." Having been bluffed in a major way, Madison would grit her teeth to stop herself from showing any emotions. On the inside, she was furious. He did this repeatedly to try to get Madison to go on tilt. She struggled to stay calm and ignore his antics, by taking deep breaths and reminding herself to stay the course. In return, she would turn over the winning hand two times in a row, then she would show a bluff to get back at Shep. *Payback's a blonde*, she thought to herself.

On the hands that were played with a flop, and possibly the turn and river cards, Shep would change his methodology each time. His technique was likened to that of a major league baseball pitcher, changing from fastballs to curves to sliders in order to keep Madison off guard. She kept up with him though, adjusting her play to counteract his game.

The remainder of the game would probably last about two hours, give or take a little. Madison and Shep seemed to be winning an equal number of pots, but it was Madison winning the largest ones; and with such a large lead, it looked like Madison would easily win the tournament.

Sometime after the first hour, Shep had pocket sixes against Madison's queens that tipped the tournament in his favor. The flop contained a six, giving him a set and becoming the leader.

The ladies let her down, and Shep doubled up, whittling away Madison's lead. She was wounded but not out.

The chip lead went back and forth well into the second hour until the two players ramped up the action. One of them would raise pre-flop, met with a re-raise, and once again, met with a third raise. The gap between the stacks was widening under this scenario.

It was past midnight, and they were well into the second hour. Madison had pocket tens and appropriately raised. Shep reraised her. Madison, feeling she had a strong hand and wasn't going to be bullied, reraised him. Shep, in a show of machismo or possibly because he had great cards, reraised Madison. *What could he possibly have?* she wondered. *Is he trying to run over me, or does he have pocket aces?* She sat motionless trying to figure out her next move and not give Shep a clue.

I've got too many chips in this pot to give up now, she reasoned and decided to go all in. Shep too easily called the all-in bet. This hand would be the determining factor in deciding the winner.

Since the two players were all in, both were required to turn over their cards. Madison turned over her pocket tens against Shep's suited ace and eight of spades, the dead man's hand, named after Wild Bill Hickok. Madison shook her head in disbelief that Shep would call her bet with a hand like that. It was known to symbolize bad luck. Legend has it that this was the hand Wild Bill was holding while playing poker when he was gunned down in a saloon in Deadwood, South Dakota, in 1876. Madison's pocket pair was a 51 percent favorite over Shep's cards, and whether or not the myth held up would remain to be seen.

The flop came out, and so far, Madison had the best hand. The turn was dealt. It was an ace. Shep was now in the lead, but with one more card to go, anything could happen.

Madison had one last chance to make a set and take down the tournament. She closed her eyes, afraid to look. Her stomach was in her throat, and she felt the dealer was taking his sweet time dealing her fate. She wanted to scream at him to hurry up, but that would be incredibly inappropriate. On average, the river card had been kind to Madison. Was it going to be that way now? She prayed.

The last card came out. It was a seven. She was devastated. The onlookers clapped and cheered Shep, the winner. Madison was numb but automatically went over to Shep to give him a hug and say congratulations. Shep was now surrounded by the tournament director, a photographer, and several other people involved in the running of the tournament. Madison slipped away to give Shep the spotlight he was due.

Chapter 32

Madison couldn't get her front door open fast enough. Once inside, she dropped her backpack on the floor and ran up to her bedroom. Tears started forming in her eyes and quickly made their way down to her chin. Heartbroken, she climbed two steps at a time to get to her bedroom. By the time she reached her bed, she was sobbing so hard she could hardly breathe.

She lay on her stomach, her face buried in her pillow, wailing and wailing and wailing, almost causing herself to pass out. After minutes of nonstop crying, she lifted her head and rolled onto her back. She stopped crying for a split second, and then the wailing started all over again. This went on for a half hour until, exhausted, the tears ceased to come. She looked up at the pattern in her ceiling through blurry eyes while thoughts began to fill her head. There was only one other time she felt this awful and that was when she left Shep for good. It was a replay of feeling her world had come to an end.

But this time, she felt she didn't have the strength to go through the process of putting things behind her and moving forward. Madison didn't know how she could face Nikolai and tell him she didn't have his money. The typical person would be outraged and probably sue Madison. Nikolai was not typical, nor reasonable, in his response to situations involving money. His behavior was more extreme than the norm and could be classified as deviant.

Madison's attitude was one of defeat, and every thought she had was more negative than the last. She was on a downward spiral with each passing minute while trying to figure out a solution. Feelings of hopelessness and being overwhelmed took her over. She worried about Nikolai's threats and blamed herself for being a terrible businesswoman as if the missing money was her fault. She began to feel that her life was worthless, and her thoughts turned to suicide. She knew all too well that suicide was a selfish act, and it left the loved ones behind feeling guilty. She learned that lesson years earlier when her father killed himself. Cathy and Shep came to mind, but since she wasn't thinking rationally, Madison only cared about ending her pain. The stress of her financial problems coupled with her life-threatening seizures and the loss of Frank was taking its toll on her.

She went into her closet and pulled out all her purses from the top shelf and threw them on the floor. A shoebox was exposed; she brought it down and went back into her bedroom and sat in the chair in the corner of the room. Madison took off the lid and pulled out a Smith & Wesson nine- millimeter gun that belonged to her father. She had totally forgotten that she had it until this moment. Madison loaded the magazine with bullets and put it in the gun, then racked it to put a bullet in the chamber. She set the loaded pistol on the table next to her and lowered her head to her hands in prayer.

When she finished praying, she took the gun in hand. "Am I sure I really want to do this?" she asked out loud. She heard a voice say "No." The voice startled her, and she became alarmed that someone might be in the house. Madison yelled out, "Who's there?" She got up from her chair and went to the top of the stairs to look down. Of course, there was no answer, and no one was there. Madison turned around and went back to her room and sat down. "I guess it's my subconscious mind talking to me," she said. Hearing the word *no* made Madison think twice about what she was going to do. She took the magazine out of the gun and emptied the bullet from the chamber before putting it back in the box and replacing it on the shelf.

By now, it was three in the morning, and Madison was beaten down. She put on her pajamas and went to bed thinking she would deal with whatever was going to happen when she woke up.

Chapter 33

Ring, ring, ring. Madison's phone was ringing ever so loudly that it woke her up. It was a few minutes after nine. Half awake, she reached over and grabbed her cell to answer it with a groggy "Hello?"

"Hello, I'm calling for Madison Mitchell," a female voice on the other end said.

"This is she," Madison replied.

"Madison, hi, this is Gwen over at the bank." Madison was thinking that she probably overdrew her account and that was the reason for Gwen's call. "I need to talk to you about your business account."

Definitely not prepared to deal with the shortages, Madison asked if she could call Gwen back. "This will only take a minute, and I think you'd want to know right away." Gwen's words sounded ominous, putting pressure on Madison to hear her out.

"Yes, what's it about?" Madison asked. She didn't really want to hear Gwen's answer, knowing it was bad news. "Can you come in the bank this morning?" Gwen asked.

"This morning? Can't you tell me over the phone?" Madison wondered how serious it must be if the bank manager had to call first thing in the morning needing to see her in person. *Am I going to get arrested?* she privately thought.

"It would be best not to discuss it over the phone," Gwen advised her.

Madison was becoming annoyed as a way of deflecting her worry that not only was she getting bad news, but it had to be delivered in person.

"Okay, but I'll need about an hour," she told Gwen.

"That'll be fine. I'll see you then."

Madison slowly got up from her bed to get ready to meet the banker. "When it rains, it pours," she said to herself.

Still under doctor's orders not to drive, Madison ignored it and drove herself to the bank to meet with Gwen and deal with another disaster.

Madison went up to the receptionist and told her that she was there to see the bank manager, Gwen. The receptionist picked up the phone to inform Gwen of her arrival. "She'll be right out," the receptionist stated.

A smiling and overly friendly Gwen came out and thanked Madison for coming down so promptly. They went into Gwen's private office. Gwen shut the door behind her and offered Madison a cup of coffee or some water. Madison felt she was being served up her last meal. She was anxious to get on with business and simply asked what was so important that Gwen couldn't tell her over the phone.

Gwen cleared her throat and began. "If you recall, about a month ago, your business account was overdrawn two hundred and fifty thousand dollars."

Madison, always one to make light of her troubles, was not in a joking mood. She responded seriously, "Yes, I recall that day very clearly."

Gwen continued on, "The account was cleared out by a bank check written by your business partner, Frank Jensen—"

Madison still retained her characteristic tendency to interrupt. "Yeah, I know. Do I owe bank fees?" Madison asked.

Gwen ignored the interruption and once again cleared her throat, this time taking a sip of water. It appeared to Madison that Gwen was visibly nervous, and couldn't understand why. *Aren't I supposed to be the nervous one?* she silently asked herself.

Gwen picked back up. "Frank came in to withdraw two hundred and fifty thousand dollars and then wanted a cashier's check made out to him."

"Yes, check number nine-nine-nine," Madison chimed in. Madison looked at her watch, becoming acutely aware that she was going to have bigger problems on her hands in a couple of hours when she's unable to deliver the funds to Nikolai and his lawyer at closing.

"We were short-staffed that day and had a trainee on the window. She did everything properly, well, almost. She asked to see Frank's driver's license, and when she printed out the cashier's check, she asked for my approval, which, of course, I gave since I knew Frank as well as I know you." Madison was getting impatient with the recap of the events of the day that changed her life forever and almost caused her to do away with herself.

"It wasn't until yesterday, late Thursday evening, that I got the call from our accounting department. The bank withdrawal check had Frank's personal account number on it, but it hadn't been withdrawn on his account. Instead, Libby, the teller, took it out of the business account and then proceeded to give Frank the cashier's check."

Astonished, Madison jumped up and asked, "What are you saying?"

Gwen asked her to please calm down and take her seat. Madison wasn't about to take orders from her and remained standing. Gwen could feel the ire coming from Madison and took a step back, not sure what Madison might do. "What I'm trying to say is that there was a bank error, and the money should have never been taken out of your account. I want to offer you my deepest apology, and the bank is going to give you free checking for a year and a free safe deposit box. We don't want you to sue the bank."

Madison couldn't believe her ears. She was *saved*.

"The money's been restored to your business account. I'm terribly sorry, and it goes without saying, Libby is no longer employed with us," Gwen told her.

Madison was furious, and in a raised voice, said, "I don't care about free checking or any of that. I just want my money back."

"It's in your account," Gwen reassured her.

Madison didn't know where to begin. "Okay," Madison told her and took a deep sigh of relief. "There is one thing I need you to do right this minute." Madison demanded, "I need a cashier's check made out to Capital Investment Company for two hundred and fifty thousand dollars."

"I'm on it. Please wait here, and I'll be back shortly with your check," Gwen said and immediately headed out her office door.

Madison sat down. A tear rolled down her cheek. She was feeling as though she had been pardoned one minute before being executed. She began to settle down and knew the next step was to call Nikolai's office to tell him that she would be at the closing on time with the cashier's check. He wasn't in, but the secretary told Madison she would give him the message. Gwen returned with Madison's check, once again apologizing and saying that the bank appreciated her as a customer.

Madison wasn't interested in any apology and contemplated dropping them for all the aggravation they had caused her by their stupidity. No longer feeling distressed, she took the check and said goodbye.

Madison had plenty of time to make the closing but chose to head over early and drop off the check. She put on her favorite Pandora station while driving and, for the first time in weeks, felt everything was going to be okay. Her mood had improved a thousand percent from yesterday, and slowly, Madison's mojo was coming back.

She arrived at the closing attorney's office and delivered the cashier's check promptly. The receptionist gave her a receipt, and afraid of running into Nikolai, Madison hurried out of the building. She headed home and was eager to get her life back on track. Her first order of business was to write Nikolai a letter and fire him as her client.

Chapter 34

It was Friday, the start of the weekend, and Madison was very much in need of a break from all the drama in her life. She gave Cathy a call to see if she was available to go to the wine country, but unfortunately, since it was at the last moment, Cathy had plans already. Madison felt it wouldn't be any fun going to the wineries alone, and Shep came to mind.

She wondered why she hadn't heard from him and figured that he was headed back to Las Vegas. She definitely wasn't going to call him figuring it was best to add closure to their interactions and put another situation to rest.

Madison knew of a great spa in Sonoma that would be totally relaxing and the perfect place to go even if it was alone. She called the hotel to make a reservation and lucked out. A guest had canceled a few minutes prior, and Madison was able to book the last room. The weather was clear and sunny, and it was a beautiful day for a drive. Madison packed a bag and did some things around the house to get ready for the drive up north. It was early afternoon before she got on the road. The trip would take a minimum of ten hours, and without a care, Madison figured she would stop along the way and finish the trip the next day. She chose to drive up the Pacific Highway because it would be the most scenic route.

Madison had been driving for about six hours when it started getting too dark to continue on. She had made it as far as the Monterey Peninsula on Highway One, high up on the cliffs of California. It was a treacherous road to travel at nighttime. There were no lights or guard rails, and if a car went over the cliff, it was a three-hundred foot drop to the Pacific Ocean.

She was close to Carmel-by-the-Sea, a seaside resort with quintessential places to stay. Madison made her way into town and drove down Ocean Avenue, looking for a place to spend the night. She came upon an inn that stood out from all the other hotels and bed and breakfasts. It was a Victorian Painted Lady with a wraparound porch that looked so inviting. Madison pulled into the carriage porch attached to the house where long ago horse and buggies had stopped to let their passengers out. She left her suitcase in the car in case there wasn't a vacancy and sauntered up to the front desk, admiring the antique decor of the lobby.

The hotel desk clerk, dressed in old-fashioned attire consisting of a striped vest with a black jacket and a bowtie, greeted Madison. "Good evening, Madam, how can I be of service to you this lovely evening?" he asked.

Madison smiled, enjoying the ambience and throwback to good old-fashioned hospitality. "I would like a room please, if you have one."

The desk clerk checked his computer, a reminder that it was still the twenty-first century. "Yes, we have availability. I have a lovely room with a king-size bed or a room with two queens. How many are traveling in your party?' he asked politely.

"It's just me," Madison said with a note of sadness in her voice. "The king bed will do," she added.

"I'll need to see your driver's license, and I'll send someone to get your bags," the desk clerk told her. Madison reached into her purse to get her wallet with her driver's license.

There was loud laughter coming from a room adjacent to the lobby. Madison looked to see where it was coming from, but her view was blocked by a large white column. The clerk informed her that the bar was beyond the column, and she was welcome to take a peek while he filled out the paperwork.

"Maybe later," Madison responded. The laughter was that of a woman and was getting louder. Once again, Madison turned to see whom the infectious laugh belonged to. Madison saw a very attractive blonde walking arm in arm with a man. He was hidden from view by the oversized column. Madison watched them happily strolling past the column and down the hall. By now, she could see the gentleman who was escorting the woman. Unbelievable! It was Shep. Madison quickly turned her head in hopes of not being noticed. The desk clerk patiently said to Madison, "Whenever you're ready, Madam."

She looked at the clerk and didn't know what to say; all she knew was that she had to get out of there fast and hoped Shep hadn't seen her. Madison looked inside her wallet and proceeded to tell the clerk that she left her license in the car and needed to fetch it. She rapidly exited the lobby and got in her car and raced away.

It was too late and too dark to drive back to LA, something Madison wanted to do very badly. She knew she was stuck on the Monterey Peninsula, so she headed north and planned to stop at the nearest town with a hotel. All during the drive, Madison screamed out loud and cursed Shep, calling him every foul word in the dictionary. She felt anger more than hurt. Having suffered so much pain in the preceding two days, anger was the only emotion she had left.

Madison saw a motel sign flashing "vacancy," and knowing that Shep would never be caught dead in one, she chose to spend the night there.

She checked in and climbed the stairs to the second level to go to her room. It smelled musty, and the beds were rock hard, but she didn't care. Madison sat there like a lump on a log. She couldn't bring herself to cry; she had done enough crying when she lost the tournament and feared for her life.

Her anger turned to rage as she replayed the scene in her head of the beautiful blonde laughing and enjoying herself, her arm tightly wrapped around Shep. The feeling of betrayal was beyond words. "How could he do this to me? 'Oh, baby, baby, I love you.' Bullshit, motherfucker."

It was the first time in years that Madison had used words like that. They used to roll off her tongue so easily in her poker-playing days when every other word was a cuss word. Cleaning up her language was the first step in redefining her life. But sometimes proper language wasn't enough to express one's self, and this wasn't the time for Madison to care about etiquette. Shep had hurt her more than before, and feeling inflamed, she wanted to destroy him once and for all.

She immediately blocked his number on her phone and, being irrational, considered moving from LA so that he couldn't find her. Her next thought was that moving would be more of a hardship on her and would probably have no effect on Shep. She got a hold of herself and, changing gears, stopped for a moment. "No, I'm not going to change my life for him or waste another moment thinking about him. Getting on with my life will be the best revenge." So unlike in the past when Madison would have cried all night or stayed awake, she went to sleep.

Chapter 35

When morning came, Madison was planning to drive home. Getting out of bed, she couldn't help but think about Shep and the woman on his arm, laughing and having a good time. "She was probably headed to his room to sleep with him," Madison said to herself. The thought of him with another woman made her furious and solidified her commitment to never see or hear from him again.

She took off her pajamas and threw them on the bed so she could take a shower and leave as fast as possible. She turned on the water and waited till it was hot enough to step in. The hot water falling over her head felt good and had a calming effect. Madison let it run for several minutes before washing her body. The water made her think about how good a hot tub would feel and what she would be missing by not going to the spa. "I've paid for it, I might as well go there and enjoy myself. Having a good time will be therapeutic, and I can forget about Shep," she reasoned.

The sun was shining as it always did in California, making the drive pleasant and the scenery from the hotel to Sonoma even more beautiful. She played music on the way to Sonoma to help keep her mood elevated, but she could still feel the hurt below the surface.

Madison checked in to the spa hotel and went directly to her room to change into workout clothes. She was going to take a steam before the hot stone massage she had booked with her reservation. After the massage, she went to the hot tub then relaxed in the spa lounge while sipping herbal tea. She was totally relaxed, and when Shep's name popped into her head, she simply told herself, "I'm not going to think about him right now" and continued enjoying the sensations of peace and well-being.

By the time Madison finished in the spa, it was close to dinner time. She went back to her room to get dressed and throw some makeup on to go eat. Madison was struck by the beauty of the dining room as she was escorted to a table. The dining room was octagonal in shape and totally enclosed by large windows with arches at the top. The ceiling was vaulted with simple scrolls of painted green vines and a single huge chandelier made up of five tiers of yellow glass, hung in the middle. Lalique wall sconces provided extra light. The room overlooked a beautiful English garden containing numerous varieties of flowers and plants. The two-tiered fountain in the middle of the room made a sound like a babbling brook, adding to the mood of the room.

The restaurant offered both a vegetarian menu and a traditional one. Madison chose a filet mignon and a glass of cabernet to go along with dinner. Still sailing off the good feelings from her massage, she managed to enjoy a relaxing dinner in the serenity of her surroundings, forgetting all about Shep for the evening.

After dinner, Madison attended a mediation class that was being offered to all guests of the spa. Soon after, she went to bed and had a very deep, uninterrupted sleep.

The next morning when Madison woke up, she was surprised at how well rested she felt. Wondering what she should do that day, she thought that since she was in the wine country, she should go to some of the vineyards for wine tasting. While at breakfast, she Googled wineries and chose four that she had not been to in the past.

Madison finished her meal and emptied her coffee cup before taking a leisurely walk around the garden. It was too early to leave for the wineries, but eventually she left to visit the first winery on her list. They had released an award-winning chardonnay for sale, and Madison was eager to try it and maybe pick up a bottle or two. She was one of the first visitors to the tasting gallery along with two couples. Madison sampled two merlots, a pinot gris, and the much-awaited chardonnay. She purchased a case to give as gifts and to keep some for herself.

After several more tastings, Madison loaded her car and headed to her next stop on her list. She passed through the gift shop and into the winery's tasting room. Unlike the last winery that had a view into the barrel room, this tasting room was glass enclosed overlooking the vineyards.

It was a spectacular view that made her wish she lived in what is known as the Gold Coast area of California.

Here, she tasted merlots and cabs, very common wines that grow well in the region, and in addition, she sampled a Syrah; and because it was so good, she had to have more than just a taste. She purchased two bottles of that one. Madison stayed for lunch in their restaurant and ordered a glass of Syrah. She engaged in conversation with the sommelier serving the wine, learning more about the grapes and the growing conditions necessary to give the wine its raciness and pepperiness. She was having a wonderful time, and thoughts of Shep never entered her mind.

Enough time had passed between wine sampling and lunch that Madison felt it was safe to get back on the road and head on to her third pick of the day. Most of these wineries were less than a half hour apart, and most were only a ten-minute drive.

She made the drive in no time at all and arrived to find the parking lot almost completely filled. When Madison approached the winery, she was told there was a fifteen-minute wait to get in. She was not in any hurry and was willing to wait, taking a seat on a bench near the door. There were several other guests waiting also. She listened in on the conversation of a couple who had visited the winery that Madison was planning to go to next.

They raved about the wines and made mention of the gold medal Zinfandel. Madison looked forward to going there and experiencing it for herself.

While sitting and waiting, a man, about thirty- five, dressed in shorts and a T-shirt, sat down next to her. Madison could see that he was athletic by the size of his calves and his pronounced biceps sticking out from his short-sleeve shirt. He said hello to Madison and struck up a conversation, telling her that he had been to this winery before and that they were known for their Viognier wine. It was a wine that Madison was not familiar with and was eager to hear all about it, especially coming from him. He was good-looking, and she could tell that he was attracted to her. There was something about him that made Madison return the feeling.

A short while later, the door opened, and a woman came out announcing they were letting in a new group for the tasting room. Madison stood up, and Patrick, the man she had been talking to, said, "After you." The guests sidled up to the bar where the wine tasting was being held. Patrick conveniently situated himself next to Madison.

The first wine served was a Pinot Blanc, and the server talked about its flavor and body and the grapes that were combined to make this particular wine. Madison, after taking a sip, turned to Patrick and said she liked its refreshing fruit flavor.

He agreed and the server poured a second wine for everyone to sample. Patrick continued the conversation with Madison, talking about his many trips to the wine country he had taken with friends and out-of-town guests since he lived nearby in San Francisco. He was very amusing as he recounted the many stories of his adventures in the wine country. Madison laughed so hard that between all the samples of wine she had consumed and the loss of breath from laughing so much, she became light-headed.

The wine sampling ended after tasting eight or nine different wines. Madison had mentioned that she was headed to one last winery to taste their Zinfandel. Patrick asked if she minded if he met up with her there. Madison felt that would be fine since she felt an attraction toward him, and he didn't pose a threat to her.

They walked out to the parking lot together, and Patrick walked Madison to her car. She stood at the car door, purposely taking her time finding her key. She was hoping he would kiss her. Patrick wasted no time picking up on her clue and kissed her passionately. "I can still taste the wine on your lips," he said.

Madison, wanting more, playfully asked him, "Ah, but can you tell which one?" to which Patrick kissed her several more times. Things were getting heated up, and Madison realized that a winery parking lot was not the place to continue, nor should she, having just met him.

She slowly separated her lips from his and gently said, "If we're going to go to the next winery, we need to be on our way."

Madison got in her car and waited for Patrick to follow behind. The next winery was a short distance away. The parking lot was practically empty, enabling them to park next to each other. Patrick got out of his car and walked over to Madison and gave her a kiss. She kissed him back with desire. They stood there kissing for a few more minutes before he grabbed her hand and led her to the winery. He acted like he knew Madison for a long time, and she responded the same way. They ran and laughed their way into the tasting room. It was late afternoon, and there weren't any guests in the room. "Is the winery still serving?" Patrick asked the barista.

"Yes, you have about an hour," she told them.

They tasted several of the wines that were unique to the winery including the famous Zinfandel. It tasted as good as the couple she overheard talking about it said it was. The laughter continued between them, and the attraction grew stronger. They drank and talked, and Madison noticed that Patrick's face was as chiseled as Shep's. She muttered under her breath, "Screw him," and Patrick asked, "What did you say?" She howled with laughter. "Was it something I said?" Patrick asked her, worried that he offended Madison or turned her off.

She wasn't sure if he had heard her correctly or at all. "Screw 'em" Madison repeated, and that gave her an idea. "Wish they had screw-on caps so when I've been drinking too much, I can get the next bottle opened easily." Madison let out another laugh, and Patrick joined in. *Whew,* Madison thought to herself, making sure not to utter her private thoughts by mistake again.

The barista announced that she would be serving the last sampling and that if they were planning on making any purchases, the gift shop would be closing in ten minutes. Patrick and Madison sampled one last wine; it was a cabernet. After taking a swig, they looked at each other and made a face, letting each other know that they both didn't like it. Patrick tipped the server, and they left the winery together.

He walked Madison to her car and said, "I'd like to talk with you a little longer, if you aren't in a hurry." Madison said that would be okay, and he got in on the passenger side of Madison's car. They talked about the wines they had just experienced, and Madison told him that the Zinfandel was the best of all the wines they had tried.

They stopped talking for a moment. "I'd really like to kiss you again, but we've been drinking, and I don't want you to think I'm taking advantage of the situation," Patrick said in a sincere-sounding tone. Madison didn't feel that he was trying to take advantage of her at all and became a willing participant.

She had gotten to know a little bit about this man, and the vibration she got from him was that he was a gentle soul. "I would like that very much," she told him. He kissed her, followed by another and another. There in the parking lot, like two teenagers on a date, they were making out. Madison was enjoying the sensation and wasn't willing to stop, at least not yet. Their kissing went on for a good half hour until Madison expressed a need to use the restroom. All the wine she had been drinking was catching up to her. Patrick walked back with her to the winery and waited while she used the facilities. He walked her back to her car expecting to pick up where they left off. Madison told him that this would be a good time for her to head back to her hotel. He told her that he wanted to see her again and asked her for her phone number. Thinking that he was never really intending to call, she gave it to him. He leaned over and gave her a kiss, and this time, it ended with one.

Madison drove back to her hotel and when she arrived there, decided to grab a quick dinner in the café and forego the luxury of the dining room. It was a simple meal, and when she finished, she went to her room to catch up on the day's news on her iPad before going to sleep.

She had a few epiphanies during the weekend. One of them was that she was going to throw herself into her business like never before and build it up to become financially independent. The other realization was that you can never go back and recreate something that once was. She made an analogy between being an artist and her love affair with Shep. Michelangelo created one statue of David, and while he could make other statues, there would be only one David. Shep would be her one and only great love of her life, and now it was time to let him go. She felt she was wrong in thinking that she could recreate what they once had. Once again, it was a lesson learned after the experience.

She had made up her mind to leave the next day for home and had proven to herself that she could move forward and forget about Shep. She was happy that the thought of him only periodically entered her consciousness, and she was able to wipe him from her memory for some of the time. Madison wasn't going to let him ruin her life again.

Chapter 36

Arriving home by early afternoon, Madison managed to avoid getting delayed in traffic. She unpacked her bag and when finished, went directly into her office to get down to business. Her company had suffered all these past weeks, and now it was time to get serious. Madison needed to get her finances back on track if she was going to achieve success. The loss of the escrow funds put a scare into her, and she promised to never let anything like that happen again. Work offered her a secondary benefit in that it was an excellent diversion from thinking about Shep. While she was able to erase him from her memory, she knew she wouldn't be able to totally eradicate him out of her thoughts. But at least she was able to function and not feel frozen.

Madison checked her emails and listened to her messages on her office voice mail. There was a message from Detective Malachek. He wanted her to call him and set an appointment to come in to see him. She was fed up with Malachek; the last two times she went to see him at his request, he wasn't available. She was aggravated, and seeing him might just cause her to unload on him. Besides, even though Madison wanted to know who attacked her that night at the casino, she didn't want to deal with any more drama. Whatever he needed to see her about could wait till it was more convenient for her.

Madison buried herself in work over the next few days, only leaving the house to go to the grocery store. By the third day, she needed a break from the routine and to see a living soul.

She went to Rosie's for dinner and then on to Colonial Pool Room to shoot some pool. She could always find someone to play a game with. Madison rented a table and shot some practice balls. It wasn't long before a man came over and asked if she would like to play a match. That was perfectly fine with her and exactly what Madison was hoping for. He introduced himself as Gary and said he hadn't been playing much since his wife of fifty years had passed away. He went on to explain that they would shoot every Saturday night and have dinner there.

Gary racked the balls and said, "Ladies first," letting Madison take the first shot. She sunk a solid in a pocket. "Looks like you're stripes," she said, referring to which balls he would have to get in. She missed sinking another ball, and Gary took his turn. He stood there, cue stick in hand, reminiscing.

"When we first started playing, I was the better player. Then Liz, my wife, joined a league. It wasn't long before she whooped my behind. We had a friendly competitiveness to our relationship, I guess that's what made it last." Madison could hear the melancholy in his voice, and it was obvious that he missed her dearly.

To lighten up the mood, Madison said, "Well, I'm glad you came over, and I hope to prove a worthy adversary." He gave her a smile and took his shot. They played for hours, each winning four games. They would play one more for a tiebreaker.

Madison was so very aware of Gary's fragile feelings that she sandbagged the last game and let him win. She had accomplished what she set out to do—have an evening out and some conversation.

The next morning rolled around, and Madison hopped out of bed, eager to get to work. A sense of purpose replaced her tears and anger and served to return Madison to the once very strong individual that she was. She was feeling that the worst was behind her, and new opportunities awaited.

Unlike the past, she had immediately showered and dressed and was ready for work.

She began by making her usual cup of coffee and went to her office to start her day. Her routine would be ratcheted up several notches to help her realize her desire to increase her business.

Madison took out her day timer and flipped through her notes to determine what she needed to accomplish that day.

Detective Malachek's name had appeared on the previous days' page with a note to speak with him. She made this her first order of business and immediately placed a call. He was in and able to speak with Madison, saying he wanted to see her in person.

When Madison was at the spa, she realized how over time, she had allowed people to manipulate her like Nikolai and Shep. She had come to the conclusion that she was no longer going to take any crap from anyone, and Malachek was the perfect target. "You've asked me twice to come in to see you, and both times you weren't there. I'm not driving all the way to the police station unless you can guarantee that you're going to be there for me," Madison adamantly told Malachek.

"I can't promise anything. If I get called out to investigate a homicide, then I won't be here. But you can trust I won't be stepping out for doughnuts and coffee," Malachek told her.

"Fair enough," Madison said. "What are your hours today?" Detective Malachek told her that he would be at the station till four in the afternoon. "Okay, I'll get there before then," she told Malachek, and they said goodbye.

Madison planned on getting as much work done as she could before going to see Malachek. She wasn't happy that she would have to take valuable time away, but it had to be done. She set about working, making phone calls, and utilizing the tools of a realtor's trade to find ways to get new customers and listings. She was diligently working when her doorbell rang. She got up out of her chair, peeked out her window, and answered it. It was the FedEx delivery man.

Opening her door, he said hello and asked her to sign for the two packages in his possession. One of the packages was a long thin box, marked "fragile, flowers." Madison signed while thanking him and promptly shut the door. She dreaded opening the flowers, fearing they were from Shep. She didn't want to be reminded of him, and there wasn't anything he could say to make her want to be involved with him again.

She brought down an antique cut glass vase from the kitchen cabinet that had belonged to her mother and filled it with water, preparing to put the flowers in. Even though she wanted nothing to do with him, she hated the thought of wasting something as beautiful as flowers. She opened the box to find a dozen pink roses, her favorite color. She took the card out of the envelope, expecting to see some drivel that said, "I love you, blah blah blah, Shep." It wasn't from him. To her surprise, it was from Patrick. "Madison, enjoyed meeting you and spending time together. I hope I will see more of you. Patrick."

Madison didn't see this coming. She smiled and was delighted. There was still a second package to open. She took out her kitchen scissors to cut open the cardboard box. Inside was a bottle of Zinfandel with another note. "Think of me when you drink it," signed, Patrick. "Wow!" Madison said out loud. "What a romantic." She placed the wine in her wine rack and carried the flowers into her office and put them on her desk.

It was going to be hard to focus on work and not on Patrick, but she was determined to stay on track. She moved the vase to a bookcase to prevent them from distracting her.

Madison spent the remainder of the day making a marketing plan and on administrative duties. She had been working nonstop. Madison looked at her watch and discovered that it was quarter to four in the afternoon, not enough time to drive to the police station. She placed a call to Malachek and apologized for not being able to meet with him but promised to be there first thing in the morning.

Malachek justifiably gave her flack. "And you were concerned that I wouldn't be here. Get your butt down here tomorrow. I have some news to share with you." Madison reassured him that she would be there bright and early.

After a quick trip to the kitchen for a bottle of water, she continued working into the early hours of the evening and only stopped to have dinner. She fixed herself a salad, trying to lose the two pounds she had gained over the weekend from all the rich food she ate and the wine she had consumed.

Madison had accomplished a great deal that day, obtaining leads on listings and potential property management clients. She felt she deserved to take the few remaining hours in the evening off and watch a movie before going to sleep.

She surfed the movie channels and settled on a comedy. Madison belly-laughed her way through the movie, but at one point, her attention had turned to Shep. Even though she didn't want to hear from him, she couldn't understand how he didn't even try to get in touch with her. The lack of communication or effort to see her made her feel bitter. The more she thought about him, the more incensed she grew.

She went downstairs to her office to retrieve the flowers Patrick had sent her. She brought them upstairs to her bedroom and placed them on her nightstand. She looked at them, recalling Patrick with pleasure, especially his hot kisses. Feeling less angry, she went to bed hoping to dream about him.

Chapter 37

Madison quickly dressed and guzzled down a cup of coffee. She had to get down to the police station to see Malachek first thing that morning. She had put him off long enough and felt now was as good a time as any to deal with the attack and get it over with.

She arrived at the station in a timely manner and asked to see Detective Malachek. This time, he came out to personally greet her and showed her to his office.

He started the conversation asking, "How you feeling?"

Madison shrugged her shoulders as if to say, "I'd rather be somewhere else other than here," and answered, "I'm fine. Thanks for asking."

"Well, let's get started," he said. "I want you to tell me what happened the night at the casino, everything you can remember, no matter how unimportant you think it is." It was a replay from the first time she had met him and was asked to recall the attack at Frank's condo.

"Okay, I can do that, I know the drill," Madison said. "I was at the casino, playing poker. I'd been there for many hours, was doing well, and there was an interesting guy next to me. He was talking about what he did for a living, and I was intrigued so we kept talking, and I stayed later than I'd planned to. Besides, I was winning." Malachek was looking directly into Madison's eyes; his facial expressions showed that he was actively listening.

She kept on recalling the events of that night. "I was getting tired and didn't want to be dragging in the morning like I do when I go to bed too late, so I said good night and cashed in my chips and went to leave. Oh, my friend was so engrossed in playing cards that I didn't want to disturb him and take him away from his game to walk me out. Stupid me."

Madison paused for a second. "Do you have any coffee? I've only had one cup this morning."

"Sure, I'll get you a cup. How do you take it?" Malachek asked her.

"Cream only, no sugar please."

Malachek left his office and returned a minute later with two cups of coffee. "I live on this stuff," he said, and they both took a drink. "Please continue," he urged her.

"Okay, so where was I?" Madison stopped a moment to remember what she was talking about. "Oh yeah. So I cashed out my chips and headed out to the parking lot to find my car. My friend had parked it for me since he was driving. At first, I was looking in the main parking lot right out front of the casino, and then I remembered I was parked in the side parking lot. I walked over to my car, keys in my hand, and was about to click open the door when I felt someone from behind me grab me."

Madison took a sip of coffee before continuing recounting the details. "I told you that I was trained in martial arts, so immediately, I went into fighting mode. I was wedged between my car and the one next to me, so I couldn't use kicks to defend myself, only my hands and arms, and then I must have slipped on something and lost my balance. That's when he got the better of me. The next thing I knew was that I was facedown on the hood of my car, and I was at a definite disadvantage." She paused to relive the incident. "It was a good thing you came along when you did, which, by the way, reminds me, what were you doing there at that moment?" Madison asked Malachek.

"I'll get to that later," he told her.

"Well, that's all there is to the story. You know the rest, you arrested him." Madison finished recalling the events of the night she was attacked outside the casino. "So who is this person, and where are they?" she asked Malachek.

He took a gulp of coffee and told Madison that they were locked up in a holding cell.

"Could you identify the attacker?" he asked her.

"No, unfortunately not. He was wearing black clothing and a ninja mask. I couldn't see his face," Madison said in response to his question.

"Are you sure it was a male?" Malachek asked her.

"I guess so. He was very strong." Malachek stood up from his seat and told Madison that "he" was a "she."

"What? I don't believe it," Madison said. "Why would a woman want to attack me?"

"I want you to wait here for a few minutes, and I'll be right back," Malachek told her, leaving Madison alone to ponder about her attacker being a woman. Madison would have never suspected a female was after her. She assumed it was a male because of the force used and wondered what the woman was after.

She drank her coffee and looked all around Malachek's office. His office was cluttered and messy and probably hadn't been dusted in a year. There were stacks of files on a cabinet, a cork board on the wall filled with papers, and a bookcase half filled with more files and one shelf containing books. Madison cocked her head sideways to try and read the titles.

The door opened, and Malachek had returned. "I want you to come with me," Malachek said and held the door open for her.

Madison got up to go along with him and asked, "Where are we going?"

"You'll see" was all he said. She followed Malachek obediently and was taken to a room with a mirror that filled one wall and chairs lined up in two rows as if readied to watch a movie. "Please take this seat." Madison was given a chair right in the middle of the front row, facing the mirror. By now she had guessed that it was a two-way mirror.

A female in an orange jumpsuit, arms behind her back and handcuffed, walked into the room on the other side of the mirror, followed by a police officer and two men in suits, one of whom was carrying a briefcase.

Madison, whispering to Malachek, asked if the woman in the jumpsuit could hear anything that was said on this side of the mirror. She was told no.

The man with the briefcase sat down, and the other man sat across from him and removed his jacket. Malachek pointed out to Madison that the man without his jacket was Detective Lewis, and the other gentleman was the woman's attorney. The officer took the prisoner's handcuffs off, and she was seated next to her attorney.

Madison could see the woman's face plain as day. It was the woman from the Starbucks near the casino. Madison stood up and screamed out in disbelief, "I recognize that woman! I saw her at the Starbucks one morning when I went to get coffee. Her name's Christine, and she's the woman who was in all my dreams. Why is she here?" Madison was shocked at seeing the woman in person again and spoke very rapidly and nonstop.

"You've confirmed what I've concluded," Malachek told her. "Are you okay?" he asked.

Madison sat back down, stunned. "I guess so."

"Let's go back to my office to talk," Malachek said, and they left together.

Madison didn't say a word on the walk back to Malachek's office. She was puzzled and was trying to put things together. The moment her butt hit the chair in his office, she fired off one question after another. Malachek, leaning against his desk, cautioned her, "Slow down. Just listen. I'll answer all of your questions in time," he told her.

"Let's go back to our very first interview. You told me about a dream you had, the one where you saw Frank Jensen dead, but there was no blood, only that his head was twisted. Do you recall those details?" Malachek asked Madison.

"Yes, I recall that. It was very upsetting."

"You also told me that day that you were proficient in the martial arts, right?"

Madison nodded her head yes. "But what's that got to do with that woman?" she asked.

"Madison, please be patient. Rome wasn't built in a day, and what I do here is not like playing the game of Clue. It takes a long time, sometimes years to solve a murder, and the clues aren't neatly laid out one after the other."

"Okay, I'll be quiet," Madison submitted.

"The second time we spoke was when you called me while you were stuck in traffic. At first, I thought you were just wanting to talk to someone to pass the time, but you called to tell me about another dream you had. You dreamt you found a blue lapis ring on the floor at Frank's apartment. Did I get that right?" he asked Madison.

"Yes," she replied.

"That's when I first suspected something wasn't kosher."

"With me?" Madison protested. "Did you think I murdered Frank and then hit myself on the head to cover up?" she questioned.

"Not quite, but the thought crossed my mind that somehow you were involved in the murder, perhaps with a partner, and something went south, and he or she caused the blow to your head.

"Look, I've been doing this for many years, and I've seen some strange things. I worked on one case where the boyfriend of the woman whose husband was killed, shot the boyfriend in the leg purposely to remove suspicion from him and to say that a struggle ensued and the boyfriend was justified in shooting the husband. So anything's possible." Madison was listening intently.

"Follow along," Malachek said to her. "We found a one-way ticket in a drawer at Jensen's apartment, right next to a picture of you and him looking very lovey-dovey. The ticket was to Costa Rica, and when I asked you if he was planning a trip or vacation, you said no, not that you were aware of. That was plausible but gave me food for thought—"

Madison had remained quiet long enough and couldn't stop herself from interrupting him. "What food for thought?" she asked sarcastically.

"Since you were his business partner, and you told me he had responsibilities for taking care of your customer's properties, he would have surely made arrangements with you to cover for him regarding a leave of absence. The facts were not jiving."

"So?" Madison asked.

Malachek reached around to grab his coffee cup sitting on his desk. "You'll have to excuse me a moment. I'm going to the men's room then to get my caffeine fix. Can I get you anything?"

Madison was anxious to hear about Christine and growing more impatient by the minute. "No, I don't want anything. I just wish you'd hurry up to the point," she boldly told him.

"I'll be right back, and I'll do my best to wrap things up."

Malachek returned, coffee cup in one hand and a bottle of water for Madison. "Ah, that's good," Malachek said, taking a sip of his coffee. "All right, let me get on with it. You wanted to know why I was there at the casino the exact moment you were attacked."

"Yes, definitely," Madison said, practically falling off the edge of her seat in anticipation of his answer.

"Okay, as I said, several things didn't add up. You were correct when you said from your dream that Frank was dead, but there was no blood. That was because he died from injuries sustained from a neck lock, sometimes called a neck crank." Madison was familiar with the term but remained silent while Malachek explained in detail. "A neck lock is a type of spinal lock that when it's used on the neck, it can cause the neck to extend or rotate beyond the neck's normal capacity."

Malachek put one hand on his face and the other one on the back of his head and demonstrated the move, twisting his head ever so slightly while speaking. "It's done by pulling or twisting the head further beyond its natural rotation, causing the skull to separate from the spine and can lead to death."

Madison got the gruesome picture. "It's not an easy maneuver to do and takes a great deal of strength unless the victim and the perpetrator are in a position to achieve the crank. When you told me that you knew martial arts, I made a mental note but didn't rule it in that you could utilize the move for the reasons I stated. Usually only people who engage in sports, like wrestling, would know how to do it. I had no reason to suspect you.

"Fast forward to the day you called me to say that you saw a blue lapis ring in your dream. On a hunch, we'd gone back to Jensen's place and combed it, looking for clues. My men scoured the place, looking in every nook and cranny including the obvious places, and lo and behold, under the nightstand, one of my officers found a ring.

You guessed it—it was a blue lapis ring. That's when it crossed my mind somehow you were involved in Jensen's murder."

Madison stood up and yelled, "I didn't kill Frank! How could you say such a thing? I'm outta here."

Malachek threw his hands up to get her attention and in a deep, commanding voice said, "Madison, I didn't say you killed him. Now please sit down and let me finish. Sit down." Like a trained dog, Madison sat down in her chair.

"Take a drink of water and calm down," he told her, acting more like somebody's father rather than a detective.

"You asked me why I was at the casino the night you were attacked, and that's what I'm trying to get you to understand."

Madison's phone rang. She reached into her purse to see who was calling her. "Hey, Cathy, how are you?" she asked.

"Good. Sorry I couldn't go with you to the wine country last weekend. I had plans. Remember that lawyer you met at dinner, the one I'm seeing?" Cathy asked.

"Yes," Madison answered.

"Well, he took me to Palm Springs to meet his parents."

"That's fabulous. I'd love to hear all about it, but not right now, I'm in a very important appointment." Madison didn't want to be rude to her best friend. "Can I call you later or tomorrow?" Madison asked.

"Sure, honey, that works for me. Love you, talk to you later."

"Sorry," Madison said to Malachek. "I'll turn off my phone so we won't be interrupted again," she said.

"That'll be a good idea." Malachek continued with his story. "One night over a beer with Hal, a retired buddy of mine who's also a detective, we got to talking about the Jensen case. We started putting the facts together and had to come up with a motive.

"The showstopper was you. The cause of death, your martial arts ability, and mostly your knowledge of the facts that only the murderer could have known. You were either disclosing them, disguised as a dream to exonerate yourself, or you were feeling guilty and your conscience was needing to get those feelings out. I've seen that before."

All the while Malachek was talking, Madison had made up her mind not to say a word. She knew that being considered a murder suspect was serious business, and when push came to shove, she was able to stifle her desire to cut in.

"I put a tail on you to see where you went and what you were up to, hoping you'd slip up. Most killers do at some point in time. That's why I was Johnny on the spot at the casino. Then the attack happened, and I had to blow my cover and rescue you."

"Thank you for that," she said, then added "I guess." She thought to herself that it sounded odd, like she was thanking him for suspecting her and being there.

"So am I under arrest?" she asked.

"No, you're not," Malachek said. "You've been doing well to keep quiet, keep it up, and things will become clear." Madison breathed a sigh of relief.

"We brought the person in who attacked you, and when we removed the mask, that's when we discovered your attacker was a woman. We brought her to that room you saw her in earlier and questioned her. There were several odd things about her. First off, she wore a blue lapis ring on her middle finger. Lots of women wear blue lapis, so that didn't raise any red flags. On her other arm, she had a heart-shaped tattoo.

"From where I was sitting, I could easily tell it was an old one 'cause the colors were faded. When I took a closer look, I saw that there was new ink above the arrow and below it in the middle of the heart. The initials FJ had recently been tattooed in red ink.

"It was too coincidental, this woman with the long brunette wavy hair you described in your dreams, the ring, the tattoo. There was no way you could have known this unless you were psychic, and then a thought popped into my head. One of the detectives on our force had consulted a psychic in the past as a last resort to solve a case. He swears by her. Ms. Alley is a psychic detective and has some kind of license to practice so she doesn't become a suspect. She's helped him solve a couple of cases, missing persons, embezzlement, things like that. I don't subscribe to it, the jury's still out in my opinion. But

I thought it was worth investigating to see if there was anything to it. Yeah, turns out it's real." Madison hung on his every word.

"I was able to hold Christine, the woman who attacked you, all this time on suspicion of murder. We interviewed her over a period of days and wore her down. Her story was inconsistent and constantly changed that she finally cracked." Malachek stopped to take a breath of air.

"She'd met Jensen about two months ago. They had a sexual relationship that turned into a love relationship, at least from her standpoint. Frank came up with an idea to buy a marina together in Belize and move there.

"Christine trusted in him so much that not only did she have his initials tattooed on her arm, but she invested two hundred and fifty thousand dollars with him for a half interest in the marina."

"So that's how he got all the money. Our business was good, but not that good," Madison interjected.

"What are you talking about?" Malachek asked.

"The day I got hit on the head, I had gone to Frank's to find out why two hundred and fifty thousand dollars was missing from the company bank account. I only found out the other day from the bank that when he asked for a cashier's check, the teller took it out by mistake from our escrow account and that it should have been taken out from Frank's personal account. I was wondering how he could have saved that much money. The funds didn't belong to me, and I didn't know what I was going to do. The bank eventually caught the error and credited it back to my account but not until I went through hell and back again trying to replace the money."

"Yes, that's how he got the money," Malachek said, collaborating what Madison had just told him. "He had no intention of contributing a cent of his own. In fact, we found some papers showing that he had paid for the marina in full, with a sales receipt for two hundred thousand dollars. He was planning on pocketing the rest."

Disgusted, Madison said, "What a scumbag he turned out to be."

"He must not have been very careful shoving his one-way ticket to Costa Rica in the drawer along with your picture. Christine secretly got a look inside and realized she'd been duped out of her money and assumed that he was going to go to Costa Rica with you. Instead of letting on that she knew his plan, she decided to get even. They were preparing to make love, and while he was sitting on the bed, she positioned herself behind him under the guise of stroking his hair and giving him a back rub. Frank was naked and relaxed. It was the perfect scenario to execute a neck crank and murder Frank."

"Oh my God. What a sick person. To feel such rage that you could actually kill someone. I would rather just leave and never see them again." As Madison said those words, she thought of her own situation, seeing Shep in the arms of another woman. "So that's why she was after me, she wanted to kill me out of jealousy," Madison exclaimed.

Malachek added, "That, and you might possibly identify her as the killer. She was still in the condo when you walked in, and had to prevent you from seeing her leave. You were a threat to her identity."

Madison put her hand up to her mouth and closed her eyes, thinking what a nightmare she had been through. Malachek stopped talking for a minute to let Madison absorb what he had just told her. "What's going to happen to her now?" Madison asked.

"She'll be brought up on charges, given a trial date, and if the justice system works, get prison."

"I'm not sure if I should feel sorry for Frank or for Christine or for neither of them," Madison said.

"I can understand where you're coming from. I suggest you go home and live your life as joyously as you can. Life is short and precious," Malachek advised her.

"Thank you, I will do exactly that," Madison said and then repeated, "Life is short."

She got up to leave, and Malachek was quick to stop her. "Madison, I have just one question for you."

"What's that?" Madison asked.

"Can you give me the winning lottery numbers?"

She let out a laugh and replied, "If I could predict the winning numbers, do you think I'd give them to you?" She smiled and gave him a hug.

Chapter 38

Madison was getting back to her happy-go-lucky self. She could breathe a little easier knowing that Frank's killer was caught, and the person who was after her was one and the same and was behind bars. She kept her commitment to herself to work hard to build up her business, and it was paying off. She was going to be making more money from new listings and had a new love interest on the horizon. Things were looking up.

Patrick was coming to LA to see a client and wanted to take her to dinner. It had only been two weeks since she met him, and Madison was looking forward to seeing him again. She genuinely liked him and felt that she wasn't on the rebound from Shep, who, by the way, had dropped off the radar. Now that he had won his coveted first place that he had always desired and tons of money, Madison felt that he no longer was interested in her. She felt used and refused to give him any more of her mental energy.

The weekend arrived along with Patrick. He was planning on picking Madison up at her house like an old-fashioned date. It was a lovely LA evening, and Madison suggested they sit on her patio and have a drink. She made appetizers and served Patrick the bottle of wine he had sent her. He was moved that she had saved it to share with him. They talked about work, life, and living in the Bay Area and got to know each other better. Patrick made Madison laugh and smile continuously. The two of them were never at a loss for words.

Patrick asked Madison to suggest a restaurant, perhaps her favorite. Rosie's came to mind, but she thought it wasn't cosmopolitan enough for him, coming from San Francisco. She chose a restaurant high atop a bank building, giving the best views of LA at night. They ate and drank, and Madison's affection toward Patrick grew. While Patrick recounted a story concerning one of his clients, she put her drink down. A thought had crossed her mind while she enjoyed the view.

Why did I take him here? she asked herself. *A restaurant high above the city with a view of all of LA? Is there a pattern here? I first fell for Shep atop the Voodoo Lounge high above Las Vegas.*

"Did you ever have the desire to walk out of a client's house?" Patrick asked. Madison didn't respond. She had zoned out. Patrick repeated the question. "Did you?" he asked. Still no answer from Madison. Concerned, Patrick asked, "Madison, are you okay? Madison?"

Snapping to, Madison said, "I'm sorry, what did you ask me?"

"If you ever wanted to walk away from a customer," he repeated.

Returning her attention back on Patrick, she answered him, "Yes, in fact, I did once. They were being such a butthead, I knew they'd be even more trouble when I had to present offers to them, so I just nipped my aggravation factor in the bud and told them they needed to get another agent. After six months of trying to sell their house, they called me, and I got it sold for them."

They finished dinner, and Madison invited him back to her house for an after-dinner drink. She served Amaretto to cap off the lovely evening. Madison had truly enjoyed herself and was looking forward to kissing him. This time, Madison made the first move. When she went to serve him a refill, she brought it to him and sat down beside him on the couch. Patrick was an all-American male and put down his drink and took the one from Madison's hand. He held her face in his hands and kissed her. Madison was going to go but so far. She was always a lady, and the idea of sleeping with a man after two dates was not appropriate, in her opinion.

Madison explained her position to Patrick, and he said that he respected that. She had a way of attracting men who were complete gentlemen. He gave her one last long good night kiss and promised that they would see each other again. Madison walked him to the door and, closing it behind him, she floated to bed.

Chapter 39

Patrick called Madison the next day to say how much he enjoyed having dinner with her and that he would be returning to LA in a month to see his client again. "I'll let you know exactly when that will be, closer to the date. Hope you'll be available," he said.

Madison, not one to hide her feelings, responded back, "I'll be available."

Over the next few weeks, Patrick and Madison talked frequently and emailed each other. She concentrated on her work and kept busy, attending networking events and going out to dinner with friends and colleagues.

She returned to weight-training at the gym to stay in shape but didn't go back to her martial arts classes. To change up her routine, she went to the Colonial Pool Room, hoping to see Gary. She was in luck; he was a regular and was always there. They exchanged numbers so that whenever she wanted to play, they could hook up.

Madison took joy in the smallest of things in life and made sure to laugh at least once a day or make someone else laugh. Her life was complete, and she felt fulfilled. She thought about taking a vacation in the future and that it might be nice to go with Patrick, but only if their relationship had progressed to that stage.

Several weeks later, Patrick called Madison to let her know that he wouldn't be coming down next month after all because his client was going to be away.

Disappointed, Patrick suggested that Madison come to San Francisco. He wanted to see her so badly that he offered to pay for her flight there. She was flattered and as eager to see him as he was to see her, but she declined his offer to pay. "I'd enjoy the drive," she said. She recalled the last time she made the trip, and like falling off a horse, she felt she needed to do it again to add closure to the past.

Saturday arrived, and Madison left at the crack of dawn so that she wouldn't have to drive in the dark on the Pacific Highway. She got to his apartment in North Beach by three in the afternoon. It was a very nice apartment with four large bay windows overlooking Coit Tower—a San Francisco landmark. His apartment was beautifully furnished with a white sofa, two navy-blue chairs, and a glass coffee table. There were pieces of art glass throughout the living room. Madison complimented him on his good taste, and he revealed that his ex-wife had furnished it. This was the first time that Madison had learned that he had been married before. She wondered if he had children, not that it mattered. He explained to Madison that his wife got custody of the dog, half of the savings account, and moved up to Marin County with her girlfriend. He came home early one day and found the two of them together, kissing. "There's no working that one out," he said.

Patrick offered Madison a drink and told her that he wanted to take her to his favorite restaurant for dinner. He opened up a bottle of white wine and served Madison a glass. "Would you like to see the apartment?" he asked and grabbed her overnight bag. She followed him into the master bedroom, and he put her bag on the bed then showed her the master bath.

Next, he led her into his office. "This is where I do all my great thinking," he jokingly said. Madison smiled and said that her office was her sanctuary. The kitchen was contemporary with stainless steel appliances, an apron sink, and white subway tiles for the backsplash. He had a breakfast nook with an ice-cream parlor table and two chairs. Madison had already seen the formal dining area from the living room. It was obviously a very expensive apartment.

"That's my humble abode," he told her. Madison was expecting to see a second bedroom, but that didn't happen. They returned to the living room, and Madison nervously asked, "So where are you going to sleep?"

He could see that she was uncomfortable. "I have a pullout sofa in my office."

Relieved, Madison nodded her head okay and felt a need to explain her question. "I'm not old-fashioned or anything when it comes to sex—"

"I'm sure you're not," Patrick interjected.

"It's just that…" She hesitated a moment. "If I sleep with you, I'm afraid I'll fall hard, and I want to be sure there's a next time and a next time and a next."

"Don't be afraid," he said. "I feel meeting you was very fortuitous. It seems that there's been turning points in my life where I was at the right place at the right time, and you're one of them. You're obviously very smart, beautiful to boot, and extremely ambitious. You have the motivation of a man—that's what I like best about you."

Madison felt a chill run down her spine. Her inner voice was telling her that she was turned on to him. She was glad that she could feel deep feelings for someone other than Shep.

They went out to dinner together and had a fabulous time. Afterward, he drove Madison across the Golden Gate Bridge just so she could see it at nighttime. She was having a great evening with Patrick. Once across the bridge from the city, he drove to Sausalito and found a place to park. They skipped the conversation and got right down to kissing. Madison was thinking she might break her rule this one time and become intimate with Patrick. He was thinking about how much he wanted to make love with her and sensed that Madison was ready to take things to the next level.

Unfortunately, this was not the place or the time. They heard thunder, and Patrick looked up to see a flash of lightning, followed by the sound of heavy rain pouring down. "As much as I don't want to stop, we need to get back before it gets worse," Patrick announced. He started up the car and drove away. Madison no longer had to decide what her next move would be.

The rain was coming down even harder in San Fransisco, and they both got drenched running from Patrick's car into his apartment. Madison went into the bedroom to get into dry clothing.

She wondered if she should put on a pair of jeans or her pajamas. Wishing she had brought along some sexy lingerie, she didn't know what to do. She looked at the clock on the night table and decided that it was late enough to go to sleep, so she might as well just get into her pajamas. She put on her robe and came out into the living room. Patrick walked out in a pajama bottom and no shirt. Madison stood there awkwardly, feeling frumpy in her boring bathrobe but just as attracted to him more than ever. She mustered up the courage to walk over to him and give him a sensual kiss. After one long kiss, she pulled back and said, "That's going to have to keep you. I'm going to get some sleep."

The next morning, Madison got up early and went into the kitchen to make coffee. She tried to be as quiet as possible while she looked for the coffee and the cups. Patrick appeared in the doorway. "Let me help you," he said.

Startled, Madison turned around. "I'm sorry, did I wake you?" she asked.

"I was borderline awake. Good morning."

"Good morning to you," Madison repeated.

"Did you sleep well?" he asked.

"Yes, thank you" was all Madison answered. She didn't want to rub it in that he had to sleep on an uncomfortable pullout sofa and go to bed alone.

"I thought we could go around the corner and have breakfast and maybe go to Golden Gate Park afterward," Patrick told her.

"That would be lovely," Madison said. "I would just like to get on the road by two this afternoon." Patrick was feeling frustrated but remained a gentleman and acknowledged her wishes. He took the coffee out from his freezer and started the coffeepot.

They shared conversation over a cup of coffee before going to breakfast. The place was packed with people who had the same idea as them. Luckily, the wait wasn't too long for a Sunday morning and was well worth it. The menu wasn't your typical breakfast menu, with unique dishes named after the city's sights like the Trolley Car. They were served their breakfast and talked continuously. It was amazing how Patrick and Madison never ran out of topics to talk about while they ate.

On the drive to Golden Gate Park, Patrick suggested they go horseback riding. Madison loved horses, and it had been a long time since she had ridden. "I would love to, but I'm not dressed for it," she commented.

"Yeah, sure you are, blue jeans are fine. It'll be fun," Patrick convincingly said.

"Well, I do love horses. All right, I'm in," she agreed. The next thing she knew, they were in a group, riding down the trails of the park. It would only be an hour-long trail ride, and Madison wished she could have galloped away like she used to on her uncle's farm as a child. Only back then, she rode bareback and took many a spill before learning to stay on.

By the time they returned to Patrick's apartment, it was half past two. Madison had a good time and didn't mind getting a later start than she had planned. She packed her bag and walked out into the living room. Patrick was standing, ready to walk Madison to her car and say goodbye.

He kissed her passionately, desiring more than she was willing to give him so early in their relationship. Planning to turn the tables on her, he kissed her again then said, "This will have to last you awhile." If that was meant to make her want him more, it worked. Patrick walked her to her car and told her that he would see her again on his next trip to LA.

All during her drive home, Madison played the events of the weekend over and over in her head. She loved his apartment and riding horses again. Most of all, she loved the hot kissing and wondered if she should invite him to sleep over on his next visit. Best of all, she was glad that she had gotten over Shep, and for the first time in her life, she was able to put him out of her mind totally. This was never the case as thoughts of him in the past always managed to creep into her psyche when she was getting too close to someone. The result was that she would break it off. Madison felt that this time it was different, and she was ready to commit to a new relationship.

Chapter 40

Madison spent the first part of Monday morning cleaning house and then getting down to business. Her life was falling into place. She had new clients to call and appointments to set and a new boyfriend. She was happy with her life and was moving forward.

Cathy called her and asked her out to dinner for that evening. Madison quickly said yes, especially since she hadn't seen her friend in some time and wanted to hear about her trip to Palm Springs. Madison worked all day, rarely taking breaks in anticipation of her time away from the office. Her new life included working late into the evening, but she would make an exception to have dinner with Cathy.

Madison stopped work around six to change and go out to dinner. Cathy picked the restaurant, and of course, it was going to be upscale since Cathy enjoyed the finer things in life. Madison put on a pink cocktail dress, her signature color, and heels for the occasion.

She got to the restaurant before Cathy, who arrived only seconds behind her. They kissed and hugged each other while being escorted to their table.

Cathy immediately asked Madison what she'd been up to, but Madison, ever so considerate, told Cathy that she wanted to hear about Philip, the new man in Cathy's life, and her visit to his parents' home. Cathy explained that Philip's parents moved to Palm Springs from Ohio when they retired, to be closer to Phil and his sister who lived nearby.

His parents had a cookout the first evening of her visit, and Phil's sister was there also, so Cathy got to meet her. Even though Cathy was a mature, accomplished career woman, she was nervous meeting the future in-laws. His parents were gin drinkers, and while Cathy usually drank wine, she obliged them. Not accustomed to drinking hard alcohol, Cathy lost track of how much she drank and being tipsy, to put it politely, had to go to bed early and miss the cookout. The next morning at breakfast, Cathy was so embarrassed and afraid that Phil would regret his decision to marry her. His parents were so loving that his mother gave her hug and said, "Welcome to the family." They were as compassionate and understanding as Phil was.

Upon hearing that Cathy was engaged, Madison hugged her and wished her congratulations. Cathy asked Madison to be her maid of honor and help her plan her wedding. "But of course I will," Madison assured her. The two of them screamed with joy, acting like teenagers. Madison ordered a bottle of champagne to celebrate Cathy's engagement.

She was so happy for her friend's good news and went on to share the news of her new love interest. She explained how they were just getting to know each other and hadn't been intimate yet, but that Patrick was very much a gentleman and made an effort to see and call her often.

Shortly before midnight, Madison rolled into bed, having celebrated the evening with her friend. Madison hoped the champagne wouldn't catch up with her the next morning, making her regret drinking so much the night before.

Chapter 41

Madison made herself a cup of coffee, showered, and dressed in preparation to start work early. Luckily, the champagne had no lasting effect on her, and Madison felt fine the next morning. She made herself a slice of toast and grabbed her coffee and was walking into her office when the doorbell rang. She put her toast and coffee down on the center hall table then peered out the front bedroom window, expecting to see a FedEx truck delivering her Amazon order. There was no truck, so she answered the door to see who was there. It was Shep. She attempted to slam the door on him, but Shep put up his hand and pushed it open. "Madison," he said firmly.

"Get out! I don't want to see you!" she shouted.

He had made his way inside, and closing the door behind him, he said, "I can understand."

"No, you don't!" Madison yelled at him.

"All's fair in poker, and I'm sorry I busted you out," Shep said.

"I don't care about that!" Madison shouted back. She was not going to remain calm no matter what he said or did. To say she was angry didn't begin to scratch the surface in describing the emotions she was feeling at that moment.

"I want to talk with you. I've got some news," he said.

"I really don't care what you have to say. There's nothing you could tell me that would interest me," she protested.

"If you're not angry over losing the tournament to me, then what's bothering you?" Shep asked. The two of them stood in her hallway yelling at each other.

"I'm not getting involved with you," Madison responded.

"And why is that?" Shep shot back.

"What the f—do you care?" She almost used the curse word but caught herself, feeling the swear word packed more punch.

"I do care," he said. "What's going on here?" Shep was very puzzled by her behavior. "Is it because I haven't been in touch with you till now?" he asked, looking for an answer as to why she was acting so hostile toward him.

"I've met someone new," Madison blurted out.

Feeling thrown under the bus, Shep shouted at her, "So that's it! You met someone new, or maybe you were screwing him behind my back while we were seeing each other."

"You're one to talk!" Madison volleyed back.

"I'm one to talk? What the hell are you talking about?" he questioned. "I never cheated on you, past or present," he bragged.

"*Really?*" Madison asked, drawing out the word to emphasize it and show her disbelief. "You're going to add insult to injury?" Their shouting became louder and louder, drowning each other out.

Realizing it wasn't good for her health to become so agitated, Madison picked up her toast and coffee and walked away. To help her gain control of her emotions, she sat down on the sofa and took a bite of her toast. "I was in the middle of having breakfast, and I have a lot of work to do. Can you leave now?" she asked him in a composed voice.

"No, I'm not going anywhere," he said and took a seat across from her. Hoping he would eventually leave when he didn't get what he came for, Madison offered him a cup of coffee. The thought crossed her mind to kill him with kindness and acting pleasant instead of crazed would aggravate the stink out of him. Madison was good at psychological warfare, a skill she learned from playing poker—and perhaps she could exact a small amount of retribution at the same time.

"Yes, I'll have a cup. I've been driving all night just to get here. Now I understand why you blocked my calls." Shep was settling down also but was deeply hurt. Madison returned and handed Shep a cup of coffee.

"Where did you meet this guy?" he wanted to know.

"Does it really matter?" Madison asked. "Do you really want the details?"

"Yes," he said. "I want to know what I'm up against." Shep was being territorial and wasn't going give her up so easily.

"If I tell you, will you leave then?" Madison asked.

"Yes, I'll leave," he answered.

"Well then, here it goes. After the tournament, I felt I needed some time away." Embarrassed and afraid that he might have her committed, she wasn't going to mention anything about her suicide attempt. "I called Cathy to see if she wanted to go with me to the wine country, but she already had plans. I wasn't going to go alone, and the thought of staying home was, well, boring.

Then I remembered this great spa that I had read about and felt that it would be a perfect getaway even solo. So I packed my bag and left late Friday afternoon and drove up the coast. I always loved that drive except when it gets dark." She was calming down while she pictured the Pacific Highway in her mind and the beauty of the cliffs running parallel to the Pacific Ocean. "It was late, and the sun was going down, and I was getting a little scared, driving in the dark. I had reached Carmel-by-the-Sea and decided to stop there."

Shep put down his coffee cup; he knew where this was going. "I looked for a quaint place to stay although all the places are special," she said. She was surprisingly unperturbed while recounting the night of her betrayal by Shep. She focused on the pleasant parts and hadn't yet mentioned seeing him with another woman.

"I suppose you stayed at the Painted Lady?" Shep asked.

"Yes, how did you know?"

"It's the kind of place you'd pick," he said, smiling. He lost all concern about the new man in Madison's life.

"Did you see me there?" Madison asked.

"No, why would I see you there?" he asked her.

"You're such a liar. You saw me, and I saw you with another woman. Why are you doing this to me?" Madison was becoming angry all over again.

"Do what to you?" Shep asked.

242

"I saw you arm in arm with another woman, and you were headed up to your room to sleep with her, and you're accusing me of being unfaithful?" She was going to blow a stack and yelled at him, "You are such a scumbag! All men are scumbags." The *all* was in reference to Frank, recalling his betrayal.

"So that's it?" Shep was astonished. "You were never planning on talking to me again or to find out why I was with another woman? Do I really mean that little to you?" he questioned.

Madison shouted at him, "Okay, so I'll ask. As if that'll make you feel better in a perverted way. Who was that woman?"

Shep was quick to reply, "That was my sister-in-law."

"On your arm?" Madison asked. "So you're sleeping with your brother's wife?"

"Madison. Get a hold of yourself. I'd never do a thing like that to my brother or to you. I love you," Shep said.

Still doubting him, Madison asked, "Then where was your brother?"

"Annette, my sister-in-law, and I had a drink in the bar with Erik. He was paying the bill, and I was walking her to the elevator where we were going to wait for him."

Madison felt like a fool, all the wasted anger and emotions. *If only I had communicated with him, all this could have been avoided,* she thought to herself. She almost burst out in tears.

"Now tell me about this new boyfriend," Shep demanded.

"What's his name, and did you sleep with him?" Shep needed to know where he stood with Madison.

"His name is Patrick, and I met him in the wine country, and no, I didn't sleep with him. There! Satisfied?" She paused for a moment.

"That's what I needed to know," Shep said.

She stood up to show him to the door and asked, "So will you leave now?"

"No, not until I tell you why I came here and where I've been, other than Carmel.

It was Madison's turn to put the screws to him and pushed for answers to her questions. "What were you doing in Carmel? And how come I didn't hear from you till now?" she asked him.

"If you'll sit back down and calm yourself, I'll tell you."

Madison sat down and said to him, "Okay, I'm listening."

"Do you think you can remain quiet long enough to let me get out the whole story and not interrupt the way you usually do?"

"I won't interrupt, just get on with it." Madison was still very hurt that he hadn't made an effort before now to contact her, but she was going to allow him his day in court.

"My brother Erik's business partner suddenly passed away. He was only in his early forties, a marathoner, picture of health. He flew out to the coast to attend the funeral and wanted to see me. I suggested Carmel. He was telling me that if he didn't replace his partner's position, his business could go down the tubes.

"The position requires someone who is totally trustworthy with the necessary skill set. That's a tall order to fill, and replacing Tom won't be an easy task. I know because I used to do it."

"You used to work with your brother? I didn't know that," Madison interjected.

"Hush," Shep told her. "I've been spending the last couple of weeks getting my own house in order and my priorities straight. That's where you come in." Shep got up from the couch and walked over to Madison and sat next to her. He put his arms around her and turned her toward him. "Madison, will you marry me?" he asked.

Madison was never expecting that. She sat there like a deaf mute. Shep had caught her off guard, and Madison didn't know what to think or to say. Then her gut began to do the talking for her.

"I would marry you only if you gave up playing poker, and I can't ask you to do that. It would be like cutting off your arms and legs for me."

Shep released his hold on Madison and said, "Yes, you're right." Madison bowed her head down, her heart broken, knowing it was the best thing for both of them. There was a deafening silence between them. Madison was about to get up from the sofa and walk Shep to the door when he took hold of her hand. "But I can survive without my limbs. If I let you get away a second time, I would be cutting out my heart, and without that, I couldn't survive. Erik asked me—no, let me rephrase that—*begged* me to join him in the family business. I told him I would let him know. What should I tell him?"

Madison couldn't control herself any longer. She burst out crying, and Shep hugged her so hard while wiping away the tears rolling down her face with his shirt. Slowly, Madison stopped crying.

"I have something you need to know about me," Madison said in a serious voice. She pulled back from Shep. Then she removed her wig, exposing her bald head. "I have epilepsy." She turned her head to the left to expose a long scar on the right side of her skull. "I had brain surgery to stop the seizures, but I still need to take medicine."

Shep, astounded by her revelation, told her, "You're more beautiful to me than ever." Then adding levity to a dramatic situation, he said, "Hey, blue eyes, we match," referring to his cleanly shaved head. Madison let out a little laugh, appreciating his humor.

"I'm still waiting for an answer," Shep said. "What should I tell Erik?"

Madison wiped the remaining tears from her cheek. She took a deep breath before responding, "I can't make that decision for you."

T H E   E N D

About the Author

Though D.G. Partington has been writing since she was a teenager, *An Empty Seat*, is her first published novel. The author wanted to bring to the forefront a woman's struggle to be respected by men as equals, oftentimes putting her own interests second, especially in a relationship. She illustrates women's desires to break free from the control and influence of the men in their lives. The inspiration for the story is drawn from her own experiences as well as those of the women she has met over the years. D.G. hopes you enjoy reading her novel as much as she enjoyed writing it.

CPSIA information can be obtained
at www.ICGtesting.com
Printed in the USA
BVHW080936010521
606268BV00005B/69